FIC Irela
Ireland, Justina.
Wayseeker /

KE - Apr 2025

BY JUSTINA IRELAND

STAR WARS: THE HIGH REPUBLIC
Defy the Storm (with Tessa Gratton)
Path of Deceit (with Tessa Gratton)
A Test of Courage
Out of the Shadows
Mission to Disaster

STAR WARS
Spark of the Resistance

DREAD NATION
Dread Nation
Deathless Divide

CHAOS & FLAME (WITH TESSA GRATTON)
Chaos & Flame
Blood & Fury

STANDALONE
Rust in the Root
Promise of Shadows
Vengeance Bound

STAR WARS
THE ACOLYTE
WAYSEEKER

STAR WARS
THE ACOLYTE
WAYSEEKER

JUSTINA IRELAND

RANDOM HOUSE
WORLDS

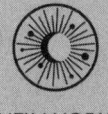

NEW YORK

Random House Worlds
An imprint of Random House
A division of Penguin Random House LLC
1745 Broadway, New York, NY 10019
randomhousebooks.com
penguinrandomhouse.com

Copyright © 2025 by Lucasfilm Ltd. & ® or ™ where indicated. All rights reserved.
Excerpt from *Star Wars: The High Republic: Light of the Jedi* by Charles Soule
copyright © 2021 by Lucasfilm Ltd. & ® or ™ where indicated.
All rights reserved.

Penguin Random House values and supports copyright. Copyright fuels creativity, encourages diverse voices, promotes free speech, and creates a vibrant culture. Thank you for buying an authorized edition of this book and for complying with copyright laws by not reproducing, scanning, or distributing any part of it in any form without permission. You are supporting writers and allowing Penguin Random House to continue to publish books for every reader. Please note that no part of this book may be used or reproduced in any manner for the purpose of training artificial intelligence technologies or systems.

RANDOM HOUSE is a registered trademark, and RANDOM HOUSE WORLDS and colophon are trademarks of Penguin Random House LLC.

Hardback ISBN 978-0-593-87443-1
Ebook ISBN 978-0-593-87444-8

Printed in Canada

2 4 6 8 9 7 5 3 1

First Edition

BOOK TEAM: Production editor: Abby Duval • Managing editor: Susan Seeman • Production manager: Erich Schoeneweiss • Copy editor: Laura Jorstad • Proofreaders: Rachael Clements, J. J. Evans, Taylor McGowan, Laura Petrella, Natalie Richman

Book design by Elizabeth A. D. Eno

The authorized representative in the EU for product safety and compliance is Penguin Random House Ireland, Morrison Chambers, 32 Nassau Street, Dublin D02 YH68, Ireland.
https://eu-contact.penguin.ie.

For Eric, who has been there since the beginning.
You are my light.

THE STAR WARS NOVELS TIMELINE

THE HIGH REPUBLIC

Convergence
The Battle of Jedha
Cataclysm

Light of the Jedi
The Rising Storm
Tempest Runner
The Fallen Star
The Eye of Darkness
Temptation of the Force
Tempest Breaker
Trials of the Jedi

Wayseeker: An Acolyte Novel

Dooku: Jedi Lost
Master and Apprentice
The Living Force

I — THE PHANTOM MENACE

Mace Windu: The Glass Abyss

II — ATTACK OF THE CLONES

Inquisitor: Rise of the Red Blade
Brotherhood
The Thrawn Ascendancy Trilogy
Dark Disciple: A Clone Wars Novel

III — REVENGE OF THE SITH

Reign of the Empire: The Mask of Fear
Catalyst: A Rogue One Novel
Lords of the Sith
Tarkin
Jedi: Battle Scars

SOLO

Thrawn
A New Dawn: A Rebels Novel
Thrawn: Alliances
Thrawn: Treason

ROGUE ONE

IV — A NEW HOPE

Battlefront II: Inferno Squad
Heir to the Jedi
Doctor Aphra
Battlefront: Twilight Company

V — THE EMPIRE STRIKES BACK

VI — RETURN OF THE JEDI

The Princess and the Scoundrel
The Alphabet Squadron Trilogy
The Aftermath Trilogy
Last Shot

Shadow of the Sith
Bloodline
Phasma
Canto Bight

VII — THE FORCE AWAKENS

VIII — THE LAST JEDI

Resistance Reborn
Galaxy's Edge: Black Spire

IX — THE RISE OF SKYWALKER

A long time ago in a galaxy far, far away....

STAR WARS
THE ACOLYTE
WAYSEEKER

Chapter One

I adjusted my perch on the narrow outcropping of cobalt-hued rock overlooking the Bernerine Pass, the most direct way into Norna, the capital city of Cerifisis. And I waited.

It is a truth galactically known that where there is something of worth, there are those who will do anything to acquire it, either through honest work or through thievery and violence. As a Jedi Master, I had seen this firsthand throughout my life. I had seen humans fight over ore on Grandak and Hutts farm glaka root on Jero with the help of massive labor forces. The farther I traveled across the galaxy, the more the axiom held true.

And the work was rarely the issue.

Which was why the Force had brought me to Cerifisis, a planet plagued by piracy. As a Wayseeker, I let the whims of the Force decide my next stop, or rather J-6's next stop, since the droid did much of the flying of the *Cantaros*. I disliked piloting on my own—hyperspace had a way of pulling me into Force-powered visions, which were more often than not unwelcome—but with a droid copilot I had managed to navigate the galaxy just fine, spending the past few years doing everything from helping bring in the harvest on Tiikae to corralling a bloom of fire lizards on Targusian. They were small, simple acts that just made life better for the inhabitants of their respective planets. For the people who benefited, they could be life changing. That was the point: The tiniest of efforts, when applied in the correct place, could be magnified into huge gains.

And that was why, during my tenure as a Jedi, I had returned time and again to being a Wayseeker. Spreading the light of the Jedi across the galaxy was the point of the Order. Yes, we could protect and defend those who could not help themselves, and that was always an honorable undertaking, but sometimes it was best to just help out in whatever way a Jedi could. And so I traveled where the Force led me, all in the hope of making the galaxy a better place.

This time, the Force had guided me to the otherwise peaceful planet of Cerifisis, which was currently plagued by pirates stealing rations. That was the reason I perched on an outcropping, looking out over the vast azure-hued landscape, waiting for the sign of movement that would indicate it was time to act.

For the past few months on Cerifisis, the Strafes had been raiding the critical supply caravans that stocked the capital city of Norna, and it was beginning to have a real impact. Food was short, and if the marauders weren't stopped, the entire population would starve. The Strafes' villainy was a slow, creeping poison, and one that had already been proven lethal as people wasted away to nothing.

I had known none of this when I arrived on the planet. J-6 and I had merely stopped on Cerifisis to refuel—and because I wanted to see its magnificent blue sands after hearing about them from a hauler who regularly delivered foodstuffs to the planet. During our layover, a worker at the dockyard had told me of the attacks and the threat of starvation incapacitating the capital. I had immediately gone to the mayor of Norna to offer my assistance, hastening my steps when I saw the lines of people waiting for rations. The sight of children crying, hungry because there was too little to fill their bellies, would have moved anyone. But even without the obvious suffering, offering my assistance was just the right thing to do. I didn't outwardly subscribe to the common thought within the Order that the Jedi had to hold themselves separate from their emotions, neutral in a galaxy where most actions were anything but. Not that I was given to intense emotions, but the Jedi were *of* the galaxy. We belonged out and about in it.

And I would never stand idly by while people were in pain, especially if there was something to be done about their suffering. So there I stood, on an outcropping above the narrow pass. The mayor's hand-picked security team stood a few meters behind me, watching me with a mixture of awe and wariness. Whether it was because I was a Jedi or because I was a Mirialan—my green skin a far cry from the humans who made up the majority of the planet's population and likewise the security team around me—I didn't know. I had been told repeatedly that neither Jedi nor Mirialans made it very often to the far-flung corner of the galaxy that contained Cerifisis, a way of explaining away the distrustful glances and rude stares I had endured in my short time on the planet. But I also didn't care. I didn't need to make friends. I just had to help.

"What do you think, Jedi Vernestra Rwoh?" Kavil, the mayor's brother and leader of the security team, called to me. A tall, rangy human with a shock of white-blond hair and a permanent sunburn from the merciless Cerifisis sun, he was the most skeptical of my ability to stop the pirates. That didn't bother me in the least. I liked surprising those who doubted me.

"We attack the Strafes when they come after the caravan. No one was told of this delivery, correct?"

"No one outside the Council of Elders." Kavil scowled. "This is a waste of time."

I allowed myself a small smile, despite the frustration clear in every line of Kavil's body. "Only if the pirates don't show."

Kavil's sour expression did not shift. "You truly think one of our own is working with the Strafes while children starve?"

"The capacity for selfishness and cruelty exists everywhere across the galaxy," I said, my amusement fading. Why did so many people believe they were beyond such things? It made no sense. Especially here.

Yet I understood Kavil's wariness and his doubt. He wanted to believe that the people he'd chosen to surround himself with were somehow better than others, even when they weren't. But that was no concern of mine. It was not my place to convince him that injustice existed in every corner of the galaxy.

It was much better to show him.

The growl of hauler engines wrenched me from my thoughts, and I pulled down the goggles perched on top of my head before pulling up the scarf wrapped around my throat. Cerifisis was currently in its dry season, and a fine blue dust rose up in all directions as the convoy approached the pass. That was one of the reasons the supply deliveries were so critical. For half the year, the bright-red sun was closer due to Cerifisis's orbit, while rain was nonexistent, meaning that food could not be grown. The planet's infrastructure was not yet advanced enough to allow year-round farming, so the government had resources shipped in from Hetzal.

Now I just had to make sure the supplies got to their intended target.

In the valley below, the haulers approached, massive vehicles that carried thousands of crates on the flatbeds that made up the rear three-quarters of each. These vehicles were necessary because of the electromagnetic fields that surrounded Norna. It was impossible to fly into the city itself, since the radiant energy caused engines to sputter out suddenly. The city had been established in its current location because the water available underground supported the population during the dry season. Relocating it had been discussed throughout the years but always discarded. I suspected that the city's inimical effect on machinery actually made the residents—most of whom had lived through armed conflict—feel safe. There was no way to approach

Norna without being detected. Even landspeeders were risky. The haulers would stop about ten kilometers outside the city, and there the cargo would be transferred to carts pulled by beasts of burden, a slow and arduous process that everyone had come to accept as normal.

This process was one of the many reasons the pirates had been so successful in stealing cargo time and time again. It left too many opportunities for theft. Still, despite many discussions with the mayor and her security team, it seemed to be the best way to bring the much-needed supplies into the city. This left the citizens with only one solution: direct confrontation.

The convoy of haulers had nearly finished traversing the canyon, the azure dust plumes of their passage clogging the air and making visibility difficult. Behind me, Kavil sighed in relief.

"See? Your worries were unfounded, Jedi."

The scarf covering my face hid the amusement I felt when the whine of speeder bike engines joined the growl of the haulers. A lesser person would be smug, but I had been doing this dance for far longer than any of the people around me. I only found humor in the predictability of pirates. Their lack of originality was a delight.

Cries of alarm began to sound in the valley, and I pointed downward.

"Follow me as you will," I shouted. Then I stepped over the edge into the valley below.

There was a trail from the top of the ridge that switchbacked on itself until it reached the valley floor. I ignored the trail, reaching for the Force and using it to guide my way as my feet slid down the steep slope, a direct path that was much quicker than the established one. Dust bloomed behind me like a plumed tail. I heard a few exclamations from comrades now far behind me, but I ignored them, landing sure-footed at my destination. The settlers of Cerifisis, as well as the Strafes, were about to see just how effective a lone Jedi could be.

Leaving my lightsaber tucked into my belt—I was hoping I wouldn't have to use it—I plunged into the fray. It was difficult to see exactly what was going on, since the dust had not yet settled from the trio of haulers, which had all come lurching to a halt. A speeder bike whipped past me, and the sound of blasterfire was everywhere. There were at least a dozen speeder bikes, some carrying two passengers. I ran toward the lead hauler. A group of pirates had swarmed it and were working to pull the driver from within, their speeders idling nearby. As I sprinted, I raised my hand, launching the pirates crawling over the exterior of the hauler into the air with the Force. I wasn't careful, either. These were people who did not mind if children starved and who looked to have already killed one of the drivers. I would not be overly cautious in granting them mercy that they did not see fit to even consider.

The billowing dirt added an element of surprise to my attack, since the masked pirates were too busy attempting to steal the cargo to pay my arrival any mind. With the Force, I plucked the few remaining marauders off the vehicle one by one, like picking bloodmites off a bantha. Once the pirates had been removed, I held my hand out toward the trio of speeder bikes idling nearby, using the Force to crush their engines, ensuring that at least this initial group of thieves would have no method of escape.

I jumped onto the hauler, locking eyes with the driver just long enough to realize that the Nautolan woman had drawn a blaster and was pointing it right at me. I twisted away, the blaster bolt flying through the windshield and singeing the edge of my robes. Better than my face.

When I turned back, the Nautolan stared at me with wide, inky eyes and an expression of shock. "Get out of here!" I yelled, and she nodded, the hauler lurching forward as she engaged the engines. I leapt onto the roof, running up and over the back of the cargo containers. One down, two to go.

A flurry of blaster bolts flew my way, signaling that the rest of the pirates had finally noticed my arrival. I threw off my outer robes, using the moment of distraction to flip through the air while drawing my lightsaber. I powered it up and thumbed the bezel, twisting it so the purple plasma blade fell away into the deadly cascade of my lightwhip.

The Strafes would know the might of a Jedi.

The blaster bolts found a new trajectory as I spun the whip around my body, using the angles and an intuition granted by the Force to ricochet the bolts back in the direction they had come from. Cries of pain echoed toward me, and I took advantage of a momentary hesitation by a pirate on my left to use the lightwhip, snapping it so that their hand was neatly severed from their body, the wound instantly cauterizing.

That caused most of the pirates to drop their weapons and run away toward the rear vehicle, while a particularly stubborn duo redoubled their efforts. I lazily swirled the lightwhip around my body, biding my time as I waited for their blasters to overheat and seize, which they did.

Predictable.

I used the Force to lift the two pirates high into the air and then released them so that they crashed back to the ground with hollow thumps. Then I crushed their blasters with the Force as well. The last thing I wanted was a blaster bolt in the back.

I twisted the bezel of my lightsaber once more, solidifying the blade and using it to slice through the speeder bike closest to me. Not just because it was fun to show these cowardly crooks what a lightsaber could do, but also because I wanted to send them a message: *This could be you. Surrender and stop being foolish.*

To their credit, the remainder of the pirates surrounding the rear hauler took the object lesson to heart, running back the way they had come. Some had to triple up on their speeder bikes, chasing after their compatriots so as to not be left behind. The retreating whine was a relief. I had injured enough of these fools for one day.

It was nice when people made things easy.

I leapt up onto the second hauler to check on the driver, but the blast burn in the center of their chest and their wide staring eyes confirmed that the human was dead. I leapt down and made my way to the last remaining hauler, kicking blasters away from the pirates writhing on the ground in pain. I did not bother to stop and render aid. I had to check on the third driver first.

I spotted the last driver cowering among the nearby rocks. On seeing me, the Pantoran came over, gushing his thanks in a language I did not understand.

I smiled and took his hands into mine. "Go back to your truck. The danger has passed," I answered in Galactic Basic.

"Thank you, Jedi," he said, regaining some of his composure. By the time he climbed back aboard his hauler, there came the sound of footsteps behind me, and I spun around to see Kavil and his security team approaching. He held out my robes, and I took them.

"Lady Jedi," he said, giving me a deep bow of respect. "I was wrong to doubt you."

I inclined my head slightly in acknowledgment of his apology. "Let's put that in the past," I said, shaking most of the dust from my robes before donning them once more. "Now begins the hard part."

"The hard part?" he echoed, looking around the casualties strewn about the valley in disbelief.

"Yes," I said. "Now we must see if we can convince one of our many prisoners to talk."

Chapter Two

Light-years away on Coruscant, Jedi Knight Indara stepped lightly through the halls of the Jedi Temple, intent on her destination. She hopped around younglings and smiled at Padawans gossiping, but nothing about her outward appearance revealed the turmoil swirling around in her middle. She had been summoned by the Jedi High Council, and that was either a good thing or a very, very bad thing.

Indara hoped it was good. But there was something that made her believe that perhaps she was being overly optimistic. After all, she was a perfectly serviceable archivist, far below the notice of the Council unless there was research to be done. And research requests rarely required an in-person audience.

So as she approached the turbolifts that would take her to the level that held the Council Chamber, she had very much decided that the summons was nothing to be excited about.

Someone called Indara's name, and she turned toward the sound, stopping short of running over a line of younglings being escorted to their next lesson. Far down the hallway, moving forward with a measured pace, was Master Yaddle, her green face split in its characteristic smile. As she moved through the hallway, younglings and Padawans alike turned toward the diminutive Jedi Master as though she were a faraway sun and they were hungry for her light. Master Yaddle had a way about her. She exuded such a sense of peace that it was impossible for anyone not to relax in the elder Jedi's presence, and Indara was no exception. She felt her inner turmoil calm as the Jedi Master approached.

"Master Yaddle, I have been meaning to come see you," Indara said, her voice steadier than she'd expected. A shock of dark-brown hair fell over Indara's eyes, and she hastily pushed it back. She'd been hoping to get into the city for a haircut but had become deeply distracted by her current line of research, stories of a long-ago battle on Tevu from when Yaddle was still a Padawan. The planet was planning a celebration on the upcoming anniversary—a flashy, ostentatious spectacle as befitted a place dedicated to high-end tourism—and Indara had been horrified by the reports from back then as well as the many redactions and contradictions that now existed in the archives. She'd wanted to speak to Master Yaddle about the findings, since the elder Jedi had been there, but she found herself now more concerned with why the Jedi High Council had requested her presence than with the experiences of a few Jedi in a battle, most of whom were long dead.

Suddenly, Indara realized her summoning before the Council could be tied to her research on Tevu, and she chided herself for not making an effort to seek out Master Yaddle sooner. She always liked to ask for forgiveness rather than permission, but in this case it may have been a mistake.

"Indara. It is good to see you. Come, the Council is waiting."

Master Yaddle stepped into the turbolift, and Indara followed, reluctant to share a lift with the Jedi Master when she was not quite sure what the summons had been about. The silence between them was awkward, and when they reached the spire where the Jedi High Council Chamber resided, Indara could no longer hold her tongue.

"Master Yaddle, is this about Tevu? I want you to understand that I was going to send my findings through the proper channels. I was just finalizing my thesis and my thoughts on the best way to discuss any failure on the Jedi's part—or rather not failure but perhaps a lack of patience?"

Master Yaddle smiled at Indara and shook her head but did not answer the question. She set off at a pace that should not have been possible given her short stature, and Indara had to hurry to keep up, talking faster to say her piece before they reached their destination: "Perhaps the better phrase is lack of clarity? Not really sure the term I want to use there... Either way, I still have a lot of work to do before my research is going to be ready for review, so I hope you don't think I'm setting out to condemn you—I mean, you were just a Padawan! I was just making sure that everything was, um, fact-checked."

Master Yaddle did a mere half turn toward Indara as she spoke, never once slowing her steps, so that by the time Indara finished her defense of her process, she was a bit out of breath.

But Yaddle just chuckled. "Child, the battle on Tevu is ancient history, even for me. That is not our concern today. We have a mission for you, but it will be best if I allow the Council to explain."

By that point, they'd reached the Jedi Council Chamber, and Indara froze as Yaddle continued, entering the room and leaving the younger Jedi behind.

"A mission?" Indara said. A tingle started in her toes and began to work its way to the top of her head, like a crackle of electricity. Indara had always seen the Force as energy, sparking through the galaxy and connecting everything and everyone, and when she got excited or overly worried, it was normal for her to feel that same sizzle of energy pulsing through her.

A mission? It couldn't be.

She still didn't feel ready.

Indara swallowed hard, trying to keep her anxiousness off her face as she stepped into the room. Before she'd taken the position as an archivist, she'd traveled the galaxy as a Padawan alongside her master, saving endangered tomes and learning all that she could about various cultures, most especially their fighting forms. But that was before the disaster that had stolen Indara's confidence in her abilities. For the last year, Indara had not left Coruscant, working instead in the archives, researching. When her request to be assigned to the Jedi Temple on Coruscant had been granted, she'd felt a deep sense of relief. That was for the best. Coruscant was the safest place to be.

And her time before being a Jedi? She had been dropped at the Temple mere days after her birth, so there was no *before the Order* for her. There was only the Order and Coruscant.

The idea of having to go back out in the galaxy gave Indara pause. What if she was no longer the Jedi the Order needed her to be? She had only been knighted a year ago, and at twenty-six she felt like the galaxy was more confusing than it had ever been.

"Jedi Knight Indara, please step forward." Jedi Master Oppo Rancisis, his long white hair tidied up into a bun on the top of his head, beckoned Indara closer with a taloned hand. Master Yoda and Master Yaddle sat on either side of him. Master Niko Jiro, a slim human with pale skin and a halo of wild, dark curls, was the only other Jedi High Council Member in attendance. They gave Indara a kind smile of encouragement. The remaining seats sat empty.

Indara stepped into the center of the room, folding her hands in front of her so that she could better channel the inner peace that befitted a Jedi and not the swirling mass of nerves her midsection had become. She took a deep breath and let it out. "Masters, I await your request."

Indara could feel all the eyes in the room upon her, the energy of the Council's gazes crackling across her skin. But the feeling only gave her strength. She was worried, but she could do this. They had chosen her for a reason, had sent for *her* over all the other Jedi Knights assigned to any number of tasks within the main Temple. She could show them she was worthy. Because she was.

The Jedi High Council did not make mistakes.

"Called you here, we have, for an important reason," Master Yoda said, nodding as he looked to his colleagues. "Jedi Master Vernestra Rwoh."

Indara blinked. She had heard the name before. Of course she had. There were few Jedi—from the smallest youngling to the most ambitious master—who did not know the name Vernestra Rwoh. She was a force unto herself, dedicated and calm, her exploits legendary.

"I— Did you want me to research Master Rwoh's most recent log entries?" Indara was surprised at the sense of disappointment she felt. Had she really wanted to be out in the galaxy again, courting danger in the name of the greater good? Her uncertainty about her own emotions was surprising, but at least if she had to be stuck in the Jedi Temple, she would be spending her time doing something exciting. Vernestra Rwoh was a Wayseeker, out in the galaxy doing as the Force willed. Her reports were sent to the Temple at irregular intervals, and Indara had spent some of her own personal time reading through the missives as though they were the latest entry in a holodrama. Just hearing the name conjured up images of Vernestra Rwoh in her younger days, fighting pirates, liberating planets from despots, helping with harvests, saving innocents, just about anything one could think of. Even for a Mirialan—a people who lived much longer lives than humans—Vernestra had accomplished a lot.

And if the Jedi High Council wanted her to spend her time summarizing the exploits of one of the greatest Jedi of their time, well... she would. Happily.

Indara had once wanted to be a Wayseeker, but she'd given up on that idea following the tragedy that had brought her back to Coruscant. And now it felt unlikely. After all, how could the Order trust her to her own devices after what had happened on Seswenna?

It had been silly to think that she was being assigned to a mission. She was becoming an accomplished archivist. Though it had been only a year, Indara was beginning to believe she belonged in the library, not out jaunting about the galaxy.

"No, child," Master Yaddle said with a small, indulgent laugh. "We don't want you to *research* her. We want you to *fetch* her from her current location and bring her back to Coruscant."

Indara blinked. She was smart. Quick. Her current supervisor had even praised the way she was able to pivot so effectively from one idea to the next within an analysis. She was far from ignorant.

But in that moment, she felt incredibly behind.

"You want me to go find a Jedi Master?" Indara said. She tried to keep the skepticism from her voice. "I . . . wouldn't it be easier to just send her a message to return?"

A chorus of laughter erupted from the Jedi Council. "The first thing you should know about Vernestra Rwoh is that she is not easily swayed from her path," Jedi Master Oppo Rancisis said. Indara did not know if that meant they had sent her a request to return and she had ignored it, or if they just thought a face-to-face request was a better route. "We have a matter that needs her personal attention, and the timing is urgent."

Indara nodded. "I understand. I thank you for thinking of me." Emotions warred within her: fear, excitement, worry. But she swallowed them all down. She didn't really want to go, but she was a Jedi. Her desires mattered very little in her service to the Order. She would simply do the same as she did when setting on any other task: try her best and hope the effort was sufficient.

Indara stood a little straighter, looking around the room so that she could remember this moment later when it came time to write in her personal datalog. "When do I leave?"

"Right now," Master Yaddle said, climbing from her seat and gesturing for Indara to follow her. "Come, I will show you to your assigned Vector and see you off."

Chapter Three

The meeting with the Council of Elders on Cerifisis was not going the way anyone had hoped.

I leaned against the wall and tried to remain unobtrusive, but my patience was wearing thin. While I understood the need for politics—some might even say I was exceptionally good at them—I had no patience for lying.

And everyone in the room was being as honest as a dockhand trying to sell a recently crashed hauler.

We had returned to Norna, the capital city of Cerifisis, after fully tending to the injured and dead. Besides the driver of one of the haulers, there had been no appreciable casualties, just a few deceased pirates. And while that was sad, as any loss of life was, they had chosen their path and walked it to the inevitable end. Which was all anyone could ask. The driver of the hauler had been cut down needlessly, cruelly. I could not feel the same level of regret for the pirates' end as I would for a person earning an honest living. I had learned in my time in the galaxy that guilt was best reserved for the things I regretted, and I did not regret defending the lives of the drivers and ensuring that provisions got to the hungry people who needed them.

Plus, there were other, more pressing matters to attend to. Such as the matter of someone within the government working with the Strafes to steal necessary supplies.

And so far, no one seemed to have any idea who it could be. Or rather, it could have been any one of the people within the room.

"Okay, let's try this again," Mayor Lansa said, pinching the bridge of her nose. The mayor was the polar opposite of her brother Kavil. Where Kavil was pale and prone to temper, Lansa was dark-skinned and calm, her full lips usually pursed in contemplation as she listened to and analyzed what was happening around her. Upon our first meeting, I thought she would have made an excellent Jedi: calm, deliberate, generous. She was a farmer and loved growing things, and she had been trying to get the Council of Elders, the primary ruling body on Cerifisis, to focus more on investing in agricultural infrastructure and less on defense. And now, with the success of the pirates, her previous ideas hung over the gathering like a cloud of smugness, even though Mayor Lansa had not said out loud the *I told you so* we could all feel. The Council of Elders had been wrong to ignore Lansa's lobbying for more growing pens, especially since their defense spending had not had any impact on their ability to stop the Strafes. It was turning out that no amount of weaponry could help a starving population, especially when they were not particularly good at wielding it.

"We told only this council and a handful of members of the security team the plans for the most recent shipment, including the route the delivery haulers would take," Lansa said, her dark gaze landing on each of the elders around the table. "So it is reasonable to deduce that either one of you shared this information with a subordinate or one of you is working with the Strafes."

The Council of Elders began shouting denials and misdirection. Normally, I eschewed participating in politics like this unless I was asked directly. I was good at politics, but that did not mean I enjoyed participating in them. These were local matters, and I felt it to be more prudent to keep my own counsel on such things, especially if I was unfamiliar with local mores. I had in the past witnessed how outsiders could influence local opinion, and the resulting fallout was never good. The last thing I wanted was for an errant comment of mine to lead to a future war. Extreme, yes, but that was exactly what had happened on Genetia more than a century ago.

A wise Jedi knew their history and learned from it.

In most cases, local politics quickly became a non-issue. I would wash my hands of the matter until the residents came to a decision, or provide insight if asked to weigh in. If I could help execute their chosen plan, I would do so until all parties involved were satisfied. And once the matter was settled, I would meditate on my next destination until I had a new location in hand, as revealed by the Force.

But in this case, the government—or at least someone within it—*was* the problem, and either way, Mayor Lansa had asked me to observe the meeting. Cerifisis elected their ruling council by region, each rural enclave voting for an elder. The term was a title only, as anyone old enough to join the planetary protection forces was eligible to run for office. And so it was colloquially known as the Council of Elders.

There were four of them, each representing one of the cardinal directions: Sera Wra from the north, a human man with snow-white hair and pale skin; Hudor Plinkythuj from the south, an ill-mannered Siniteen man with a permanent sneer who thought he was too smart to have to deal with anyone else's agenda; Panaya Po representing the east, a brown-skinned human woman with waist-length black hair and a friendly smile that seemed about as genuine as counterfeit credits; and Joleena Wasterna, a lavender-skinned Soikan woman much younger than the others, who represented the west, her silver hair braided into an ornate crown. Of the four, only Joleena seemed interested in actually working with the mayor. The rest radiated contempt and annoyance, and one did not need to be a Jedi to see that. It was clear in everything from their posture to the tone of their words when they spoke.

The mayor was elected by all the people of Cerifisis, but a few conversations with residents made it clear that the power rested in the city:

The entire population of the planet was less than a quarter million, and more than half of those people lived in Norna and its immediately adjacent areas. The mayor was the only one who could singularly veto the workings of the council, although any measure she vetoed could be raised again and put forward to a popular vote, a process that took place monthly. So it was natural for there to be tension between the countryside and the city, as well as between the Council of Elders and Mayor Lansa.

Further complicating the matter was the fact that every single person in the room, including Mayor Lansa and her brother Kavil, was being deceptive, as it usually went with politics. Part of Lansa's request that I attend the meeting was for me to evaluate how honest participants were being, and the short answer was not very truthful at all. But the longer answer was of course more complicated.

People who are familiar with the Jedi know that we sometimes have the ability, through the Force, to detect deception and even lies. But it wasn't like in the holos, where a Jedi detective could show up, read a suspect's mind, and then know exactly what happened. It was more about feeling out the truth, as though the flow of the Force ebbed and flowed differently when a person lied. The challenge was trying to figure out what was causing the ebb and flow. Because it could be *anything*.

And when it came to politics, the truth was always fungible.

So the more Mayor Lansa and the council yelled about grain taxes and land allotments, the harder it was to figure out who—if anyone—in the room was actually working with the pirates. Because a lie is only easy to uncover within people who value the truth.

And I was starting to suspect that no one in the room was particularly enamored with honesty.

"You bring a Jedi in here and then accuse us of treachery," said Elder Plinkythuj, a vein in his large head pulsing rhythmically, further highlighting the gyri and sulci visible through his skull. He wasn't nearly as put out as he was pretending, but the performance was much better than a few of the holodramas I'd watched in my life. "Why can't she just tell us who in here is lying?"

"Because you all are," I said, not bothering to hold my tongue any longer. Perhaps I'd been spending too much time with J-6, but I found my patience for their petty drama at an end. "We have been at this for nearly two hours, and in that time not a single one of you has been entirely truthful. My goal here is not to decide whether the northern wastes should be leased to an offplanet licensee, as you all seem so keen to discuss. I merely want to help you feed your population, and startlingly, no one else seems overly concerned with the people on this planet who are starving. So, Mayor Lansa, with your permission?"

Lansa was holding her head in her left hand by this point, her elbow resting on the arm of her chair. Her posture was no act. She was completely out of tolerance for her colleagues, despair in every line of her body. We had spoken at length about her feelings on the matter. Of everyone in the room, she was the one person I knew cared as much about the lost cargo as I did.

But it was with great effort that she nodded and waved, giving me the go-ahead. "Please, Master Vernestra. I do believe my attempts have met with failure."

When I had suggested pretending to use my Jedi abilities to find the traitor within the government, Lansa had been aghast. I understood lying to one's associates was bad form, but so was causing starvation. My suggestion had been to give the Council of Elders a show alluding to the powers of a Jedi. So few people knew what we could really do.

Stories of Jedi flying through the air like birds or teleporting from one place to the next were common, especially the farther one got from Coruscant. The reality was that the Jedi Order was not nearly as widespread as it had been in my youth. Many of the temples abandoned the last few decades hadn't been rebuilt, and the Order had begun to turn its attention from the frontier to the home front, preferring to focus efforts on those planets that were active members of the Republic. The effect was twofold: Those who knew the strength and honor of the Jedi were all too happy to have our help, and those who had never met a Jedi formulated outrageous ideas about our abilities, the most pervasive of which was the ability to compel a person to do something they did not want to do.

You Jedi and your mind tricks was an epithet hurled at me repeatedly, and it didn't seem to matter what the truth was. People were wont to believe what they wanted.

So why not use that to my advantage?

I took no joy in the deception. Okay, maybe it was a *little* fun. But I truly was primarily concerned with finding my way to the truth. It was a tactic I had used with younglings a few times over my career: The easiest way to find a liar was to convince them you already knew they were being deceptive. After that, their defenses would crumble with a single nudge, like spun sugar.

I stepped away from the wall I had been standing next to and made a slow circle around the outside of the table where the elders sat, letting my gaze fall and then linger on them one by one. The emotions in the room immediately spiked, and I had barely completed my circuit when there was a sound of frustration.

"Wait," Elder Joleena Wasterna said, the Soikan woman jumping to her feet. Her purple cheeks took on a ruddy hue, and she looked around the table in a combination of fear and anger. "This is unnecessary. No one has come forward to tell you who has turned traitor, because we all have."

I blinked. Now *that* was a surprise. Even to me.

The commotion around the table erupted once more, but at this point, Mayor Lansa had had enough. She leapt to her feet, slamming her hands down on the table at the same moment as the voices around her began to rise. "*Silence!*" Mayor Lansa said, her voice carrying above the conversation. "Wasterna, since you seem to be the only elder inclined to honesty in this moment, why don't you elucidate for us all."

The Soikan woman took a single worried look around the table before clearing her throat. "A few months ago, after the first shipment went missing, I got a message sent to my office. It said that I could ensure my people were fed if I shared what I knew about the upcoming shipments and the relevant security measures. I ignored it, of course. But then the shipment went missing the month after that and again after that. I noticed that the people in the eastern settlements still had plenty to eat. I asked Panaya about it, and she said that I shouldn't be so foolhardy—"

"You foolish girl. Shut your mouth now before you ruin us all," Panaya Po said, her indulgent smile turning brittle. Her body tensed even though she still reclined in her chair.

"—and that it was better that my people are fed than starve to ensure that the layabouts in the capital are fed," Joleena finished, her expression tortured. "So I responded to the message and shared information that would have been considered classified. And the next day, a food shipment was dropped in our gathering hall. No one knew where it came from or who left it there."

Joleena sank back into her seat, and there was a sense of relief on her face. Lansa looked around the table slowly, her expression landing on one elder and then the next, until they had all withered a bit under her glare.

"Is this true?" Lansa asked, her voice deadly even, a blade wrapped in softest velvet. "Have you *all* been tipping off the pirates? Sharing our defensive plans and ensuring our failure?"

The deafening silence spoke volumes.

Lansa shook her head slowly and began to laugh, the sound riding an edge of hysteria. "You've killed us. You've killed us all. How long do you think you can live out in the rough without power or fuel delivery from here in the capital? The lack of rations is having a detrimental impact on our workforce. People are unable to work because they are hungry, and the lack of nutrition is leading to higher rates of illness. I don't have enough droids to run the power grid. I'll have to enforce rolling down wattage beginning next week. During the hottest part of the hot season."

Lansa began to pace, as dangerous as a vollka sensing prey. "What will your people do when they have no cooling centers? No water pumped to them? And no food, because I will make sure you don't get another shipment of rations until everyone in Norna has been fed threefold for your treachery?"

The Council of Elders was deathly silent, and I wondered if Lansa actually had the power to do such a thing. I realized she must. Why else would the elders look like they were about to be ill? Lansa's words were no idle threat.

"This is the worst thing that could have happened to Cerifisis," Lansa said, falling back into her chair. "A government run by selfish fools."

"Well, it's actually not as bad as it could be," I said. I hadn't moved during the past few moments, enjoying the drama in a way I usually eschew. But honestly, it was a turn of events I hadn't expected. And when you are nearing a century of life, surprises are rare and worth savoring.

"How, Jedi?" Lansa said, her voice dripping with defeat. "How can this be a good thing?"

"Because we now know exactly where the pirates will be. Without the information from the council, it seems as though they would have been easily foiled. And now we will tell them whatever we wish," I said, looking at the elders so that the message was clear: *They would make amends whether they wanted to or not.* "And this time we will be waiting and ready to halt their villainy once and for all."

Chapter Four

Indara shifted in the cramped confines of the Jedi Vector and tried once more to find a way to get comfortable as the ship traveled through hyperspace. She hadn't flown a Vector in years. As an archivist, she had no reason to fly the fighters, and before that Indara's master had always opted for something more utilitarian, a choice she agreed with. She found the ships to be touchy and too responsive, great in battle but excessive for most other applications. It didn't mean she couldn't fly one. It just meant that she would much rather fly a hopper or even a smaller shuttle.

But the Council had thought it would be wise for her to fly the ship. "Difficulties, Vernestra may have found," Master Yoda had said, and the rest of the Council had agreed. It seemed common knowledge that Jedi Master Vernestra Rwoh was the type who found trouble on the regular, which just made Indara even more anxious to meet the woman. What stories could she tell, of the Nihil conflict and the Darnaburny Civil War and so many other historical events? It was one thing to hear about those things from Jedi like Master Yoda or Master Oppo Rancisis, who could lecture about the events but hadn't always been there in the midst of the fighting. But Vernestra Rwoh had been on the front lines for both events and dozens more besides. Surely she would talk about history with a bit more . . . expertise?

Or maybe not. What if looking at tragedies with a dispassionate gaze was part of living for so long? Humans never reached the lifespans of Mirialans, so their perspectives were much different. Even so, Indara had interviewed so many other Jedi about so many things, but never one who was promoted to Knighthood at age fifteen.

The longer Indara thought about what Vernestra Rwoh might be like, the more nervous she became. And, coincidentally, the further from the truth her imaginings strayed.

Indara dozed. She woke, watched a few holos, ate a grain-and-protein bar, and then meditated until the ping of the ship preparing to exit hyperspace pulled her from her thoughts. Once the serene blue streaming past the viewport snapped to black, Indara began the process of dropping from the hyperspace ring so that she could visit the small nearby planet that was her first stop: Haileap.

Which was also, coincidentally, Vernestra Rwoh's first assignment as a young Jedi Knight. Indara had read through the entirety of Vernestra's histories long ago. When she'd mapped out the fastest route to the Jedi Master's last known location, Cerifisis, and noted that there were two choices for a rest stop—Haileap and Eiram—the choice had been clear. And although Indara had long wanted to see Eiram and one of the birthplaces of the Nihil conflict, she opted for visiting a place Master Rwoh had once lived and worked. She wasn't sure why, except she had a feeling it might give her an idea of the best way to approach the Jedi when they finally met.

Plus, there was no way Indara could have made the flight to Cerifisis directly without at least one stop to use the restroom.

She set the Vector down on a landing pad among tall marblewood trees, their swirled bark a beautiful contrast of light and dark, before following a dried-sediment path to the dockyards. The architecture was in an older style, muddy-looking domes and sandy-hued exteriors, with storefronts surrounding a central courtyard that hosted a meager number of vendor stalls. Port Haileap had not grown much in the decades since the former Jedi temple was first established there, the entire shopping complex comprising a couple of gambling dens, a few eateries, and a Republic storage house for confiscated cargo. There were living quarters as well, and a few other buildings that didn't outwardly proclaim their uses, but for the most part it was the kind of place where people stopped only long enough to refuel before heading on their way.

Indara used the bathroom and went to the nearest market to buy some fresh fruit before wandering the space and seeing what little there was to see. It wasn't much, and less than an hour after her arrival, Indara realized that the stop had been silly beyond the ability to stretch her legs. There would've been far more to see on Eiram. Still, there was something charming about the place, and Indara realized that perhaps for all of her trepidation she had missed this just a bit, the simple act of experiencing something *new*.

She was heading back to her ship when an Ugnaught wearing an ugly floral housedress and an apron waved her down from the door of a gambling hall. "Jedi! Will you try your luck? Kimnol's Gambling Hall has the best odds on rykestra and the tastiest food in all of Port Haileap."

Indara waved the woman off with an apologetic smile, but the Ugnaught was not so easily swayed. "Perhaps you would like to hear tales of days gone by and the Jedi who once defended this wonderful locale? Or maybe I can tempt you with a frosty mug of chapa ale."

Indara was about to refuse once more, but then she saw the Ugnaught look into the tavern with an expression somewhere between worry and fear, her brows drawn down and the set of her lips beneath her wrinkled, upturned nose conveying the emotions. Indara followed the woman's gaze but could see nothing within the gloom of the establishment, the light of the courtyard penetrating only a meter or so past the threshold. Still, it seemed like there might be some kind of trouble.

Indara smiled wide, her face hurting from the effort. She wanted to project calm and a sort of cluelessness so that if there was trouble, no one would expect her to handle it. "An ale sounds delightful."

"Wonderful!" the Ugnaught said, clapping her hands together and gesturing for Indara to follow. "Come, come! I have the perfect table for you."

The Ugnaught led Indara to a booth in the corner and rapped the table's surface, which was not the cleanest. She noticed and hastily wiped it down with a bar rag tucked into the pocket of her apron before gesturing toward the seat once more. "Sit, sit! I will bring you ale and my famous root vegetable pastry. Today we have gerla tubers and bantha cheese."

Before Indara could object to the food—she was hungry but rarely ate dairy—the woman was gone, leaving Indara to sit back in the booth and take in her surroundings.

The tavern was dark, only a few chemical lamps chasing away the gloom. The place smelled of old ale and the secretions of numerous species, with the scent of cooked food overlaying all of it. It was no different from any other dockside bar. There were a few gambling tables in the back, the rykestra the Ugnaught had mentioned as well as sabacc and other games Indara was unfamiliar with. A droid played music in one corner, the hammered dulcimer kicking up a racket that wasn't the most pleasing but also wasn't terrible. The most interesting items in the space were an extremely well-dressed man and a disheveled woman arguing in low voices in a booth along one wall. They were so out of place in the tavern that it was hard not to notice them.

The pale-skinned human man's robes cascaded down his body, as though he'd draped the fabric on his shoulders and let it decide how it wished to hang from there. As he moved, talking with his hands to his companion, the material shifted as well so that it looked to be a living creature wrapping his body. It was clearly an expensive garment, and it only served to make his companion—a human woman with dark skin and a curly halo of artificially bright-blue hair—look even shabbier in her meknek's coveralls. From the tones of their voices, the two were arguing about something. Indara heard "Payment" and "You won't cheat me" but couldn't understand much more than that.

Were the pair the reason the Ugnaught had invited Indara into the tavern? That didn't make much sense. She saw little reason to intervene.

But she had no sooner completed this thought than the woman jumped to her feet, a blaster seeming to appear in her hand like magic.

"You son of a flower snake!" the woman yelled, her blaster leveled at the gentleman across from her in the booth. "You're trying to cheat me. I know what I got!"

The man didn't move, didn't even seem put out about having a blaster pointed at his face. If anything, he appeared amused by the turn of events, as though this had been one of many outcomes he had seen coming.

Whatever the man replied was drowned out by the ambient noise of the bar. He held his hands out in supplication, as though asking the woman to be reasonable, and the terrified look that came over her face had Indara sitting up straight and focusing in on the unusual couple. There was definitely something off.

The woman's eyes went wide, and she looked to the door. Indara followed her gaze just in time to see the entrance of a shaggy, ivory-hued Gigoran missing an eye. He held a repeating blaster in his massive, fur-covered arms. Indara could feel her own horror at seeing someone holding a weapon that was usually mounted to a landspeeder, and so in less than a breath she was on her feet drawing her lightsaber and reaching for the Force.

Time seemed to slow. Indara felt her robes swirl around her as she leapt into the space between the Gigoran and the rest of the bar, her connection to the Force crackling across her skin like a static shock. She had no sooner powered up the verdant blade of her lightsaber than the Gigoran began firing, not just at the woman arguing with the flamboyantly dressed man but at everyone else in the tavern as well.

Indara met the blaster bolts with the plasma blade of her lightsaber, sending the shots flying up and away harmlessly in a blur of green as she worked faster than she ever had before, each blaster bolt from the Gigoran's repeater a chance for someone to die. Indara had never wielded her lightsaber in such a manner before, and definitely had not used it defensively for the past year. But just because she was out of practice did not mean that she was untrained. She had spent far more time sparring and testing herself in the training rooms than any other Jedi Knight, and her muscles knew the drills, knew the movements. Her connection to the Force lent her enough foresight to anticipate where the next blaster bolt would go. Her blade was there at not just the right moment but also the correct *angle* so that the bolts harmlessly embedded themselves in the thick overhead beam that supported the ceiling.

It would have been far easier to just kill the attacker, but something in Indara balked at the wanton waste of a life. She did not know why the Gigoran was firing into the bar, and part of her craved an answer. But more than that, she didn't want to have to take a life unless she was forced to.

It took the Gigoran firing far too long to realize that he wouldn't be able to best the Jedi, and when the realization sank in, he roared and swung the barrel at her. Indara jumped backward before bringing her lightsaber up and across the barrel, cutting it in half and melting the opening. When he lunged at Indara, she held her hand up and pushed, sending him tumbling backward out the door.

There was a rush of air, and Indara turned her head to see the well-dressed man running from the bar after the Gigoran, looking over his shoulder wide-eyed as they went. Indara turned to where the woman had stood to see her gone. The only sign that she'd ever been there was a blue wig on the floor, a disguise of some sort.

Indara stood alone in the bar, blinking. A burning smell came from above, and she looked up to see a few dozen blaster burns across the ceiling and the main support beam, telling her the last few moments had not been some kind of fever dream.

The Ugnaught returned at that moment, appearing from wherever she'd gone to ground when the shooting began. She wore an approximation of a smile on her face, but there was clear relief in her eyes. She carried a tray with a frosty mug of some foamy drink and a plate with a large pastry that smelled too good to pass up. "For you, Jedi! On the house."

Chapter Five

After the council meeting finally ended, I made my way back to my quarters in a nearby guesthouse. All I wanted was a hot shower, a few quiet moments in my darkened room to meditate, and my bed. I had a massive headache from listening to the politicians argue all afternoon, and my robes were still covered in blue dust from my adventures the day before. I longed for clean clothes and a little peace and quiet.

Which was why I couldn't quite swallow my groan of disappointment when I stepped into my sitting room and saw the owner of the guesthouse there, waiting patiently for me while J-6 gave the woman the droid equivalent of a disapproving glare.

"Oh good, Vern, you're back," J-6 said. The droid pointed a rose-gold finger at the owner of the guest quarters, an older Togruta woman named Capaskie who was a bit too nosy for my taste but still not the worst landlord I'd ever had. There wasn't much in the sitting room: a low gray sofa, a matching chair, and a table that took up the rest of the space. Capaskie had parked her generous frame on the couch. J-6 continued, "It seems you have an urgent message, but she won't tell me what it is, because, and I quote, 'Droids can make mistakes.' "

J-6 rounded on me, pointing to herself in indignation that I knew for a fact droids could not feel. "When have I *ever* made a mistake?" she asked.

I forced a smile and waved her off. "Well, I'm here now. So the Lady Capaskie can give me the message herself."

Capaskie stood and gave me a holo-emitter with an inclination of her head. "I'll send over dinner when you're ready." And then she took her leave without once turning to look at J-6, her shoulders stiff in the way most people were after a run-in with my droid. J-6 was not what I would have called sociable, and while it worked for me, it was definitely a problem for others more often than I liked to admit.

When she was gone, I exhaled loudly. "Jay-Six. I'm going to need you to take about twenty percent off the top."

"Twenty percent off the top of *what*?" J-6 demanded.

I moved past her to place the emitter on the table in the middle of the sitting room, taking the seat Capaskie had vacated only moments earlier. "The attitude. You know, at some point someone somewhere is going to realize you're a bit freewheeling for a machine and start asking questions about why you're capable of self-determination and emotions. And I'm not sure what they'll do when they hear the answers."

J-6 snorted, or at least gave her approximation of a snort, a sound she somehow made with her vocabulator to convey disdain. "Who's going to mess with me, the Techno Union? I'd like to see them try."

I ignored her and focused on activating the holo-emitter.

Immediately, Master Yaddle appeared, and I sighed as her blue-hued hologram began to speak. "Vernestra. It is time to come home."

I waved my hand over the holo to immediately stop the recording and took a deep breath, letting it out slowly. "Jay-Six. Make sure the ship is ready to leave at a moment's notice. Rations fully stocked. Fueled up. Every update the navicomputer may need. And I am asking you to do that because I know you are a good friend who has never made a mistake as long as I've known you." It did me no good to have J-6 in a mood.

She made a chuffing sound like laughter. "You are still too soft, Jedi Master Vernestra Rwoh," she said, then left for the dockyard to do as I asked. What she meant by that, I had no idea.

I waved my hand again, and Master Yaddle began speaking once more. "I know you must have gotten at least a couple of these messages."

It was true. There had been at least three messages that I had received and discarded, and probably more besides that. One of the benefits of traveling was it was sometimes difficult to receive messages, especially if one were to, say, deactivate the receiver on one's shipboard comm.

From the emitter on the table, Yaddle continued. "You may be stubborn, but you are also a stickler for protocol. So I will reiterate what I've told you in every other message I have sent your way: You must return to the Jedi Temple on Coruscant. You have been away for nearly a decade now, with only the briefest of stops on Coruscant. It is time for you to return. You're a Jedi Master, and the Order has need of your experience and expertise here."

My stomach was in knots. I took a deep breath and let it out. I didn't know I could still be nervous at my age, yet here I was, as anxious as the morning I underwent my Jedi trials. Nothing like a summons from the Jedi High Council to make me feel fifteen again. Sweat slicked my palms, and I rubbed them down the legs of my robes and tried to focus on what Master Yaddle was saying.

"The Council had hoped that you would come to the conclusion it was time to return to Coruscant on your own. Indeed, we have been more than lenient at this point. We have been downright *indulgent.* We are sending a Jedi Knight named Indara to come find you. If you do not return with Indara, you will be disobeying a direct order from the Council. See you soon, Vernestra."

After a moment, the message began to replay, and the pounding in my head took up a two-beat counterpoint. I rubbed my temples for a moment before standing, stripping off my outer robes, dropping them next to the front door, and reaching for the Force as I lay back so that I was levitating a scant meter above the floor. I let the Force wash over me like a spring-fed pool, using it to anchor myself in place while I pondered Master Yaddle's words.

I'd discovered the odd use of the Force while visiting a trio of Jedi on Krugan, a frozen landscape with only a few months of temperate weather each year. They complained about how cold the floors could be and jokingly said they never meditated without levitating. I didn't really consider floating and breathing meditating, because it still required an active connection to my body that I found to be different from my meditation within the Force. But the posture was great for deeply thinking about a problem.

Such as returning to the Jedi Temple on Coruscant.

When I was promoted to master, I had some idea of the requirements of the rank, but I would be lying if I said I was ready to step into the role with my whole heart. Teaching, I enjoyed. I'd even enjoyed instructing younglings, though they could be incredibly silly creatures. In addition, I'd had a number of Padawans over the years, each of them different and yet the same in their devotion to learning. And I'd enjoyed mentoring them, right up until my last Padawan, whom I'd failed in so many ways . . .

No matter what other tasks I'd undertaken—and there had been many—the memory of that failure rose up again and again until I'd finally decided to take some time away from the Order.

It had been a good time to step away. I did not enjoy the many ways politics interfered with the pure intentions of being a Jedi, and I found its encroachments stifling. The Republic was a demanding mistress. What had been a useful relationship during the Nihil conflict had morphed into something I found less mutually beneficial, and although the Order did not work closely with the Senate on every matter, it seemed that the Republic wanted more access to the work of the Jedi than I was comfortable with. I did not see that changing in the foreseeable future. I didn't mind advising on strong security plans when I was working with a small rural village, trying to protect against marauders. I had a much bigger problem when it was a kingdom trying to put down righteous dissent.

The Jedi were at their best when they were free to be the light in the galaxy, and although I was not nearly as old as many of the elders on the Jedi High Council, I could feel the shift in the winds. So if protecting the vulnerable in the galaxy was no longer a priority for the Order, I would continue to make it mine. I would be the light my former master, Stellan Gios, had always urged me to be. And the Force would provide my path.

But here was the end of my freedom—and delivered by Master Yaddle, the Jedi who had urged me to go spend time Wayseeking when she sensed the restlessness in my heart so many years ago. And the Jedi Council was right: There were things I could do to help the Order on Coruscant. Still, I chafed at the thought of working with the Republic: attending cocktail parties and elegant dinners in celebration of that senator or this recently passed act, endless meetings and advising, and so much double-talk that I couldn't be sure if we were discussing politics or selling rights to swampland. It didn't matter that I excelled in such situations, able to navigate them in a way that promised nothing while everyone left satisfied. My talents were better used in *direct* action. Physical sparring, not verbal. And now for nearly a decade, a time that was both too long and too short, I had done my best for the people of the galaxy every day by being present.

How could I do that when I returned to Coruscant? No one cared about another farm bill passing. Most times those new laws and funding never even helped the average person, only the politicians and corporations who'd been advocating for them in the first place.

I took a deep breath and let it out. I could be upset, but in the end nothing would change. So I had to make sure that I could do one last thing to spread light, and that would be defeating the Strafes and breaking the pirates' hold over Cerifisis.

I put my foot down and levered myself upright, gathering up my robes so that they could be washed. Tomorrow we would find the Strafes, and the pirates would regret stealing food rations from the people of Cerifisis. Already a plan was brewing, one that would be quick and effective and result in the least amount of suffering.

The Strafes would rue the day they stole food from hungry children. The Force would see to that.

And then I would return to whatever was waiting for me on Coruscant.

Chapter Six

Nilsson Summach, an unrepentant spicehead and casual weapons dealer, leaned back in the soft couch in the gathering area of his pleasure cruiser and listened as his underlings tried to explain how they'd botched the easiest deal to fall into their laps in years. It was such a preposterous story that Nilsson was having trouble following it. And the amount of spice he'd smoked in the past hour had nothing to do with it.

"Wait, okay, back to what you just told me," Nilsson said, tapping out the spent char of his pocket pipe and refilling it with a sparkling lavender powder from a vial. Lake Country Daydreams, it was called. He was going to need the pleasant haze of a quality Naboo spice to get through the load of bantha fodder the Gigoran and the human were peddling.

Well, just the human. The Gigoran didn't talk all that much.

"You went to Haileap like I asked," Nilsson said, weighing each word as it came out of his mouth, as though speech had form and shape as well as sound. "You had a drink. Was it an ale?"

Dashon, the pale-skinned human of the pair, blinked, not expecting the question. "Uh, no. I had wine."

"What kind?" Nilsson asked.

"What?" Dashon looked at the Gigoran, as if the big furry bloke were going to help him dig his way out of this one. Nilsson already knew that Hinra didn't like Dashon. It was why he'd sent them together in the first place. People couldn't plot against you if they were too busy fighting.

"What. Kind. Of. Wine. Did. You. Get?" Nilsson said, packing the spice tight in the bowl of the pipe before putting the setup to the side. He had a feeling he was going to need it after the conversation was finished. He could already feel a fine temper welling up in his chest, burning like a bright sun.

"Oh, Pelisisi green. It was, uh, all that they had."

"Did you talk to the nice Ugnaught lady who runs the establishment? Orna?" Nilsson said, his gaze now locked on Dashon. Nilsson knew his gaze was off-putting to humans. It was because his mother—one of his human father's many wives—had been half Kuranu, and he'd inherited her pupil-less eyes, though his were green. It was the only part of him that didn't appear human—his lank brown hair and brown, freckled skin were utterly unremarkable—and in moments like this, his people sometimes forgot that there were two halves that made up his whole. He was a complicated man who lived his life one day at a time. And today was not about getting ripped on spice.

Today was about all the money he'd just lost on a very important, very *simple* deal.

"Um, no, we did not. We met the contact, tried to complete the exchange, and she balked," Dashon said, the words coming out in a rush. Beads of sweat had appeared on his brow in the retelling, and Nilsson found them fascinating, the way they just sat on Dashon's face, giving away his nervousness.

"Mmm-hmmm. Did you think to offer the woman more money? She destroyed a lab that cost me more than the entire worth of your planet. Do you really think I was concerned about getting a *bargain* at this point?"

"Uh, ah, we tried that. But then she was just mad, and she pulled a blaster, and then the big guy here came in and—"

"Did you skip a part?" Nilsson asked, tapping his chin. "Last time you told me something about a Jedi."

Dashon swallowed, the prominent nodule in his throat bobbing. "Yes! But that was after. There was. A Jedi. Like you said, a human woman, pale skin, dark hair. When the Gigoran came in with the repeating blaster, she was there going *whoom whoom whoom*!"

Dashon began to act like he was swinging one of the laser swords the Jedi preferred, and Nilsson decided he was out of patience for the ostentatious man. He'd been hired as a favor, and he'd been nothing but ballast weighing them down. It was time to shed some deadweight.

It helped that Nilsson didn't like him very much.

"The Gigoran's name is Hinra, you waste of oxygen." Nilsson waved to Hinra, and the Gigoran moved incredibly fast, grabbing Dashon by the neck and breaking it in a single fluid movement. That was why Nilsson preferred to hire Gigorans. They didn't talk so much, and they were fast for their size. And of all the help he had ever hired, Hinra was the most ruthless and the most loyal.

"Was he telling the truth?" Nilsson asked, picking up his pipe once more when Dashon's body stopped twitching. Hinra nodded and gave an affirmative in chirps and growls. The Gigoran preferred to go without a vocalizer, which was fine because Nilsson knew enough to get by. And what the giant, white-furred man was saying was nothing good. Ruinous, even. Nilsson sighed.

"Grizela!" Nilsson yelled, and a beautiful Pantoran woman with a complex set of scrolling facial tattoos appeared, datapad held at the ready. She wore a skintight bodysuit in bright white, a lovely contrast with her blue skin, the filmy overdress making her look as though she were ready for a grand gala. It was a waste of a beautiful outfit, since no one but Nilsson would see it in their orbit around Haileap. And Nilsson might have been an unrepentant hedonist, but he never indulged in his appetites with his employees.

"Nilsson. How can I assist you? Is the spice not to your liking?" she said, before turning and seeing Dashon's prone body. "Ah. We need to hire again." She began to type on her datapad. "Should I reach out to some of my associates with the cartels?"

"No, we're going to stick to in-house promotions this time," Nilsson said with a sigh. He found the business part of his empire to be incredibly boring, which was why he left so much of it to Grizela. She had a much better head for such things.

"Ah, in that case, I recommend Londa from our team on Genetia. She's already en route after brokering a deal there and has been known to be quite handy with a blaster. But not trigger-happy, which I know is something you hate, Hinra," Grizela said, addressing that last part to the Gigoran standing nearby. He grunted in agreement.

"Fine. Have Londa meet Hinra on Haileap and see if we can find out where our scientist friend has gotten to. We need her for the next stage of distribution. And kill anyone she may have spoken to. I can't have competition out there peddling knockoffs when we have the real thing. And wear your kriffing vocalizer this time, Hinra. You're going to have to talk to Orna, throw a few credits her way, make nice. Her tavern is a good place for wheeling and dealing, and I won't have one of my few spots burned because you and the space refuse there got it all shot up. *Alafahimntich?*" Nilsson asked, switching to his own native language for the confirmation. He wanted Hinra to know he was serious.

The Gigoran bowed and was beginning to leave when Nilsson stopped him. "Hey. Take that with you and drop it out the refuse chute. I'm not trying to have my ship stink like dead human."

Hinra bowed dramatically, making Nilsson laugh. But the Gigoran slung Dashon's corpse over his shoulder and left the gathering area, following the order despite his wordless sarcasm.

Grizela still stood nearby. "Anything else?"

Nilsson nodded. "Yeah. Get a file together with everything we know about that scientist. Friends, enemies, anyone she's talked to in the past year since she took our contract. If we can't find her, we're going to have to take drastic measures. I won't let this project be ruined, you understand? This is my family's legacy."

Grizela nodded and departed, leaving Nilsson alone. There were only the soft sounds of a water feature plinking away sonorously in the corner, a device Grizela had acquired to calm his nerves. It had the opposite effect. It made him feel like each moment of his life was dripping away, wasted. Thinking about time made Nilsson anxious. Of course, that could have just been the lack of spice in his system.

Nilsson lit the bowl of spice with a fire iron before hitting a button on the command panel in the arm of his recliner. There came a hiss and then the crackle of static as the call connected before a human man appeared in shades of hologram blue.

"Nilly! What is it, friend? You have called at a most inauspicious time."

"Garn. Your cousin, Dashon, ran off with some of my best guns and a kilo of spice," Nilsson said, the lie effortless. He was annoyed that he'd done a favor for a friend and, in the end, lost time and effort. There was a price to such things. Garn should understand that. It was silly to vouch for family when they were inept, but Garn had never had to do much to make his way in the galaxy. It was past time he learned about opportunity cost.

Nilsson had given him an opportunity, and now there was a cost involved.

He took a deep puff of the pipe, holding the smoke in his lungs until his eyes watered and the colors in his vision started to shift. Garn said nothing during the entire pause, and when Nilsson exhaled, he smiled. Garn's fear nearly crackled through the distance. The man might be a fool, but he understood that Nilsson's mirth never preceded anything good.

"So tell me, Senator. What are you going to do to make it up to me?"

Chapter Seven

When I woke the next morning, I was ready for whatever the day brought me. I sent J-6 to speak to Lansa as soon as I rose, asking for a meeting at the mayor's earliest convenience. An idea had been percolating in my brain, but over my evening meal it had sprung into my mind fully formed, and now that I could see all the moving parts, I knew exactly what needed to be done.

But I could not and would not do it alone.

When I rose, I practiced my forms, moving through them slowly at first to warm up and then quicker after my muscles were feeling loose. It was a routine I did every morning. I would usually go for a run once my muscles were warm, but today I needed to meditate. Center myself. The holo from the Council—and Yaddle's good-natured scolding therein—had unsettled me enough that I could sense I wouldn't be at my best today without recentering my thoughts and intentions and feelings. My actions were always deliberate, and I had always prided myself on being logical, even when my emotions were involved. I knew this sometimes led to people thinking I was cold or unemotional, and that outside perspective hadn't gotten any better as I'd gotten older.

Especially since I eschewed visiting Coruscant too often. But keeping myself grounded, centered, rational—well, it was why I'd been successful as a Jedi. The galaxy might tilt and sway with upheaval and change, but I—like the Force—was constant. An island in a raging sea.

When it came to failure or loss, I always acknowledged the emotion, let it wash over me, and grieved as I needed to. And then I put it aside, not letting it drive my actions. Some of the younger Jedi had taken that lesson to mean emotions and the connections they engendered were bad, and my heart hurt that they thought that cutting themselves off from connection was the way to be successful as a Jedi. Our connection with others gave us purpose as Jedi, but we could not let their fear become ours, and we could not let our personal worries drive our actions. That, to me, had always been the true meaning of the balance we Jedi strove toward: living without fear, loving and embracing the grief that ultimately came when such a strong connection was lost. The sweet and the bitter, forever entangled.

It was a simple lesson that was impossible to learn, and I had been trying for decades.

And for those times when the lesson was hard to remember, I bolstered my training through meditation. There was nothing like letting my body fall away and connecting to the cosmic Force to remind myself that I was nothing and everything all at once.

I did not want my worry over the Jedi High Council's emissary or my annoyance with Cerifisis's Council of Elders to impact my choices on that day, so a little focused meditation was in order. It wasn't the difference between success and failure, but it was the difference between turmoil and acceptance. No matter what happened today, I would accept it as every living creature must, but being centered meant that the outcome would not weigh on me in quite the same way.

That, of course, had not always been my perspective on things. But I was older and far wiser than I had once been. Or, at least, that was what I told myself.

But I had no sooner taken up my position in the courtyard behind my lodgings—legs crossed, eyes shut, breathing even, and the early-morning sun already punishingly hot—than I heard the door to my quarters open and close. I had expected the rhythmic clomping that signaled J-6's return from speaking with Lansa. What I had not expected were the soft footfalls that accompanied the droid's steps. I opened my eyes to see not just J-6 but also a Jedi Knight, a feminine human with pale skin and dark hair pulled back from her face haphazardly. She was somewhere between her late twenties and early thirties as far as I could tell—I was always uncertain when it came to human ages—but there was an air about her that made her seem younger. A confident veneer, but her movements betrayed an uncertainty, something awkward and hesitant. It was in every line of her body. She carried herself like she was unsure whether she should be or even deserved to be there, and her robes were incredibly pristine. Most Jedi had stains and fraying on their clothing, the marks of missions undertaken and completed. Her robes looked like they'd just been issued by the quartermaster, and she moved within them as though she wasn't used to their weight.

It surprised me. I had been expecting Yaddle to send someone with the demeanor of one who would not take no for an answer, a hardy tree of a Jedi—someone like Burryaga or Porter, who had been ancient even when I was a Padawan. Someone I knew from the old days.

But instead Yaddle and the Jedi High Council had sent a sapling.

Oh, this was going to be *fun*.

"Master Vernestra Rwoh," the young woman said, her voice carrying an emotion I couldn't name. Excitement? Nervousness? Annoyance? "I am Jedi Knight Indara. And I am here to escort you back to Coruscant at the request of the Jedi Council. You must come with me."

I smiled, a genuine, cheek-splitting expression. A bubble of laughter burbled up, and I had to clear my throat to keep it from fully escaping. Here I had been a bit worried that I would be forced to choose between my promise to the people of Cerifisis and my responsibilities to the

Order. But now that concern melted away. Indara was clearly a Jedi who *needed* adventure, who would benefit from helping me defeat the Strafes. The poor thing was so pale I wondered if they kept her down in the labs at the Temple. When was the last time she had used her lightsaber? It wasn't uncommon for some of the more scholarly Jedi to be incredibly rusty with their forms. Especially now that the galaxy as a whole was much more peaceful than it had been in my youth.

I almost owed the poor Jedi before me a bit of an escapade. A good story to share in her downtime at the tavern. Something that would be worth a few drinks for the telling. And if Yaddle asked why it had taken us so long to return to Coruscant, I would tell her just that.

I stood, feeling lighter than I had since getting Yaddle's holo. "Jedi Knight Indara. Have you ever fought pirates?"

The poor women blinked, her scowl instantaneous. "Of course. I'm a Jedi Knight, not a Padawan."

I tilted my head. Perhaps I had misread the woman. But I really didn't think so. There was something about her that felt untried; I just had to get to the root of it. "So why do your robes look so . . . untouched?"

She glanced down at her clothing and shrugged. "Because I'm an archivist? And I like my things to be tidy?"

"Not an excuse, but definitely a reason." I was intrigued by her. I had always liked puzzling out the unknown, and people were never the mystery they wanted to be.

I walked past Indara and J-6 into my quarters and picked up my robes from where they lay across the back of a chair. They were clean, meaning J-6 had actually laundered them without me having to ask. I turned toward the droid, who was watching the scene unfold with her arms crossed. "Jay-Six, were you able to get in touch with Lansa?"

"Yes. She's expecting you at any moment," the droid said.

"Feel like shooting pirates today?"

The droid groaned. Coming from a vocabulator, the sound was as disturbing as one might think, part wheeze and part low-voiced hum. "My holodrama comes on in an hour. Do you really need help?"

Indara's dark brows folded down together in confusion at the droid's snarky reply, and I gave J-6 my best smile. "I suppose not with Indara now here. Tender our thanks to the Lady Capaskie for her hospitality and pack my things. I'll meet you at the ship. We'll leave as soon as we've settled this problem with the pirates."

I turned back to Indara, who stood with her arms crossed. "You let your droid do as she pleases?" she asked. It was a valid question. There weren't many droids who could refuse a task. But there was something else to the question as well, a sort of defiance, as though she wanted to take control of the entire situation but wasn't sure how.

That was something I could work with.

"Sometimes the easier path is just that, easier," I said with a grin. "Let's go, Jedi Knight Indara. Today we are going to fight some pirates. Especially since it's long past time you got those robes dirty."

Chapter Eight

Indara crouched in the back of the covered hauler, sweat dripping along her brow and soaking her underarms, almost as distracting as the hum of annoyance she felt at having been pushed around by Jedi Master Vernestra Rwoh. Next to her, the Mirialan sat on the floor, eyes closed, legs crossed. The lantern keeping the space lit revealed that not a centimeter of Vernestra's chin-length hair was out of place. Indara couldn't even tell if the older Jedi could feel the heat or her pointed stares of dislike. She was pretty sure that the older woman didn't care what she thought one way or another. Vernestra looked cool, calm, and collected, while Indara felt like the Force was punishing her for some unknown infraction with heat and a bone-jarring ride atop an empty crate that had once held pickled fish.

Of course, there was also the small voice in the back of her mind that said this wasn't a punishment at all, but an exciting opportunity to work with a Jedi whose reputation bordered on heroic. That voice was quickly quashed when Indara recalled their conversation from a few hours before.

Were all Wayseekers so kriffing unlikable? Indara hoped not.

The plan for dealing with the Strafes was appallingly simple: The Jedi would ride in the back of the covered hauler while the next "cargo"—really just a bunch of empty shipping containers scrounged up from around the dockyards—was delivered. When the convoy was beset, they would let the Strafes take the shipment, allowing the Jedi to discover their hideout and stop them once and for all. When Indara had asked why they weren't hiding in one of the containers, Vernestra had condescendingly tapped one of the empty crates, which were quite small. She then launched into what could only be called a lecture about understanding pirates and the way they preferred to work. Apparently the Strafes liked to steal the haulers as well, dismantling them and selling the scavenged parts on the secondary market. When Indara had wondered why it was so hard to catch such localized pirates, Vernestra had explained that the security forces had tried the ruse before but the pirates hadn't attacked the convoy that day, warned away by one or all of the Council of Elders. This time they would convince the pirates that the shipment—off schedule and delivered by none other than Kavil, head of security—was larger and more valuable than any previous due to the increasing desperation of the city's populace.

As off-putting as Indara found Vernestra Rwoh, something about the way she carried herself was impressive, even imposing, though she was of an average height and build. Perhaps it was the way she answered every question as though the answer were obvious, or the way the six diamonds tattooed on the outside of her eyes in two lines of three crinkled when she was listening to someone speak, as though she was waiting for the inevitable lie. Or maybe it was the way a smile played across her lips when she found something amusing, even though the smile never quite broke free. Whatever it was, Indara wanted to find a way to bottle it for herself. But perhaps in a dose that was less obnoxious.

"How are you faring, Indara?"

Indara pulled herself from her musings to see Vernestra watching her, a single eyebrow arched. Indara forced a smile. "I'm brilliant."

"You're sweating."

"I'm human. We do that a lot," Indara said, letting out an exasperated sigh. There was a strange chuffing sound. Indara realized Vernestra was laughing.

"Mirialans sweat as well, but that is not what I meant. Do you know how to use the Force to help regulate your body temperature? I don't remember if they teach that at the Temple or not. It has been a while."

Indara shook her head, sweat dripping into her eyes. She rubbed it away with the back of her hand. "I don't think so. Besides, I have a feeling you're going to tell me anyway." She chafed at the idea that she was still a younger Jedi relying on Temple teachings. Sure, she hadn't been out on any missions for a while, but she was a Jedi Knight! Hadn't she just faced down a Gigoran with a repeating blaster and lived to tell?

Vernestra didn't seem to sense Indara's ire. Or if she did, she chose to ignore it. "Okay, here is what you are going to do," the elder Jedi said. "First, sit on the floor. If we stop quickly, you'll fall off that empty crate and right onto your face. Good. Now, think of the place where your body touches the metal. It will be hot, but that is to be expected. What you are going to do is imagine your connection to the Force drawing out the extra heat in your body and bleeding it away. Push it away with each breath until you start to feel some relief. Oh, and drink water. Using the Force will make you feel more comfortable, but it will not really change your body temperature. Well, at least not until you are accomplished in the technique. It has been said that some Jedi have used it to survive the extreme temperatures of space without a suit, but I think that may just be a myth."

Indara stared at Vernestra as she pondered the possibility of Jedi walking through space without an environment suit. She wanted to ask if the elder Jedi had tried the feat herself, but she wasn't really in the mood for another lecture. Still, for a moment Indara saw a glimpse of the girl she had read about, the intrepid Jedi who had taken on Drengir and the Nihil at an age when most Padawans were still polishing their lightsaber skills. Testing wild theories about the Force seemed like something that version of Vernestra Rwoh would do.

Vernestra saw Indara staring and raised her eyebrows. "Are you not going to at least try? Or are you just going to sit on the floor and create puddles for the next couple of hours?"

Indara shook away her distraction and gritted her teeth to bite back a sharp reply. She pulled her lower spine in, sitting up straight and tall as she closed her eyes and felt the heat of the hauler through her robes where her buttocks connected to the floor. She began to breathe and thought about pushing away the heat, bleeding it off into the hauler. After a few breaths, she frowned. It did feel like it was getting colder. Or maybe she was just distracted and not noticing the heat as much.

There was a jolt, and she lurched forward while Vernestra remained exactly where she was, eyes closed in peaceful repose. If Indara had still been sitting on the crate, there was no doubt she would've fallen off. Indara opened her mouth to speak, and Vernestra put a green finger to her lips before pointing up. Sure enough, shouting came from outside the hauler.

The Strafes had found the convoy.

There came the muted sounds of blasterfire and then another lurch as the hauler began moving once more, this time much faster and more erratically than before. Vernestra gave a nod and stood. Indara followed her lead.

"I have a feeling that the Strafes have their hideout nearby," Vernestra said, snuffing the chemlight. "So now we prepare ourselves. When they open the doors, I will go first."

Indara climbed to her feet, her heart pounding. She drew her lightsaber, letting the hilt warm in her hand. She was nervous, but she was also in disbelief. No matter how she felt about the woman, she was on a mission with Vernestra Rwoh! That was an amazing story for any Jedi to be able to tell. Sure, it was probably unsanctioned—Master Yaddle had asked her to leave as soon as she found Master Rwoh, implying that they needed to return quickly—but this was still exciting. Especially since they would be able to help so many people. Indara realized that even though she'd been uncertain about leaving the archives, she had missed this part of her life as a Jedi.

"How does this compare to fighting the Nihil?" she asked, and she could sense Vernestra turning toward her in the dark of the compartment. They still traveled over the landscape, hitting a bump every now and then that was jarring, but Indara found herself more in tune with the moment than with her own inner turmoil. She was an archivist. Investigating was endemic to her nature.

"It doesn't," Vernestra finally answered, her voice soft. Indara couldn't see the older woman's expression, but she could hear a tendril of sadness in her words. "And I say that not because fighting the Nihil was harder, even though it was. I've fought numerous thieves and marauders since my youth, but the Nihil were different because I was fighting them for *me*. I fought to defend the people and places that I loved, in addition to fighting because I felt it was the right thing to do. Now the battle is only that of a Jedi, and it just doesn't compare. And I still have not figured out whether that is a good thing or not."

Indara had nothing to say to that. It seemed too honest, and it left her feeling deeply uncomfortable, although she was not sure why. So she did what she always did when she felt unsure: She kept her mouth shut.

Long minutes passed before the hauler slowed to a stop and the voices outside grew louder once more, even though the words were indistinguishable. It was too dark for Indara to see much of anything, and her heart pounded in her chest, not from fear, but from excitement. There was safety in the predictable, but there was also boredom.

Indara was definitely not bored now.

The *vwoom* of Vernestra powering up her lightsaber drew Indara's gaze, the vibrant violet glow revealing the stone-faced visage of the elder Jedi. If Vernestra was nervous or even a bit unsettled, there was nothing in her expression that revealed it. Her serenity in the face of certain violence only irked Indara once more.

"It doesn't seem as though our friends are in any hurry to open the door, so slight change of plans. Follow my lead. Try to stay at least a meter back and out of the range of my whip."

Indara didn't get a chance to respond. Vernestra held up her hand, using the Force to push the hatch off its hinges, the metallic panel landing somewhere a few meters away. And then the elder Jedi was gone, the echoing shouts of surprise from the pirates filtering into the truck in her absence.

Indara took a deep breath and stepped forward, only to freeze at the sight before her, her mouth falling open just a bit. The hauler was parked in a large cavern, and at least four other haulers in various states of being dismantled occupied the rest of the space. The rocks were a beautiful deep blue, and the chemlights arrayed around the cavern picked out bits of sparkle from within the rock.

But it wasn't the majesty of the cavern that had given Indara pause. Her surprise was entirely due to how Vernestra was making her way through the space. It took Indara a moment to realize that what she was watching was *really* happening, and it wasn't a fever dream. She had seen lightsaber demonstrations and archival recordings of Jedi in the field, but she'd never been in a pitched battle herself. So she wasn't expecting the way Vernestra Rwoh *flowed* around the cavern, neutralizing each threat as it appeared. The woman never stopped moving. One moment she was flipping to avoid a series of blaster bolts, and the next she was twisting the bezel of her lightsaber to release the whip, taking out the blasters of three pirates before spinning and using the Force to shove back a couple who were charging her. Indara was in awe.

But then a blaster bolt went flying past her cheek, uncomfortably warm and entirely too close, and she snapped into action.

Indara jumped down from the back of the hauler and entered the fray.

It would have been easy to be overwhelmed—there were at least two dozen pirates bearing down on them—but as she had back in the tavern, Indara reached for the Force and let go, feeling the connection to everything and releasing the nervousness and fear that came with her too-human flesh. A blaster bolt flew toward her, and she twisted her wrist slightly, deflecting the bolt back at the pirate who had fired it.

The person—Indara had only the briefest impression of sandy rags and a rebreather—fell and did not move.

But she didn't have time to mourn the senseless loss of life. She had a Jedi Master to follow.

Indara cut her own swath of destruction through the space, deflecting blaster bolt after blaster bolt back at the perfect angle, precise and deadly. She hated to kill so indiscriminately, but she didn't have a choice. She also didn't have a lightwhip to use against multiple aggressors at a time, so she focused on making sure every single flick of her wrist or swing of her arm counted.

Indara followed the path Vernestra had taken, glancing around as she moved. The pirates' hideout was spacious but did not appear to provide many avenues of attack, since Indara saw only two corridors entering the main cavern: one large enough to accommodate vehicles, which seemed to lead back outside, and a narrower, person-sized tunnel that likely led deeper into the cave. It was a good system for defense, unless one had the terrible misfortune of being trapped trying to defend the space from a couple of Jedi.

Indara used the Force to pick up a human woman charging her with a vibroblade and throw her across the room into some crates. A few more blaster bolts were deflected back at the people who fired them, and the next thing Indara knew, it was eerily silent. The only sound was her heartbeat in her ears.

"Are you good?" Vernestra called from across the space.

Not a single pirate remained standing, and Indara felt a keen sense of frustration. What a waste. They should have surrendered as soon as they saw the lightsabers. Why did people always think they could best the Jedi?

"I'm fine," Indara said, powering down her blade. "I just wish . . . I wish there had been another way."

"So do I. In all my years, that feeling of senselessness? That's never changed," she said, the mask of cool efficiency slipping for a moment, just as it had in the dark of the hauler compartment. But when Indara looked again, the Jedi Master had tight rein over her emotions once more. "We need to find whoever is in charge."

"How do you know it isn't one of them?" Indara said, pointing to the bodies that littered the space.

"The boots," Vernestra said. At Indara's puzzled look, she explained, "No one here has nice boots. The leader always has nice boots, good clothes. It's common for whoever is in charge to pay themselves first and take the largest share. Not a lot of fairness in piracy."

Indara followed behind Vernestra as she headed toward the smaller hallway leading away from the cave. As they walked across the cavern, Indara realized that the space truly was a garage of sorts. Beyond what she'd seen from the back of the hauler were a couple of other haulers stripped down to their frames as well as scattered cargo containers, the remnants of previous jobs. As they made their way down the narrow hallway, the chemlights gave way to complete and utter darkness, and when Vernestra powered up her lightsaber once more, Indara followed her lead, the purple and green glows of their blades the only light to see by.

They'd gone only about thirty meters when chemlights appeared in the walls, and both of the Jedi doused their lightsabers in response. Voices grew audible, not coming toward them but echoing down the stone hallway.

"A Jedi? Are you sure? You'd better not be about one of your hallucinations again."

"No, I'm serious. I swear! They killed the rest of the crew. We need to get out of here!"

"Nonsense. Jedi don't scare me."

Vernestra gave Indara a quick nod and took off running the rest of the way on quiet feet. Indara followed, wondering if maybe there was a smarter option than just rushing into danger, but then they were standing in a room filled with smoke, a couple of Devaronians smoking spice in long-handled pipes. They were barely visible through the thick haze, and Indara couldn't help but cough.

Vernestra powered up her lightsaber and pointed it at the men. "Who is in charge here?"

"I am," said a voice to the right, and Indara turned to see a Toydarian flying nearby, his long nose bearing an ugly scar. "And I really hate Jedi."

Indara powered up her lightsaber just as the Toydarian reached for a bangle dangling from his wrist. He gestured toward the Jedi, and Indara watched in horror as her lightsaber powered down entirely on its own, Vernestra's doing the same.

"Jedi think they've uncovered every secret of the galaxy," the Toydarian said with a sneer. "I never get tired of the expressions on your fool Jedi faces whenever you're proven wrong."

Indara couldn't believe that her lightsaber was now useless, and she cast about for what to do next. Vernestra reacted more quickly, flipping her lightsaber hilt at the Toydarian, hitting him right in his very sensitive nose before using the Force to recall the hilt and tuck it safely in her belt. The Toydarian yelped and tried to fly away as, behind Indara, the Devaronians scrambled to their feet, the spice they'd smoked making them clumsy.

"Time to improvise," Vernestra said to Indara before running toward the Toydarian, launching herself into the air, and grabbing his feet as he attempted to flee. Indara picked up a metal dish near the Devaronians and threw it at them, spice flying through the air. The pair dropped their pipes and tried to save the dish, but Indara grabbed it first and used it to knock out one and then the other Devaronian. The physical violence was a bit unsettling, but a glance at the blasters on the table before the two men was a stark reminder that this truly was a life-or-death situation.

When Indara turned back around, Vernestra had her knee in the Toydarian's back and was using a length of wire to subdue him. When she stood, she was grinning like a youngling who'd just levitated for the first time. She turned to Indara.

"Excellent work, Jedi. Now let's go outside and wait for the security teams."

"Wait, what was that? The way my lightsaber just went out? Was that . . . I've never heard of such a thing."

Vernestra's expression grew tight before relaxing once more. "Not here. We can discuss this later, once we're off Cerifisis. Understood? Right now I think we both could use some fresh air."

Indara nodded, lightheaded. She didn't know if it was the spice smoke permeating the air or the reality of what they'd just done, but she couldn't help but feel a bit of euphoria.

She felt more alive than she had in months.

"Fresh air sounds like a great idea," she said and led the way back from whence they came.

※

It took another couple of hours before the security teams were fully briefed, the remaining pirates rounded up, and what was left of the supply shipments accounted for. Indara absorbed it all from the sidelines, watching Vernestra move from one task to another like a battle-hardened general. It occurred to her that maybe that was exactly what Vernestra was. Her file stated that she had been a Wayseeker for over a decade, and this was only her most recent foray into such a vocation. Before that she had undertaken a number of tasks that were sealed to all but the High Council, and Indara wondered how many of those missions had been something akin to what they'd just done: a single Jedi defying the odds in the name of a people who had no other hope.

Even though they'd handled the pirates, Indara still felt a deep sense of unease. She was trying not to think too much about the way her lightsaber had just fizzled out in the midst of a pitched battle. Despite her outward calm, she was impatient for the explanation Vernestra had promised her, one that apparently would only come once they were away from the people of Cerifisis. Indara wondered if it had been some Force technique she'd never heard of, but that didn't make any kind of sense. Why would a Jedi willingly power down their lightsaber in such a fashion? Not only was it unfair, but it seemed like a strange way to pull an opponent off balance.

And she didn't want to delve too deeply into the matter with Vernestra. Indara had just met the older Jedi, but the woman had an air of secrecy about her. Indara had the strange feeling that if a subject was broached that Vernestra did not want to discuss, she would simply refuse to answer, and that was not a theory Indara wanted to prove one way or the other. It was a long ride back to Coruscant, and Indara did not want her time spent with the Jedi Master to take on an even more awkward cast. The trip had already been eventful enough.

"Okay, I think we're all set here," Vernestra said, walking up with a placid expression on her face. The abject joy that Indara had witnessed in the caves while Vernestra was fighting the pirates was gone, once more replaced by the coolly polite Jedi. "Kavil is going to give us a ride to my ship. I assume the Council sent you with a Vector?"

Indara nodded. "Master Vernestra, if you would like to fly the Vector back, I can ride with your droid to Coruscant."

Vernestra grimaced before she managed to gain control of her expression. "I'd prefer to fly in the *Cantaros,* but you're welcome to ride with Jay-Six and me. There's plenty of room aboard, and the ship is much more comfortable than a Vector. That, I can promise you."

Indara wanted to say no. She had the feeling that the elder Jedi expected her to decline. Perhaps that was why she forced a smile and said, "Thank you, I'd vastly prefer that. I find the Vectors . . . cramped."

"How many have you crashed?"

Indara blinked. "Um . . . none?"

Vernestra laughed, the sound lilting. "That just means you haven't been flying them long enough. We'll head to the *Cantaros.* When we get aboard, you should call Master Yaddle and request to have someone pick up the Vector and let her know we're on our way. Otherwise she's likely to send another annoyed holo and a few more Jedi after us."

Indara knew she was missing something. Vernestra seemed brusquely efficient, but something about the way she was speaking made Indara feel like the Mirialan was debating whether or not to share something, some bit of information. Whatever it was, she obviously came to a decision, because she nodded.

"Yes, you flying with us will be fine. Much better than flying in the Vector," Vernestra said, mostly to herself.

Indara didn't think she was imagining the slight worry in Vernestra's frown, but then the Jedi Master was walking away, and Indara had no chance to ask what was amiss.

Regardless, Indara was so relieved to not have to fly the Vector back that she would have concurred with just about anything the elder Jedi said. It would be nice to return to Coruscant aboard a ship with a bathroom.

It was only after the matter had been settled that Indara wondered why she'd been sent after the elder Jedi if she'd gotten Master Yaddle's missives.

Surely Vernestra Rwoh wasn't avoiding her responsibilities as a Jedi Master?

The reality was just a bit unthinkable.

Chapter Nine

As soon as we were safely ensconced on the *Cantaros,* J-6 piloting us directly to Coruscant, I showed Indara to the extra sleeping quarters, then made my way to my own and locked the door so that I would remain undisturbed. It had been a while since I'd taken a trip through hyperspace, which meant it had been a while since I'd had the chance to experience a vision. I was long past due.

Especially after the moment with the Toydarian in the caves and the device that I'd only heard rumors of long ago. A weapon that could nullify lightsabers, disabling them and leaving a Jedi vulnerable. It was supposed to be a device lost to time. And here it was, popping up on a small backwater planet no one had heard of.

It was beginning to seem more and more likely that the Force had led me to Cerifisis because of the nullifier the Toydarian possessed, and finding it had left me feeling unmoored. No Force vision had brought me to Cerifisis, but the Force had clearly wanted me there even if the decisions had felt like my own.

It was honestly a bit unsettling. There was a comfort in the unpredictability of the Force when people across the galaxy were so predictable.

A balance, so to speak. But if the Force was directing toward some larger purpose, I liked to know that. Especially since it meant I needed to discover what it was sooner rather than later.

Force warnings that were ignored aged poorly.

When I was younger, I'd hated the possibility of having a vision, and I still found the way my subconsciousness could be yanked into this musing or that unsettling. But as I'd gotten older, I'd learned to listen to the warnings and to drive them toward a more logical conclusion, no matter how cryptic they might be. The Force *usually* moved in mysterious ways, but I found that if I was willing to listen, the paths and patterns became a bit clearer. And my visions were just about as close to communing directly with the Force as a Jedi could get.

The device secreted within my robes felt like an omen, the first piece in a much larger puzzle. The key was now figuring out whether this was a task I would need to undertake or whether it was a matter to be brought to the Jedi High Council and left to them. Neither prospect made me happy, but there was only so much I could do when the Force decided to move purposefully. So I might as well get a bit of rest and see what my immediate future might hold.

I stowed my robes in the closet, stripping down to just the tunic and trousers that I preferred. The closet also contained a number of other clothing choices: civilian garb for when it was better not to be recognized as a Jedi, coveralls for ship repairs, and formal dress for the times formality was required, which had been surprisingly often over the past decade. There was also a set of immaculate white robes that I would change into before I entered the Temple, adhering to protocol even when I found it suffocating.

I thought of Indara's pristine robes and smiled. The Jedi Knight still hadn't realized that her robe now had three new holes, all of them courtesy of blaster bolts that had gotten a bit close. Her lightsaber work was so sloppy, it was a miracle the woman hadn't been hit. I would have to say something to Master Yaddle. Really, the Order should be better prepared. One of the reasons I had left Coruscant was because it felt like the Order of my youth, the one that had adapted and could rise to any challenge, was becoming more and more a memory and less a reality. But that was not Indara's fault and was a matter for another day.

I had more pressing issues. Because someone was making lightsaber nullifiers, and if one could be found in the hands of pirates on a backwater planet like Cerifisis, how long until someone like the Hutts or the Zygerrian slavers or any of the crime syndicates got hold of one? The prospect was terrifying.

I removed my boots and my belt, including my very empty canteen and lightsaber. I stowed my lightsaber on the decorative stand on my desk—a gift from the same former Padawan who had become the namesake for my ship—and lay back on my bed, letting the tension melt away from each muscle as I relaxed into the foam of the pallet. It would be too easy to fall asleep, or at least try to. But the reality was that if there was a hyperspace vision waiting for me, I would have no rest until it was received.

I had started having visions of possible futures during trips through hyperspace when I was just a young Padawan. At first they terrified me, and I worried that there was something wrong with me, that perhaps somehow I had tapped into the dark side of the Force. But my Jedi Master, Stellan Gios, had assured me that my Force visions were a gift, even if they didn't feel that way at times. Decades later, I still wasn't sure I agreed with his assessment, but as I grew older, I became accustomed to them and took precautions to ensure they didn't endanger those around me, such as having J-6 fly the *Cantaros* long distances rather than flying myself.

So, accepting that a vision was more likely than not, I closed my eyes, began breathing deeply, and let go.

Entering a vision was different every time. Sometimes it felt like falling, a sudden drop into the strange and odd. But this time it was like being carried on a wave, a gentle rocking that reminded me of the time I'd gone boating on Trask. And when I opened my eyes, I was indeed in a boat, a small rustic thing with oars as opposed to engines.

Sitting across from me, his garb that of a simple fisherman, complete with a large floppy hat, was my former master: Stellan Gios, the Fallen Star.

Only it wasn't really Stellan. I knew that. He'd been dead for decades, his final act of heroism enough for him to have several monuments erected to him by the peoples of the planets Eiram and E'ronoh. Still, it was hard to see him, his pale skin tanned and peeling, a primitive fishing pole extending over the water. He had a beard, just like the last time I'd seen him, and under his hat his hair was too long, as though he'd been lost at sea.

"Vern," he said, his voice gravelly as though from disuse. "It has been a while."

"You never called me Vern," I told the vision, pulling my outstretched legs in and causing the boat to rock. Stellan Not Stellan inclined his head in acknowledgment.

"Vernestra, then. You would remember something like that better than I would. After all, I'm not real."

One of the things no one ever tells you is how contrary visions can be. Every single aspect of the scene had been cobbled together by my brain. I knew that. I had read up on Force visions, and the majority of scholars believed that they were nothing more than the brain reading fluctuations and variations in the Force, ripples created by upheaval somewhere in the timeline of the galaxy. Given the frequency of my visions, I'd even spent years with various Jedi scholars trying to understand how best to use what I saw in an organized manner, but every effort failed. My visions seemed to work on a logic that defied explanation, as so many things relating to the Force often did.

I had concluded that it was not for me to understand just how my visions worked, but rather to accept that they existed and use them to the best of my ability. It was the easiest way to keep from going mad.

But just because my brain was connecting to the Force or dredging up memories to interpret the will of the Force did not mean the visions were straightforward and to the point. My mind liked to drag up memories that ranged from painful to bittersweet, and it was just my good luck that Stellan was a welcome sight, his death so far in the past that I no longer felt the pang of loss when I saw him.

"Why are we fishing?" I asked Stellan.

He grinned, the expression wide and open. "What better way to find something that is lost to the waters of time than to go fishing for it? I've been here for decades, looking for it. I never should have let it go, to be honest."

"What did you lose?" I asked.

Stellan shook his head. "You'll see soon enough. You already have, to be honest. But you were so young last time, how would you have known how important it was? Anyway, I just came to give you this."

Stellan handed me the pole, a flimsy thing that felt too fragile to do much of anything.

"Go fishing. The path begins on the frozen seas."

I looked down at the pole, and when I blinked I was back in my quarters, lying on the bunk, my lightsaber in my hand. A glance through the viewport revealed that we were still in hyperspace. I wasn't certain what had pulled me from the vision until there was a gentle knock at my door. J-6 would never disturb me, so the visitor must be Indara.

I placed my lightsaber back in the holder on my desk and opened the door. Indara stood there, conflict playing across her face. Whatever had brought her to my door was no light matter.

Before she could speak, I said, "You want to talk about what happened in the cave."

She blinked. "Yes, uh, Master Vernestra. I'm sorry to bother you. You asked me to wait till we were aboard the ship. It's been weighing on me, and I thought perhaps, with your experience, you might have some idea as to what occurred."

I sighed. This would not be an easy conversation, but Indara deserved to know the whole of the matter. The Council would as soon as I returned, anyway. And as faithful as I was to the Order, I did not always trust the Council to make the best decisions. Not because they were bad at their jobs, but because too often they were more concerned with diplomacy than with action.

"Why don't we go to the galley and have a cup of tea?" I'd found that most difficult conversations were easier if had over tea. And this would be trying indeed.

Indara nodded and stepped back to allow me to leave my cabin. I led the way through the narrow corridor of my ship to the galley.

Someone had put hot water on already, most likely J-6. She knew that I often needed tea after a vision, and the simple forethought of the droid warmed me. I prepared two cups quickly and set one before Indara where she sat at the galley table, a small thing that really sat only two comfortably but could accommodate four if people were willing to squeeze into the banquette seating. Once I had settled myself, I closed my eyes and took a moment, searching for where to begin.

The beginning was best.

"How much do you know about the Nihil conflict?" I asked.

Indara sat up a little straighter. "I've studied it extensively. I've even written several analyses of the initial Jedi response in the aftermath of the incident on Valo. I've mostly been interested in the initial Emergences and—"

I raised my hand to forestall anything more. "I only ask because it seems as though the Order was quick to forget the failures of our leadership during that time. And since you're young, I wasn't sure how much you'd been exposed to, even as an archivist."

Color rose high in Indara's cheeks. "Yes, well, I happen to have written my first treatise on the actions of the Order during the Nihil conflict and how the casualties could have been avoided at key junctures."

I laughed, and Indara's expression became even stormier. The Jedi Knight didn't like me, and this conversation was unlikely to change her mind. "Hindsight is an amazing gift," I said. "But I assure you this is about a much smaller, less remembered event that I only knew about much later.

"Toward the early days of the conflict, before the Republic and the Jedi Order understood the true magnitude of things, the chancellor of the era, Lina Soh, decided to have a grand galactic fair on the planet of Valo."

Indara nodded. "The Nihil attacked and disrupted the event, correct?"

"Yes, but it is not the Nihil we're concerned about. This revolves around a device, a footnote in the reports from the time by the Jedi who saw the weapon. It was called a nullifier, a weapon that could disrupt blasters and lightsabers. A few of the Order's investigators were sent out to follow up on the weapon in the aftermath of the events on Valo, but it turned out that there were more pressing issues, so the matter was put to rest.

"Over the past few decades, there have been sporadic reports of the device throughout the galaxy—stories of weapons suddenly misfiring, lightsabers going dark, the gamut. But each time, the sightings were investigated and couldn't be substantiated. Today is the first time I've seen the impact of a nullifier myself."

"Really?" Indara said, skepticism furrowing her dark brows. "You seemed . . . unfazed."

I smiled. "I've seen a lot. Very few events surprise me anymore. And those that do, well, let's just say I haven't lost at sabacc in a very long time."

"So is this where you advise me against taking the matter to the Council when we return?" Indara asked. There was a hard set to her expression. I knew how she felt. My annoyance with the politics and procedures of the Order had been one of the things that sent me on my path as a Wayseeker, and I had disliked watching the failures of my elders when I was a younger Jedi as well. It was too easy with the folly of youth to condemn that which seemed wrong, especially when one had no context for the choices made by another.

"No. But I do think that once we report it to the Order, we're unlikely to hear anything further."

Indara nodded, not agreeing with me but not disagreeing, either.

"It's too bad we cannot show them the device so they can see the impact of it themselves. Maybe then they would believe us."

I smiled. It was a simple idea, and a good one at that. Perhaps...

"The Jedi Masters on the High Council have their own opinions and goals, and in my years in the Order, I've disagreed with their decision-making as often as I've agreed with it," I finally said. A plan was beginning to form, and I had no worries of any possible repercussions. But I would not bring an innocent into my machinations. "But you are a Jedi Knight, and an archivist at that. You should feel free to conduct yourself in the manner you see fit."

Indara seemed surprised at my pronouncement. "I thought you found me sheltered and inept."

The blunt statement took me so much by surprise that I laughed out loud. Indara sipped her tea while studying me over the rim of her cup. She had an edge, and that made me like her a bit more.

"Sheltered, yes. Young? Definitely. Inept? No. You handled yourself admirably when we went up against the pirates. Your lightsaber forms could use some work, but that's merely a matter of practice. I do think that the Order letting you waste your youth on cataloging the accomplishments of long-gone Jedi is a disservice. Jedi should be out in the galaxy, not hiding away in temples." I sighed and shrugged. "But I suppose that is just one of the many ways the Order has changed in my lifetime."

"No. You're right," Indara said, her eyes downcast. "I suppose I should have pushed harder for an assignment away from Coruscant." It felt less an honest admission than a redirect to keep me from pressing the matter. Interesting.

I stood and patted her hand where it rested on the table. "When we return, you should do just that. I do believe your scholarship would benefit if you spent more time out in the galaxy. Context is everything, and no matter how many histories you read, you'll never truly understand what it means to be a Jedi until you are among the people of the galaxy, protecting the light."

I took my empty cup to the sonic scrubber and set it on a rack. "Try to get some rest. I have no doubt that the Council will request our presence as soon as we touch down on Coruscant. Even Jedi Masters tend to be as impatient as younglings when they have their mind set to a task."

With that, I took my leave, intent on finding my own rest.

It wasn't until I woke, the ship gently touching down in the docking bays in the Jedi Temple, that I thought to consider whether the vision of Stellan could have anything to do with the nullifier Indara and I had encountered on Cerifisis.

And where the path would lead me if it did.

Chapter Ten

Neral's moon was supposed to be fun, a pleasure moon where no one much bothered to regulate anything. There were gambling halls and dens of iniquity where one could get anything—and anyone—one desired. Nilsson had been a few times and had always had a great time. This visit was different.

This trip was leaving him positively murderous.

He sat in his favorite spice den, the Marauder's Secret, which was about as clandestine as the broadcast of a new adventure holo. It was a place where everyone gathered: senators, actors, singers, information brokers, and even important scientists. Spice was the great equalizer. Even though the Republic had done everything it could to limit production and consumption, on Neral's moon, spice still flowed as freely as alcohol. Nilsson had already partaken of a particularly good blend from Banchii, even though he'd had no clue they even mined spice on that out-of-the-way patch of dirt. He was going to have to reassess his love of spice from the Chommell sector if this kept up.

As Nilsson finished what was in his pipe, he glanced around the hazy space. There were low couches in shades of deep blue and purple, and beaded curtains gave the impression of privacy in the main area, though rooms were available for those who wanted a truly private experience. Nilsson usually liked having a private room, but he was supposed to meet Garn, and the senator was already jumpy enough. The public option was always preferable when he was meeting with people from the Republic. It was nice to remind them that they had more to fear than he did. After all, he was just a spoiled spicehead living off Daddy's riches. There were few people in the galaxy who knew what he was truly about.

And every single one of those owed him more favors than he could count.

Just thinking of Garn had Nilsson draining his wineglass and pulling up the electronic menu for his next round. After the complete and utter disaster of Haileap, Nilsson had thought that things could not get worse. But that was before he'd received the holo from Hinra, the image grainy because of the distance but the mechanical voice of the vocalizer the Gigoran wore unmistakable.

"The seller ran as soon as we left. The tavern owner said she was headed to Dalna. We are en route."

Dalna. A terrible place to try to find someone. Too many tourists coming at all hours of the day and night for the planet's famed waterfalls, not to mention the pleasure cruises that stopped by for day trips. The woman could be anywhere in the galaxy, and now he'd never find her and get the prototype he'd spent so much on. There were few things Nilsson hated more than losing money. It was why he never gambled. The risk was never worth the reward.

A protocol droid designed to look like a human female with over-embellished hips and a comically painted face sashayed over. "How are you doing? Can I get you anything?" she purred through her vocabulator. "We have a few offerings that aren't on the menu."

"Is that so?" Nilsson asked.

The droid tittered, the sound unnerving even though it was meant to sound flirtatious. He'd never understood the appeal of a droid programmed to flirt. Did it really improve customer service? He far preferred living servers. At least then the banter felt genuine.

"Yes," the droid said, interrupting his wayward thoughts. "We have something available for just about every taste. There is even a premium spice from Kilner's Seventh Moon that is highly recommended."

At that moment, Nilsson spied Garn making his way through the milling crowd to the corner booth where he sat. "Not now. I'm conducting business," he told the droid, waving her away.

She turned on her heel and swayed over to another table, where a group of drunken Twi'leks laughed and swatted the droid on the hindquarters. *Vile,* Nilsson thought, punching in an order for a fresh bottle of wine and more spice, not the stuff the droid had recommended but something called Starfall Express, one of the pricey engineered strains. He would do his ordering from the terminal and leave the droid to attend to the rowdy party drinking their weight in ale.

"Nilly! How have you been?" Garn said, sliding into the opposite side of the booth. Anyone who didn't know the senator might have thought the human was completely relaxed, but Nilsson had known Garn since the two of them were in boarding school. The man's pasty complexion and slicked-down yellow hair were flawless, but the sweat glimmering along his hairline and on his upper lip was unmistakable. If Garn were to remove his jacket to expose the silkensteen shirt underneath, there would be pools of sweat under his arms as well.

"Kriffed, Garn. I'm completely and utterly kriffed. And all because of your foolish cousin."

Garn blinked and laughed hollowly as he sat down. "Ah, come on, it can't be that bad, can it? How much could he have stolen? Two, maybe three hundred credits?"

The wine arrived, the bottle in a chiller and the serving droid carrying two glasses as well as a dish of Starfall Express. Nilsson took the bottle from the tray as well as the spice and a single glass. Then he sent the serving droid away, the slight deliberate.

He slowly pulled the wine from the chiller, pouring some into his glass and savoring it. It was an excellent vintage, almost as good as some of the wine he had liberated from his father's own wine stores in the past. "Garn, I'm going to need you to increase that figure a hundredfold."

Garn swallowed. "I—he stole two hundred thousand credits from you? You can't be serious. I just . . . how?"

Nilsson waited a beat to let the panic fully set in for Garn before pulling a holo-emitter from his pocket. "Do you remember the scientist I found a few months back to help me improve my grandmother's design? The one I set up with a lab through a number of proxy corporations?" Nilsson tapped the holo-emitter to reveal the image of a human woman, her wild black curls and deep-brown skin appearing in bluescale. It shouldn't be so annoying to see someone who had betrayed him, but it was. Nilsson could feel his ire rising. It had honestly just been a terrible week, and someone should be held responsible.

Right now, that someone was Garn, whether he was actually to blame or not.

"This is Florinda Jackard. A scientist. She was working with Dashon to steal from me. The device they stole is worth hundreds of thousands of credits. Millions even. It's worth more than every single blaster and disruptor that I've shipped for you over the past three years. Garn, this is not an insult I can let go unacknowledged. This is just—well, it's *rude*. And you know how I feel about those with a lack of manners."

The story, of course, was a complete and utter lie. But the more Nilsson said that Dashon had been working with Florinda, the more he actually began to believe it. Just because it *wasn't* true didn't mean it *couldn't* be.

At the nearby table, the group of Twi'leks had tired of harassing the pleasure droid and begun calling out to some of the other hospitality workers in the nightclub, particularly a human man who wore little more than a pair of bright-purple fringed shorts. Nilsson watched them for a moment, his ire growing as they shouted at the poor man dancing on one of the corner stages, their shouts becoming less suggestive and more aggressive.

"Excuse me for a moment," Nilsson said, emptying the rest of the wine into his glass before placing the bottle back in the chiller and locking it into the device. And then he stood, surprisingly steady considering the amount of spice he'd smoked, grabbed the bottle within the chiller, and made his way over to the table full of Twi'leks.

"Excuse me, gentlemen," he said. The men ignored him, so he rapped the flat of his hand on their table, making their glasses jump and a few fall over.

"Cha, what's your damage, brub?" one of the Twi'lek men said.

"I find your behavior tedious, and it would be lovely if you'd leave off the poor dancing boy over there. Let him earn his credits in peace."

The men laughed, switching to Twi'leki to throw a few slurs his way, as though he would speak such a coarse language. This was why he didn't care for Twi'leks. Coarse and rude, the entire lot of them.

"Yeah, why don't you go get shoved out of an air lock, eh?" one of the men said. "You got no business with us."

"Lovely. Well, I did try to warn you."

Nilsson brought the wine bottle—still locked into the weighty chiller—up and around quickly, the chiller cracking against the skull of the nearest man, then grabbed the lekku of the next closest and slammed the man's face into the table. The remaining two men, sitting in the back of the booth, attempted to get up and intervene, but Nilsson had already leapt onto the tabletop. He looked like a human, but he wasn't, the latent strength of his Kuranu ancestors giving him an unexpected edge in any fight. Especially a fight that wasn't fair.

Nilsson kicked a glass toward the nearest man before swinging the chiller-and-bottle combination at the remaining man. By this time, screams had gone up in the establishment. Nilsson jumped off the table, dropping the wine bottle still locked in the chiller before smoothing the ropy locs of his brown hair and straightening the tunic he wore. He was pleased to see he hadn't gotten any Twi'lek blood on the thing. It was new, after all.

He sauntered back to his table as security droids came to clean up the mess he'd made. The manager of the establishment, a Kage with golden eyes that glimmered even in the low light, came over. Nilsson gave him a bow.

"I apologize for the disturbance. I was just taking my leave. Perhaps this will cover the mess?"

Nilsson flipped a hundred-credit coin at the man and waited just long enough for his eyes to widen and for him to give a curt nod before turning back to Garn.

"Apologies, old friend. But it seems like I have to be going. Oh, keep the holo-emitter. You have two weeks to find Florinda. Don't let me down."

And then Nilsson grabbed his glass of wine and the dish of spice and took his leave.

He had better places to be anyhow.

Chapter Eleven

Indara did not wait for Master Rwoh. Rather, as soon as the *Cantaros* had landed, she said her farewells, departed down the boarding ramp, and headed right to Master Yaddle's living quarters within the complex.

When Indara entered, the older Jedi was seeing to a strange plant on a shelf, one of many around the room. This one was something bright blue with tiny green flowers.

"A lonyuip," Master Yaddle said at the younger Jedi's look. "They once grew quite profusely here on Coruscant, but that was long before the city grew to the size it is. Now most of them are found in museums and botanical gardens." She used a mister to spritz the flowers before setting it to the side and giving Indara a pointed look. "Some flowers only bloom in captivity. But others . . . well, they thrive in unexpected places."

"You sent me because you knew my inexperience would provoke Master Rwoh to action," Indara said, feeling less like the pretty lonyuip and more like the spiky phloxos taking up one shadowy corner. "She returned with me to the Temple because you made her curious." Indara hated that she'd been nothing more than a tool for a game beyond her understanding. She'd thought she'd been chosen because she was a hard worker and an excellent archivist. And now...

It felt like the Jedi Masters were laughing, but it was at her expense.

"Vernestra has always loved a challenge, and you bear the unique distinction of being one of the few Jedi Knights who would not buckle under her withering gaze," Master Yaddle said, picking the mister back up and turning to the rest of her plants. "You were the perfect choice to provoke her to action. Besides, the Council has let you hide in the archives for the past year. Have you never wondered why that is?"

Indara blinked. "I haven't been *hiding*. I've been busy. I had to do the treatise on the Nihil conflict, and then on the Hyperspace Rush, and then there was the new research...you know this."

"I know that you are a highly capable Jedi who has buried herself in the past after a tragedy," Yaddle said, setting the mister on a side table, which immediately retracted into the wall. "I know that you have never requested to be placed on the mission roster despite your colleagues urging you to. And I know that you have never fully dealt with the trauma you lived through on Seswenna."

"That's...that's not fair. Or true," Indara said, feeling as though she were a Padawan again. "I just...I've been busy. It's only been a year, not ten."

Yaddle turned her full attention to Indara. "Mmm-hmmm. So how was it?"

"How was what?"

"Fighting the pirates on Cerifisis? Vernestra has always had an uncanny ability to find people in the most desperate of situations and help them."

Indara grimaced. "I have to admit...I enjoyed it. Not just helping the people but...all of it. Well, not Master Rwoh. With all respect for her accomplishments, the woman is overbearing to say the least." The Jedi Master said nothing, letting the silence stretch on until Indara sighed deeply. "Okay, you're right. I'm just...I think maybe I got stuck. And I hate that I still don't quite know why." Indara didn't want to think about why she'd been hesitant to leave the archives. It was sometimes easier to move forward than to look backward, and this was one of those times.

"I know," Master Yaddle said, heading toward the door. "I'm the one who suggested to the rest of the Council that we send you on this mission. Now we must head to the main training room. Master Vernestra will not hesitate to make an entrance, and we should be there for the show."

Indara frowned. "Is Master Rwoh's audience not before the Jedi High Council?"

"Oh, it is. But she requested that the meeting be open to all, so it was moved to the larger training room. I expect there will be quite the crowd. It is not every day that a Jedi who has been gone more than a decade returns, much less requests an open forum. You won't want to miss it."

Indara thought perhaps Master Yaddle was being a bit sarcastic, but when they arrived there were a number of people in the room, including the Council members, and conversation buzzed. Indara had never seen the main training room so full and had to press herself into a corner.

She didn't have long to wait. Master Oppo Rancisis had just slithered into the chair set aside for him, joining Master Yoda, Master Yaddle, Master Yarael Poof, and Master Niko Jiro, who appeared amused, as though they could not wait for what was about to ensue.

The door opened, not through the automatic mechanism but through the power of the Force, as though someone was too impatient to wait for machinery. Master Vernestra strode into the Council Chamber. The conversation in the room died as she took in the assembled crowd. There was nothing in her face to indicate just how she was feeling.

"And that is how the best Jedi in the Order enters a room," murmured a Jedi near Indara, and she had to agree. Vernestra wasn't a

Council member. But there was no way of knowing that from looking at her. She'd transformed since Indara had last seen her. Her dusty robes—with their numerous tears and even a few blaster burns—were gone, pristine ivory temple robes in their place. After a moment she lowered the hood of her cloak, and a murmur went up in the room. Her hair, worn in a chin-length bob when Indara had first met her, was now gone, her head shaved clean to reveal an interlocking pattern of diamonds tattooed along her scalp that matched those in the corners of her eyes. Her gaze was hard and discerning, and Indara now understood what Yaddle had meant about needing a Jedi Knight who could stand up to the Mirialan.

If Indara had met *this* Jedi on Cerifisis, she never would have doubted her authority. She never would've balked at being told what to do in such a haughty manner. In fact, the Jedi Master Vernestra Rwoh in this room was such a far cry from the woman Indara had encountered on Cerifisis that she was having trouble reconciling the two. Every measure of playfulness that Master Vernestra had evidenced on the faraway planet was gone. This version had such a gravity that Indara couldn't help but feel a bit of awe at just being in her presence.

Even if she knew, firsthand, just how irksome the older woman could be.

"Esteemed members of the Jedi High Council, I have returned just as you requested. Jedi Master Vernestra Rwoh awaits your orders."

Indara thought there was an edge of amusement riding Vernestra's words, as though she knew she could have dodged their request for another decade and still have returned a hero.

She wasn't wrong. Few Jedi had as many accolades attached to their names as Vernestra.

Master Yarael Poof was the first to speak, the Quermian's bald head tilting on his long, alabaster, serpentine neck as he turned to peer at Vernestra. "This Council has sent several missives requesting your return over the past few years. Did you have trouble receiving them?"

Vernestra smiled, the expression serene as she inclined her head in acknowledgment of his question. "Master Yarael. My apologies. Communications on the edge of Wild Space can be sporadic and unpredictable and nearly impossible to trace. It was a good thing you sent an emissary, which is the reason I stand here today, returned at your request. Jedi Knight Indara accomplished her mission with grace and aplomb. She is a credit to the Order and to her training."

Indara felt her face heat. Did Vernestra really mean that? Or was she using her to mock the Jedi High Council? Indara couldn't tell, and judging from the chorus of murmurs that went up around the room, the rest of the gathering couldn't, either.

"Master Rwoh," Master Jiro said. Their eyes were crinkled in amusement as they spoke. "It is good to see you, and I am curious as to why you've requested a public forum. But first, tell us of your travels."

"Ah, it seems you did not receive my dispatches, so we are all victims of the unpredictability of communications over long distances," Vernestra said with a pointed look at Master Yarael. "But it would be an honor to highlight for the Council where I have been, the things I have seen, and the tasks I have undertaken."

Vernestra then began to regale the room with the stories of her adventures, and Indara realized there were many of them. The Jedi Master had helped bring in harvests, rebuild schools in the aftermath of environmental disasters, and fight pirates. So many pirates. Indara wondered if Vernestra sought out pirates to fight or if the criminals just happened to be so pervasive that it was nearly impossible not to run up against a crew of them every now and again. She had a feeling it was the latter.

Vernestra spoke at length for nearly an hour. Master Niko Jiro, Master Yaddle, and Master Yoda were clearly rapt at all she had done, but Master Oppo Rancisis was nodding off, his prodigious white beard and long hair hiding his face so that the only hint of his boredom was the bob of his topknot. Indara was reasonably certain she was the only one who noticed, as everyone else's gaze was fixed on Jedi Master Vernestra Rwoh.

She was an incredible orator, able to insert enough humor into what would've otherwise been a dry speech to keep everyone invested in her words. Well, everyone but Master Rancisis.

As Vernestra spoke, every moment of the past ten years seemed to come to life. When she talked of assisting with the annual grass shark migration on Tiikae, Indara could see the animals running across the plains and feel the hoverboard under her feet as Vernestra gently guided the creatures away from the nascent settlements, the oohs and ahhs of the assembled Jedi adding inflection points to the narrative. When Vernestra discussed meeting with the royal family on Durga and assisting in the mediation of a wedding contract, her impression of each of the players had a good number of Jedi laughing. The woman could even make judging a soup contest on Brackna sound interesting.

"And that brings me to my time on Cerifisis, which is where Jedi Knight Indara found me. I was there because a group of pirates known as the Strafes were stealing the food rations for the planet. See, Cerifisis has a dry season that means virtually no crops can be grown for around six months of the year. The government there has had to rely on food shipments from Hetzal to feed the populace, and the Strafes were stealing these shipments and selling them back to the officials in charge of the more rural areas, leaving the citizens in the city to starve. A very typical scenario when you've traveled the galaxy as much as I have.

"The thing of note here is not the activities of the pirates but what Indara and I found within the Strafes' hideout on Cerifisis. By your leave, Jedi Masters, if I may demonstrate?"

Master Yoda inclined his head to give his approval, and Vernestra pulled a simple bangle from the folds of her robes. It looked like something that could have been jewelry, but Indara knew Vernestra was about to make a very uncomfortable point. The last time she'd seen the device, the Toydarian in the caves had been wearing it.

The Mirialan gestured to Master Yaddle. "Can you assist me in a quick demonstration?"

Master Yaddle tilted her head, studying Vernestra for a moment before giving a short nod and rising. "And just what is it you need me to do?"

Vernestra flashed a tight smile. Indara recognized a direct challenge when she saw it, and she was glad it was Master Rwoh provoking the Council and not her. The Mirialan said, "Why, attack me with your lightsaber, of course."

Master Niko Jiro let loose a surprised bark of laughter, and Master Rancisis startled awake and began to bluster in indignation. "This is hardly the time or place for this sort of nonsense." He gestured a clawed hand at Master Rwoh. "You've already made this meeting enough of a spectacle. Cease this immediately!"

"Is this not a training room?" A few Jedi tittered, but Master Rancisis still scowled. "I assure you, Master Rancisis, that you will find what happens next well worth the breach in protocol," Vernestra said. "If you will allow us to continue?"

Oppo Rancisis looked around to the other Jedi Masters of the Council. Seeing that he was alone in his objections—especially since Yaddle was an active participant—he gave an annoyed wave of approval. "Fine, fine. Continue your little show."

Vernestra inclined her head like a queen thanking a visiting dignitary before turning back to Master Yaddle.

"Are you prepared, Master Rwoh?" Yaddle asked, and Indara wondered if the elder Jedi was enjoying the display as much as Vernestra seemed to be.

"Quite," the Mirialan said.

Yaddle powered up her lightsaber, the green blade casting a verdant glow on Master Rwoh's robes. Then she took a half step forward, flipping through the air, her blade on target to cleave Vernestra clean in half.

Which, of course, did not happen. Instead the blade powered down and Yaddle landed lightly on her feet, her lightsaber extinguished.

A murmur went up through the crowd as Vernestra turned back to Yaddle. "Master Yaddle, tell us, why did you power down your lightsaber?"

Yaddle smiled, the expression tight. "We both know that I did not power down my blade."

Vernestra took the bangle off her wrist and held it up for the gathered Jedi. "But the rest of the assembled Jedi do not. When Indara and I confronted the leader of the Strafes, he wore this. In a heartbeat, we found ourselves with our weapons neutralized, and we had to improvise. The rumors we have heard through the years? They're true. There is a weapon that can disrupt a lightsaber, something beyond the cortosis armor of the old histories. This device can nullify both lightsabers and blasters. The question now is this: How many criminals across the galaxy have these? And what will happen to the galaxy with the predictable escalation in weapon development in order to counteract these devices?"

The hushed silence, which had fallen over the room when Vernestra had begun talking, erupted into chaos. Jedi were exclaiming and asking questions—many of the younger Jedi didn't know the history of the device. Master Yaddle turned toward the crowd, her voice booming out over the din of Jedi debating the magnitude of Vernestra's revelation.

"Jedi. Give us the room," she said, and the Jedi who had gathered to witness Jedi Master Vernestra Rwoh's homecoming began to filter out in twos and threes. It took a long moment for everyone to leave. Quite a few went over to welcome her back personally, and Indara realized with some surprise that Vernestra seemed to be quite popular. Or infamous. She wasn't sure which was more accurate.

Indara made to take her leave as well, but Master Yoda halted her, saying, "Indara. Stay, you must."

She felt like a child trying to snag an extra pastry, and Master Rwoh's gaze landed on her. The older Jedi gave a small nod. "Master Yoda is right. This part of the story belongs to you as much as it does to me."

Indara nodded and went to stand in the center of the room, next to Vernestra, waiting for the Council to speak.

"I have to admit I am awed at your ability to make an impression, Master Rwoh," Master Jiro said, adjusting their robes. Their earlier mirth had faded considerably.

"I agree. Quite the presentation, Master Rwoh," Master Yarael said, and Vernestra laughed, even though there was no mirth to the sound.

"Is that sarcasm?"

"Are you mocking the Jedi High Council?" Master Rancisis asked.

Vernestra scoffed. "You would send Padawans and younglings out into the galaxy without the knowledge that such a device exists?" she asked. Her gaze was direct as it landed on each master. "I am not a member of this most esteemed Council, but it seems foolhardy not to share knowledge that might save a life."

"We already had knowledge of the resurgence of the four-seven nullifier created by Klerin Chekkat," Master Yaddle said, her voice even, calm. "It is why we recalled you."

"And when were you going to share this information with all the Jedi who make up the Order?" When silence greeted Master Vernestra's question, she nodded. "Ah. So I see some things remain unchanged."

Vernestra said nothing further, and Indara wondered what she meant. Indara couldn't help but notice the way a muscle in Vernestra's jaw twitched.

"It seems as though this shouldn't be kept secret, even if we aren't certain how widespread the issue may be," Indara said. It wasn't until the eyes of every Jedi Master in the room landed on her that she realized she'd spoken aloud, not merely thought her dissent. Embarrassment surged through her. The age and wisdom of the gathered masters had her feeling more like a youngling than a grown woman who had become a Jedi Knight over a year ago. "Oh, ah, forgive me, I merely meant—"

"Indara is correct," Master Yaddle said, still standing. "When will we learn that secrets serve no one and nothing but our regrets?"

Master Yarael's lips quirked with amusement, and he nodded.

"Yaddle, perhaps you should speak with Vernestra. In private." Indara thought the suggestion was strange until she saw the look Master Rwoh and Master Rancisis exchanged. It was clear the two did not care for each other, and it seemed as though Master Yarael had noticed as well or was already aware.

Master Yaddle led the way out of the room, Vernestra on her heels. It was only when the two Jedi Masters got to the door that Master Yaddle turned and looked over her shoulder. "Indara, please join us."

Indara hurried to catch up, but as she retraced her steps toward Master Yaddle's quarters, she had the feeling that perhaps she was better off forgotten in the archives.

Chapter Twelve

Being back in the Jedi Temple on Coruscant felt odd. Everything was familiar, but the faces had changed. The younglings and Padawans looked impossibly young and hopeful, fresh-faced and innocent, and something about seeing them made my heart squeeze painfully. I was nearly a century old—not antiquated by Mirialan standards—but walking through the Jedi Temple made me feel ancient. Every centimeter of the space was filled with memories of friends and mentors long gone, and the effect was a sort of nostalgia combined with homesickness. I didn't hate the Jedi Temple, but I definitely was no longer comfortable there. It was a bit like walking through a graveyard for me, and I realized that part of the reason I'd remained gone so long was that I was not very fond of the ghosts that haunted Coruscant, even if the spirits were nothing but my own fond memories. The strength of the emotion was unexpected but overall not surprising. I just hadn't thought it would feel so sharp, so fresh.

My discomfort had made me sharper with Master Rancisis than I would have liked. And yet I did not regret my honesty.

I glanced back at Indara, who looked at me as if she had stepped in a pile of something distasteful. Ah. I might not have been contrite about my honesty, but it seemed as though Indara was regretting hers. She followed along dutifully, but I had the feeling that if she could have escaped to her beloved archives, she would have at a moment's notice.

Yaddle glanced up at me, a knowing smile playing around her lips. "It will pass," she said, and at first I thought she meant my dislike of Master Rancisis or Indara's remorse. But then I realized she'd most likely sensed something of my turmoil as she continued. "The memories get better the longer you're here. It also helps to visit with the younglings. Their enthusiasm can mend any hurt." She would know. Master Yaddle had seen scores of Padawans grow old and die, some rejoining the Force before their time. I didn't understand how she managed to be so calm about her loss. Each one cut me deeply, and part of what I had enjoyed about my last decade as a Wayseeker was knowing that I would not have to watch the friends I'd made grow old and succumb to the ravages of time. For some reason, it was harder to lose the people I cared about in a natural way than it was in battle. Perhaps because the reason that it was just the way things were was so . . . unsatisfactory.

Dying for a cause, for a *reason,* had always seemed like a far better end than the natural process.

That was not attachment the way so many of the younger Jedi suckled solely on rhetoric pretended it was. That was just being in and *of* the galaxy. Sometimes it was hard to witness the end of things. No matter how natural and necessary they might be.

Master Yaddle entered her quarters ahead of me. I felt something that had tightened within me when I'd first entered the Jedi Temple loosen as I followed her, Indara trailing behind. There were only happy memories within Yaddle's personal space. I had found nothing but peace in and around the older Jedi. Her counsel had always been valuable, especially in light of my failures. She was the one who had urged me to become a Wayseeker once more, to take time and direct my energies toward improving the galaxy, spreading light when the darkness felt too close. She'd been right.

Jedi Knight Indara looked a bit like a lost tooka cat, unsure and nervous. I knew how she felt. I'd been the same as a Jedi Knight, although by her age I had already been promoted to Jedi Master. But I had spent my youth fighting pirates and creatures of legend. Indara had spent hers in a much more peaceful galaxy. The comparison wasn't fair.

Master Yaddle sat at one of three round chairs she'd moved to the center of her quarters, and gestured for us to sit. Master Yaddle's quarters were filled with plants and flowers from across the galaxy, from spiky broma flowers to the trailing fingers of Twi'lek's tears that vined around the space near the ceiling. The sheer amount of life in the space unknotted the remaining tension that had settled into my middle, and I took a deep cleansing breath and released it, steadying myself once more to be the Jedi Master I needed to be in that moment.

"How long have you and the Council known the four-seven nullifier was real?" I asked.

Master Yaddle raised a single eyebrow and leaned back in her chair, smoothing her long auburn braid with a single clawed hand as she searched for her answer. "Since Valo. In the aftermath of the disaster there, we sent someone to search for the device on Valo and later in the ruins of the Nihil stronghold Grizal. No trace of it was ever found, and Klerin Chekkat swore that the design had died with her mother."

"A century, Yaddle?" I said, the tightness in my middle returning. This time it was driven not by grief but by anger at bureaucracy. "The Council did nothing for nearly a *century?*"

Yaddle sighed in annoyance, the sound audible. "No, Vernestra. There were numerous investigations every single time there was another report of the device, no matter how specious the details. The problem is, there was never anything to be found. You cannot expect us to handle something that does not exist."

Indara cleared her throat and leaned forward. "Jedi Masters, I apologize, but could you explain what you're talking about? I've read a lot about Valo and the disaster of the Republic Fair, but while I remember a rampaging hragscythe, I do not recall any mention of a weapon that could disrupt a lightsaber."

Yaddle looked at me, and I gestured for her to continue, feeling a bit chastised after her emphatic retort. "This is the purview of the Council. I am but a humble Wayseeker here to do as commanded," I said as sweetly as possible.

Master Yaddle snorted in amusement, her annoyance already gone, before composing herself. "There is much that happened on Valo that never made it into the official report, in part because the Order was preoccupied with other matters but mostly because it was decided that the histories should only contain verifiable facts, not speculation."

I had to bite my tongue to keep from interrupting Yaddle and pointing out that eyewitness accounts were far from "speculation." But that was an old argument that I didn't feel like dredging up. It did not much matter. Most of the Jedi who had seen the nullifier were long dead.

Of course, there was also Ty Yorrick, a Tholothian and ancient by her people's standards. It would be difficult to open a line of communication with her, if she was even still alive. Ty had retired from the Order several years ago, with little fanfare or notice. Although I'd never learned just what had led to her abrupt retirement, I'd heard rumors that she'd strongly disagreed with the number of diplomatic missions the Order had taken to doing for the Galactic Senate. But these were, of course, just rumors.

Still . . . I needed to send a comm to Ty's last known location as soon as I was finished speaking with Yaddle. Perhaps there was something interesting to be had in a conversation with the old adventurer. Especially since she had worked as the personal bodyguard to Klerin Chekkat and her mother at the time.

"Either way," Master Yaddle continued, "sightings of the four-seven nullifier were something of an isolated occurrence until around fifteen years ago, when Jedi began to report a strange . . . disruption of sorts.

There were only a handful of incidents, and not a single one was substantiated. It wasn't exactly a complete darkening of lightsabers, more a flickering effect, something that could have easily been ignored or imagined, not that most Jedi are prone to flights of fancy. But it was happening often enough that the Council became concerned.

"We investigated and found it was connected to an arms dealer who had ties to Senator Jakob Garn of Thelj in the Airam sector. Nothing concrete, of course, but a lot of rumors and talk in back rooms. Garn had been accused of helping to broker the weapons deals, putting the arms dealer in touch with those who needed his merchandise. And there were rumors that this arms dealer had bragged about having a device that would give people an advantage. We questioned the senator, and he of course denied any knowledge of such a device or any connections to any arms dealers within the galaxy. The Republic did a bit of surveillance on him and found nothing amiss."

"That, or the senator managed to line enough pockets that the issue was dropped," I said. "So, long story short, until we brought you the actual device, you'd never seen one?"

"Not true," Yaddle said, a note of irritation entering her voice. "A team of our Jedi were intervening on the most recent conflict on Soika and found a weapons cache that contained two of the devices. They were completely inoperable, though. Our scientists were able to disassemble the devices but couldn't get them to work."

"So we brought you the only working nullifier," I said, correcting my earlier statement. "So we go to Soika and figure out who is manufacturing and supplying the weapons?"

"No, you go to Thelj and speak with Senator Garn," Yaddle said, speaking to me slowly as though I were a child.

I blinked at the planet name. Thelj was an icy planet with a system of living areas encapsulated by domes. The vision I'd had of Stellan had told me to look for answers beneath the ice.

I wanted to pretend it was a coincidence, but I didn't think it was.

I pulled my attention away from my thoughts and focused on

Yaddle as she spoke. "It seems as though the esteemed senator feels his life is suddenly in danger. He recently said that he's had death threats and fears for his safety, although there is some thought that he is just trying to get ahead of the inevitable consequences for his actions. Either way, he has admitted he knows who the weapons dealer is, and he has agreed to turn him over in exchange for protection and a Jedi escort. After he made this request, a new investigation was launched, and the Republic found some links between Garn's travel and places of conflict—places that saw a sudden uptick in the quality and proliferation of blasters. He has agreed to provide more details, again in exchange for safe passage, and the Republic is eager to have him return to Coruscant. It's good timing that you've found this device just as he is ready to cooperate with the Republic. So your task is to go to Thelj and bring the senator here. And, Vernestra, he asked for you by name."

I blinked, taken aback. "The senator asked for me? Why? That makes no sense."

"Apparently, Senator Garn's family was a victim of the Roundelay Trials on Ghalla. He was in one of the work camps when you helped to liberate them a couple of decades ago. He said, and I quote, 'There is only one Jedi I would trust with my life, and that is Vernestra Rwoh. If you can send her to escort me to Coruscant, I will tell you everything.'"

I could feel the weight of Indara's gaze, and a strange, unsettling feeling began to creep over me. I hate it when people feel grateful to me for something I've done, as though I'm someone special. I just do what anyone, Jedi or not, would do if they'd had the chance. I'm not a hero. I just don't like to see people suffer.

The Roundelay Trials had been a particularly brutal event, a civil war and ethnic cleansing masquerading as a legal proceeding, and the Republic had been slow to react to the tragedy, leading to the passage of a dozen bills in the aftermath of the violence. It was no surprise that the memory would be a formative one for Senator Garn.

What was surprising was that a man whose family had experienced such an event would consort with arms dealers and even become so embroiled with one that he was suspected of similar crimes. It made me curious about Garn. Just what had happened recently to get him to change his tune? I was not so foolish as to think it had anything to do with the resurgence of the nullifier. And danger was pretty standard in the arms-trading business. Something else had scared the senator enough to make him capitulate.

And if not *something* else, perhaps *someone* else.

"So I go to Thelj and find this senator. And Indara? What is her role in all of this?" I asked, my annoyance at the memory of the Roundelay Trials making my tone sharper than I'd intended.

"Indara will be there as an impartial observer and will lend assistance should you need it."

All this time Indara had been observing silently, tracking the conversation but not offering any kind of input. I had almost forgotten she was there. But when I glanced over at her, I saw an expression that echoed how I felt: disdain.

Whether her scorn was for Senator Garn, as mine was, or for the idea of continuing to travel and work with me, I was not quite sure. And I also did not care.

I laughed, the sound harsh and ugly. "You're giving me a Jedi Knight as a babysitter? Brilliant." Indara was a fine Jedi, but working with others had not become my strong suit in my old age. I liked things done a certain way, and most Jedi who were younger than me found this to be overbearing and insulting. It did not help that a large percentage of the Jedi Order fell into that category.

"Oh," Indara said, clearing her throat. A quick glance at her face revealed an expression that was part contemplation and part annoyance. She didn't seem particularly happy to be sent along with me on a mission, either. Fair enough. "Master Yaddle, are you sure that is wise?"

"Indara, I do believe it is time for you to leave the archives behind and serve the galaxy. Master Rwoh is an excellent teacher, and I am certain the two of you will learn much from each other," Yaddle said, her eyes meeting mine. "In addition, your research skills will help bring Master Rwoh up to speed, since she has missed quite a bit in the past decade."

"Indara, can you give me a moment with Master Yaddle?" I said.

It was more statement than question, and Indara's eyes narrowed before she nodded and left without a word.

Once Indara had left, I leaned back in my chair, as relaxed as I could be while in the Temple. "Why do you want me to take the librarian? It's pretty clear she doesn't care for me."

Yaddle didn't disagree. "Like you, she's been left on her own for too long. As I said, I think the two of you could learn a lot from each other."

"Perhaps, but why has she been left to her own devices for so long? The Council didn't send her on a single mission before you asked her to fetch me? How long has she been a Jedi Knight? Shouldn't she be off on her own missions, not following along on mine? None of this makes any kind of sense, Master Yaddle."

Yaddle gave me a small smile, the lines of her green face revealing nothing. "It was for the best. Anything more than that, well, perhaps you should ask Indara."

It wasn't a real answer, but I could sense it was the most I was going to get from her.

Yaddle would share only as much as she thought was useful in the moment. She was like a lot of older Jedi in that way. Trying to get anything more from her about Indara would be met with polite acknowledgment and redirection. Frustrating, but I knew when I was beaten. So I changed the subject.

"Fine. So what are you not telling me about Garn?"

Yaddle went to a nearby cabinet and pulled out a bottle of a darkbrown liquor. I raised a single eyebrow in her direction. "Are you still partial to Dalnan whiskey?" she asked, a bit too sweetly.

I smiled. "Is this a bribe?"

Yaddle laughed. "You've already been assigned your task. This is just a friendly conversation between Jedi Masters."

I leaned forward and nodded. "Let us partake of the bounty of the Force," I said, a common refrain I'd learned while on Kiszo, a small out-of-the-way planet where the Church of the Force had found a surprising foothold. Yaddle smiled, a true smile, knowing the expression.

"Did you see the geysers while you were on Kiszo?" She produced a couple of beautifully wrought glasses and poured a measure of the fine brown liquor in each before handing me one. She raised hers, and we clinked glasses before I took a sip of the whiskey, the taste sweet and floral. I sighed in appreciation.

"I did. And the canyons. It's a beautiful place. But I'm not here to share happy memories, Master Yaddle. You're sending me after Garn, and while the Roundelay Trials might have something to do with it, I'm not so easily turned by flattery to think that's the whole of the reason."

"Jedi Knight at fifteen. The pride of Master Stellan Gios, the Fallen Star. You always were too smart for your own good," Yaddle said. She nodded, as if finally coming to a decision. "I am not supposed to tell you this, but the real reason you're being sent, in addition to the request by the senator, is because you have been gone this past decade, so there is no possible conflict of interest in sending you. Three years ago, Garn and his cabal almost managed to push through the Jedi Annexation Act. You are one of the few Jedi Masters we have who was not here on Coruscant at some point to witness that difficult time."

A chill ran over my skin at the mention of the dead piece of legislation, and I drained my glass before placing it back on Yaddle's desk. The Jedi Annexation Act had been a move by a very vocal group within the Senate to claim oversight of the Jedi, by declaring the Order an official branch of the Republic instead of the separate entity it had always been. The Galactic Senate already petitioned the Order to take on its many pet causes, but the passage of the act would have yoked the Order to the Senate indefinitely, essentially making all of us little more than glorified servants.

I tapped my glass. "I'm going to need another dram while I sit with this," I said, and Yaddle filled my glass again, this pour healthier than the last.

This glass of whiskey I nursed. Yaddle shifted on her chair before sighing. "I don't really blame the senator, regardless of what I may think of his politics. This new crop of politicians are eager to prove themselves, and I don't think I have to tell you that they seem to think the Nihil conflict and the sacrifices of the Jedi are ancient history."

"If only we could all be blessed with such short memories," I said, sipping at my whiskey. The pop of flavor on my tongue was still nice, but Yaddle's revelation had ruined my enjoyment of the liquor to some extent.

"True. What to the shorter-lived species feels like ancient history to us can feel like last week."

"'Us'? Last I checked, you still had several centuries on me," I said.

Yaddle laughed. "Perhaps. But do you know how long I had to be a Padawan? Things even out." She finished her drink and cradled the glass in her hands. "Enough about the senator. It's an easy task, and when you're done, we'll discuss your new responsibilities."

"'New responsibilities'? Here I was hoping this was a singular request."

Yaddle gave me a long look. "Surely you didn't truly believe that?"

I didn't, not really. I had been hoping my visit to Coruscant would be short, but I knew better in my heart of hearts. I was a Jedi, and being an active part of the Order was the job. Even if I didn't relish the fact. "Well, as long as no one expects me to take another Padawan," I said, some of the old pain bubbling up. Yaddle cocked her head, and I finished my whiskey and stood. "And yes, I'm fine. Please don't bring it up. I still don't want to talk about it."

"The failures of our students are not our own," Yaddle said.

I sighed before turning for the door. "Perhaps." I paused and turned back to the Jedi Master once more. I had always respected Yaddle, but this was one place where our beliefs diverged. "Or . . . perhaps the failure of our students is the direct result of our own lack as mentors.

Either way, I'll fetch Indara, and we'll be on our way. I'll send a message once we have the senator."

"Welcome home, Vernestra," Master Yaddle said. I wanted to tell her Coruscant was not my home, but instead I just nodded in acknowledgment of her words.

I had a senator to secure.

Chapter Thirteen

By the time they left for Thelj, Indara had mostly come to terms with her new reality. Her quarters on the *Cantaros* were comfortable and well appointed, and she'd mostly adjusted to seeing J-6, Vernestra's droid, fly the ship. When Indara had inquired about Vernestra's own reluctance to fly, she'd smiled. "Hyperspace can be very distracting for me. You're welcome to fly if you'd prefer, but I assure you Jay-Six is a more-than-competent pilot."

The droid for her part had swiveled in the pilot's seat to give Indara a look that felt far more critical than it should have, then said, "Do not question my competence. I've been operational at least two centuries longer than you've been alive. I promise you, there is information in my circuits that you have never even considered."

And that was the end of that conversation.

Indara had decided to spend the few hours it would take to get to Thelj reading up on Senator Garn and the legislation he had once sponsored, the Jedi Annexation Act.

She had heard some rumblings about the possible law, but from her research space in the archives, it hadn't been much. She remembered a few of the Jedi discussing the possible loss of autonomy and what a mistake such an act would be, but Indara had been far more concerned with her own matters: researching and documenting a detailed history of the cultural relevance of shishi tea to the Kessarine population on Eriadu. In hindsight, it probably was not the best use of her time, but the request for the research had come from a Jedi Master about to embark on a diplomatic mission, so she'd thrown herself into the task without question.

But it would be in her best interest to dig a little deeper now, especially since Master Yaddle had been clear that this was a way in which she would contribute.

Indara was not so naïve as to think that Vernestra Rwoh was thrilled to have her along. The woman kept her emotions in check for the most part, but Indara had seen the slight tightening of her jaw when Yaddle revealed that Indara would be tagging along. It had irked Indara. Hadn't she proven herself on Cerifisis? She was a capable partner, and some part of Indara wanted the Jedi Master to recognize that. But Indara also knew that Vernestra Rwoh could have easily taken on all the pirates without her help, and that Vernestra saw her as some kind of pitiful Jedi who had spent her time hiding in the archives instead of serving the galaxy in a meaningful way.

And secretly, Indara knew Vernestra was right.

Indara had told herself she'd wanted to go on missions and be assigned to tasks outside the confines of the library. But the reality was that she had never volunteered for any of the various assignments that had been announced over the past year. Instead, she'd ducked her head and written another analysis of this obscure event or that cultural practice, or she'd taken on dozens, if not hundreds, of other small, innocuous duties. She had been a good Jedi, but not in the way that Vernestra thought mattered most: being out in the galaxy, spreading the light of the Jedi by making wrongs right.

And because of that, Indara wanted to prove to Vernestra that she was useful. It meant that until Indara got the chance to demonstrate her lightsaber abilities—*again*—she had to demonstrate her merit in other ways. Knowing the ins and outs of Senator Garn's push to make the Jedi Order beholden to the Galactic Senate seemed as good a way as any. Especially since Vernestra had not been party to any of the discussions.

And the more they knew about Garn, the better prepared they would be to deal with the man.

But Indara had not been prepared for the sheer volume of news holos, articles, and plain old senatorial inquiries into the man. The year he was elected to the Senate, he was brought up on charges of abusing his office when he forced a local shipping family to open their private hyperspace lanes for travel originating from Thelj. The next year, he was brought up on fraud charges related to a number of shady deals and half promises. And from there, it spiraled on: rumored dealings with the Hutt Cartel, known associations with bounty hunters and information brokers who had not been vetted by the Senate, rumors that he'd tried to have his brother-in-law murdered after a particularly bad fight with his wife. On and on and on it went, and as far as Indara could tell, all of it was true. Even the report that Senator Garn had sold spice in college, using the funds to pay his way through Bar'Leth University, had been confirmed by no fewer than three reliable sources and an arrest record with an image of a younger, reed-thin Garn.

Whatever the Jedi thought about this man, the reality was even worse.

What Indara could not understand was how such a man was allowed to remain in the Senate. Or why the sector he represented—a handful of once-prosperous planets now falling into decline—elected him time and again. Surely the reality combined with the rumors that swirled about the man would be enough to make any intelligent constituent rethink their senatorial representation?

Apparently not.

Indara finally realized that she'd had enough and shut down the datapad, leaning back heavily on the bunk in her quarters. She was beginning to understand why Vernestra had avoided the Order for a time. This was the kind of person the Republic thought the Jedi should save and protect? Indara hadn't researched the rest of the senators involved in trying to pass the Jedi Annexation Act, but she didn't need to. It was clear that Garn, as the bill's sponsor, intended it as a way to use the might of the Jedi for his own personal gain.

And now Indara was being sent to help bring the man safely back to Coruscant. The irony of it all made her want to swear.

Instead, she decided she needed a cup of tea. Maybe with a bit of whatever liquor might be hiding in the cabinets.

Indara was only half surprised to see Vernestra sitting at the dining table in the galley when she entered. The elder Jedi looked somehow older since they'd left Coruscant, and Indara wasn't sure if it was because of her newly shorn hair or the sudden mantle of responsibility that had been placed on the older woman's shoulders. Either way, it wasn't like Indara was going to ask. She knew better than to poke a sleeping rancor.

"Indara. Couldn't sleep?" Vernestra asked, her smile polite. There was a strange look about her eyes, somewhat there and somewhat not, and Indara wondered what it was about hyperspace that made Master Rwoh look so unsettled. Dreamy. She half wondered what answer she would get if she asked.

"I was reading up on Senator Garn. I . . . do you know anything about him?"

Vernestra snorted and pointed to a cabinet. "That conversation is going to need something stronger than tea. Small cabinet over the rehydrator. I keep a bottle of lompop liqueur there just in case."

Indara quickly found the bottle and placed it on the table before making her own cup of tea. She watched Vernestra pour a healthy amount into her cup and then hand the bottle to Indara, who dumped a much smaller amount into her own. At Vernestra's raised eyebrow, Indara shrugged. "I'm not much of a drinker."

"Neither am I. But I find sometimes on tasks like ours . . . it's fine to take a bit of the edge off." Vernestra closed her eyes and sighed before speaking again. "I have long known about Garn and his unsavory reputation. A dear friend of mine was one of the Jedi who very early on turned over information to the Galactic Senate so that charges could be brought against him, charges the Senate rejected." Vernestra opened her eyes. "So yes, I know what kind of man Senator Garn is. I don't much care, though. The Order has set me to a task, and I will accomplish it, because I am a Jedi and that is the job. But that does not mean I agree with everything they say. That is the beauty of the Order: The Force unites us, but in the end, we all have our own paths to forge."

Indara nodded. "I can see that. Can I ask you a question?"

"As long as you let me ask one in return," Vernestra said, raising her eyebrows slightly in challenge. Indara felt a bit off balance, but not in a bad way. It was more akin to when she was trying to master a new form, and feeling discomfort trying a new move before her body became comfortable with the choreography of it.

Also, for once Vernestra seemed to be talking *with* her, not *at* her, and she found the change made all the difference. Perhaps their mission together wouldn't be too onerous after all.

"Okay, fair enough. Why did you shave your head? And what do your tattoos mean? Two questions, really, but I suspect the answer is probably linked," Indara said. She gestured to the twin rows of diamonds on the outside of each eye, two rows of three. "I know those are kinship markings. I have studied Mirialan tattoos and their meanings a bit. But the diamonds on your hands and head . . . I don't remember reading anything about those."

Vernestra smiled, the expression genuine. "I shaved my head because I like to remind myself—and others, if I'm being honest—who I am, and these tattoos show that. They are my pride and joy. Each one represents someone who has thanked me for saving their life. It isn't a Mirialan practice at all, but actually belongs to the Kirnost of Kirna. They believe there is such a thing as a life debt, and when someone thanks you for saving their life, you must acknowledge the sentiment in a meaningful way, otherwise the debt can grow and eventually become a run of bad luck for the indebted person."

"So this is your way of showing that you didn't want anyone to feel like they owed you?" Indara asked, looking at the tattoos. There were so many. So many lives touched in a meaningful way by Master Rwoh. It was awe inspiring.

"No one owes me anything for what I've done. I am a Jedi. I wake every morning and choose the light of the Force. What good am I if I am not spreading that light? Which brings me to a question for you: What happened to you that the Order has let you hide away in the archives for more than a year? Did you plan to stay there forever, never taking a Padawan, avoiding missions? Yaddle hinted that there is a specific reason for the oversight. I would like for you to tell me what that is."

Indara's mouth went dry and her palms slicked with sweat, but instead of avoiding the question like she usually would have, she took a deep pull of the tea, the floral astringency of the liquor warmed and sweetened by the herbs of the hot liquid. She closed her eyes, savoring the moment of calm before she was launched headfirst back into the maelstrom of memory. "I was in the mines on Seswenna during the Farlingan Collapse. You may not have heard of it. I was there with four other Jedi. I was the only one who survived. It took them a week to find me."

For a moment, Indara was back in that dark time. "We went down there because the miners had been complaining about the work conditions and a lack of safety, holding up production. The Senate asked the Order to get involved, since the mines were crucial to the economies of a few different planets. We were supposed to be there to help keep them safe. Instead we were pinned behind some rubble. The other Jedi died instantly, but my leg was just pinned. And the Force . . . well, it wasn't much help."

Suddenly, Indara was once more trapped in the caves far below

Seswenna, the tortured cries of the miners all around her, the moans and pleading growing fainter by the day. She remembered crying, then meditating, and the waves of pain as they came and went. Unconsciousness, when it came, had been a blessing. When she was able, she drank from a nearby puddle, the only relief to her suffering.

"I don't remember them finding me. It was a droid crew they eventually sent down, more to recover the bodies and reopen the tunnel than because of the deaths. I don't remember the journey back to Coruscant or even the remembrance ceremonies for the other Jedi. I was in a bacta tank for a couple of weeks, and when I came out I was offered a chance to work in the archives until I felt ready to return to missions. I jumped on it because I couldn't help but wonder why I hadn't been . . . a better Jedi. And, well, I didn't think going on missions was a very good idea. I wanted to, but I never did. Or maybe I never wanted to and I was too afraid to admit that I was scared. Either way, here I am now."

Vernestra had listened to the story without moving, almost as though she were a statue, and when Indara finished, the older woman reached out and placed a warm hand atop Indara's frigid fingertips on the table. "I am sorry that happened to you, and I am also sorry I seem to have misjudged you. You lived through a hardship, but please know that your suffering and survival do not define you. And that will be all I will say on the matter unless you feel like sharing more. Now, since you're the archivist, tell me what you found out about Garn that might be most useful."

Indara could feel a sudden lump well in her throat, but she cleared it and nodded. "So, judging from his past and the way he uses his knowledge of relevant laws, this is not an honest request from him. I don't think he actually plans on turning himself in. He's escaped prosecution for a number of crimes and still holds a favored position on senatorial committees."

"Do you think this is a distraction of sorts?" Vernestra asked.

Indara nodded. "I looked a bit deeper into the Jedi Annexation Act that Garn sponsored. It never truly had the support it needed to pass, but it kicked up enough fuss that people stopped asking questions about Garn's investment in some very unsavory corporations. The man is the master of the misdirect. I suspect there is some piece of information that hasn't yet come to light—a bargaining chip hidden up his sleeve, so to speak. I suspect that once we get him safely to Coruscant, he has some scheme he'll put into action. The senator has spent an entire lifetime avoiding consequences, and I don't think that kind of person gives up easily. I just wish I knew why he asked for you specifically. It feels... purposeful."

"That confirms a lot of what I expected. But I do find it interesting that apparently the Order felt the bill was more dangerous than the facts seem to support."

Indara shrugged. "I don't think any Jedi relishes the thought of being forced to participate in politics. The fallout of such a thing could be disastrous for the Order."

"I could not agree more." Vernestra yawned widely before standing. She stumbled and righted herself, her gaze going distant before she turned back to Indara. "I'm going to try to get some sleep. You should, too. Travel between planets can sometimes make it difficult to rest, so if you need anything to help with that, just ask Jay-Six. She may seem gruff, but her underlying programming is that of a child care droid. She will be happy to help."

Indara somehow doubted that was the case, but she gave an acknowledging nod to Vernestra anyway. The Jedi was almost out of the room before Indara spoke up.

"Master Rwoh. You said you don't care for hyperspace. Can you share why?"

Vernestra smiled, the expression genuine, but there was no mistaking the haunted expression in her eyes. "Ah. That is an answer for another time. Rest well, Indara."

And then the Jedi Master was gone, off once again on her own business.

Chapter Fourteen

As I left the galley, I could sense the impending vision, a pressure building behind my eyes. Indara didn't notice, but I felt the unsteadiness in my gait as I made my way out of the galley and to my quarters.

The visions weren't always like that, but I supposed that perhaps something in Indara's story had triggered a sympathetic response. That, or I'd just been in hyperspace long enough that the Force had decided it was finished waiting.

Whatever the cause, I'd barely reached my cabin when my legs gave out and I collapsed. But where I should have been falling onto the floor, I instead landed in a gently rocking boat, Stellan still wearing the floppy, oversized hat that commercial fishers on Trask donned to help block the punishing sun.

"The bites are good today," he said. He held a rudimentary fishing pole, the line in the water.

"You never liked fishing," I said, "and yet this is the second time you've been here to talk about this."

The Stellan in my vision smiled. "I never had to communicate in metaphor before. And you haven't been looking."

I sighed. "I'm headed to Thelj right now. You told me the path begins on the frozen seas, and it doesn't get much frostier than Thelj."

The vision of Stellan didn't acknowledge my words. Not surprising, but frustrating all the same. The end of the pole jerked, and he pulled back on it. "Oh, it looks like a big one! I bet it's for you."

I held on to either side of the boat as Stellan struggled to reel in the fish on his line, a large thing that was bloated and dead when he pulled it into the boat. "Whew. Not much of a prize," he said with a wink.

Stellan leaned down and cut open the fish. Instead of entrails, a number of random things tumbled out of the fish's belly: a nullifier bangle just like the one I found on Cerifisis; a bouquet of flowers, impossibly alive and fresh; a handful of crystals that I didn't recognize; and a pipe used for smoking spice. He reached down and picked up the nullifier, flipping it to me. I caught it in midair.

"That seems useful. But as for the rest of this?" He gestured at the mess left behind in the boat. "You're going to have to figure it out."

At that moment the boat jostled, as though hit from below by a large creature, and I woke on the floor of my quarters. I sat up with a groan, my head throbbing. Once I had gotten my bearings, I went to my datapad and opened the file I kept just for writing down the visions I had. I had been diligently tracking my visions for decades, ever since the Nihil conflict, but in the last decade they had become more plentiful. And more aggressive, pulling me under entirely against my will in ways impossible to fight. Some of them were immediately helpful, problems worked out by my subconscious. Most were not, and I was hoping that this vision did not fall into that category.

It seemed pretty clear that my vision had been trying to tell me that there was more to this whole business with the nullifier than I thought, but I wasn't sure what any of the other items referred to. I made a note of them in my datapad. Flowers, crystals, a spice pipe. It seemed like a random collection. I rubbed my temples as a headache bloomed behind my eyes, breathing and letting go as the last remnants of the vision cleared, leaving me feeling annoyed and out of sorts.

The last time I had seen Stellan, he had told me to fish for answers below the ice. And now I had three items that were somehow linked to... what? The nullifier? It seemed they were connected, but I didn't want to read too much into the vision. Down that path could also lie folly. My hyperspace visions were rarely so direct.

A knock at my door brought me back to myself. "Yes?"

The door slid open, and Indara poked her head inside. "We've just landed on Thelj. I wasn't sure if you'd heard the landing alarm."

I hadn't, but there was no need for the other woman to know that. My visions were my own business, and I was not about to start sharing them now. I stood and nodded to Indara while clipping my lightsaber onto my belt. "Are you ready?"

She nodded and stepped back, allowing me space to lead the way off the ship and into the docking yard.

It had been a number of decades since I had been on Thelj. The planet was covered with a layer of ice, and it was only through the construction of geothermic domes that life was possible here for most species. But where Thelj had once been a marvel of engineering, it had long left that designation and begun to slide into decline.

The planet had noticeably changed since my last visit, and not for the better. The dockyards were in disrepair, paint peeling and bits of flaking metal showing through in odd places. Most of the shops in the marketplace were shuttered, out of business, or advertising space for new owners, and those that were open were little more than gambling halls or storefronts that offered droids at a discounted price. The lone tavern had a sour smell as Indara and I walked by, making our way to the hypertrain that would take us to the city proper.

"Have you been to Thelj before?" Indara asked, taking in the space with a critical frown, as though she was noting every single detail and found the whole of the place lacking, an assessment I agreed with completely.

"Decades ago. It wasn't like this then, though. Of course, change is one of the few constants in the galaxy."

"I did some reading on the planet before we arrived," Indara said as we stopped in the station, waiting for the train. "It seems the decline is directly tied to the Graf family and their dwindling reputation. Graf Enterprises once funded much of the development on the planet and employed the majority of the citizenry. When they pulled out of Thelj a couple of decades ago, there was a ripple effect. Most of the government funds have been redirected to maintaining the domes, leaving little for other improvements. Thelj has one of the fastest-declining populations in the entire Republic."

"Ah well, that is unsurprising, then. It seems the Grafs have not changed much."

Indara looked at me in surprise. "You knew them?"

"I've met a few of them in my years. While I usually hesitate to paint an entire family with the same brush, I feel very comfortable that honor and integrity are secondary to gaining wealth for that family," I said as the whir of repulsors filled the space. "I do believe that is our train."

The train was in no better repair than the rest of the dockyards, and once we climbed aboard, the vehicle took off with an unsteady lurch. Indara and I were the only ones in the car we had selected, and the timer on the wall displayed a flashing set of nines, indicating we were most likely on our own when it came to figuring out the travel time to our stop. Indara pulled a datapad from her robes, showing me the screen. "It seems as though this route will take us to the city center. The senator's office should be a short walk from there."

Normally, Jedi Order protocol would dictate that we go to the local Jedi temple and introduce ourselves before seeking out the senator, but there was no such outpost on Thelj. We were on our own. Still, that did not bother me as much as being here on Thelj in the first place, a corrupt senator once more proving that the Order needed to better work on distancing itself from the Republic—and most especially the Senate. Some of my distaste must have shown on my face, because Indara gave me a concerned look.

"Master Rwoh, are you well?"

"I'm fine. I just find this entire task distasteful," I said with a sigh. "In my experience, senators have a way of exploiting the Order for their own gain. You probably read about Senators Tia Toon and Ghirra Starros when researching the Nihil conflict. And there are others, elected people who crave not the honor of service but the opportunity for power. Those senators just see the Jedi as a valuable tool, and I'm not sure the rest of the Senate is too far behind in that philosophy. And how long does it take for the Senate—for anyone, really—to turn a tool into a *weapon*? The longer the Jedi indulge that behavior in the spirit of goodwill, the more we leave ourselves open to becoming subject to the Senate's whims. The Order has stood far longer than the Republic, and I have a feeling it will endure long beyond it as well. Politics and the Force are a terrible combination."

Indara looked at me in horror, and I laughed. "Does that philosophy strike you as radical, Indara?"

"Yes. A bit," she said. Her expression had turned pensive.

"I think you will discover that not all Jedi Masters share the same opinions. Which is how it should be. We are all on our own journeys. Luckily, you're young. You have time." It was the wrong thing to say, and I caught Indara's sour look before she could restrain it.

Ah, well, at least that was familiar.

A discordant chime sounded, the enunciators also clearly having seen better days, and the train began to judder to a stop. Perfect timing. I was beginning to slip into a lecture neither of us needed. Indara would have to figure out who she was as a Jedi on her own. And I would be better off biting my tongue until her annoyance had passed. "I do believe this is our stop."

I led the way off the train and out of the station, Indara a silent shadow behind me. Her gaze was nearly a physical weight on my back, her irritation clear. She was a fully grown adult who reminded me more of a petulant teenager, and I was reacting to that instead of remembering that she had lived a full life before our paths had crossed.

In all my time as a Wayseeker, I had only grown more distanced from ideologies of the younger Jedi. I wanted to be better at communicating with Indara, but I was beginning to wonder if it was possible.

Maybe I was just seriously out of touch with younger Jedi. How did Yaddle do it? Perhaps I would ask her for advice the next time we spoke.

We left the station and headed straight for the governmental building where Senator Garn's offices were located, Indara now at my side. We had been instructed to meet with the senator there and had even sent a message when we landed to ensure that he was still being cooperative. The response had been cordial and curt. Yes, the senator was still looking forward to receiving the Jedi. He was, after all, a man of his word. I had laughed when J-6 relayed the message, but I did love the audacity.

Now, entering one of the few buildings on Thelj that had not fallen into disrepair, I was beginning to wonder just what would be waiting for us when we arrived at the senator's office. "When we meet with Garn, let me do the talking. No matter what the facts might say about him, we must appear to take him at his word. I do not want him thinking we are going to do anything but take him back to Coruscant."

Indara gave me a look of alarm. "That is what we're doing, right? Escorting him back to Coruscant?"

"It is, but lifelong criminals like Garn tend to expect everyone to double-cross them, because that is what *they* would do. Our job is to reassure him that we are not like his cronies and that we truly do mean what we say."

"Why would he think so poorly of the Jedi?" Indara asked. For a moment, I thought she was being sarcastic, but a single glance at her face revealed that she was sincere.

Ah, to be so naïve. It had been decades since I'd been so foolish.

We entered the turbolift in silence. It was a short ride to Garn's office, which was predictably on the highest floor. A droid met us as we exited the turbolift, her mincing walk causing both Indara and me to stop short.

"Welcome to Senator Garn's office," she purred. "Please have a seat, and I will let him know you're here."

The droid spun on her heel and made her way down a back hallway, then returned after a pause. "This way, if you please."

She sashayed away and we followed, the narrow hallway opening on a receiving room with a sunken area filled with seating cushions. The space was decorated in shades of blue, from the midnight blue of the cushions to the palest ice blue of the window hangings. The room had a curious curve, the entire area set up in concentric circles. It was an unusual office, and far more opulent than the quarters of any other senator I had met, even those who came from families with wealth. The setup seemed better suited to an indolent prince than a servant of the people. Every single building we had seen on Thelj needed repair, the walls cracked and paint peeling. The sidewalks were also cracked, and trash clogged the alleys between buildings. There were a few beggars, and very few businesses were open. But Garn's office looked like the pinnacle of luxury. Judging from the appearance of Thelj, Garn was serving his own interests far more than those of his constituents.

Garn relaxed against a pile of cushions. "Jedi! Welcome, welcome!" he said, his smile wide. "Jedi Master Vernestra Rwoh, it is such an honor to see you once more. I have long wanted to thank you personally for saving my life when I was younger."

I smiled tightly and gave him a curt nod of acknowledgment. There was something instantly off-putting about the man. His white-blond hair was groomed so that not a strand moved, and his teeth were far too white to be his own. Even his face had a strange look, like he had endured too many beauty treatments. The man was inherently fake, like a counterfeit credit. If I had helped to liberate him and his family when he was a boy, I didn't remember them, and there was nothing about the man now that I found the least bit appealing—though perhaps that was just because I knew entirely too much about his unsavory actions.

But I was a Jedi and I had a job to do, and do it I would.

"Senator, thank you for the kind words. Please let me introduce Jedi Knight Indara. We are here at your request. We understand you would like a personal escort to Coruscant?"

Garn's smile never wavered, not even a muscle twitching from the effort. "Yes, yes! But first, let's sit, have a chat. We're in no rush."

"Actually we are," I said when Indara made to sit. She looked at me, and I gave her a slight headshake. "Our ship is ready to depart, so if you will gather your things, we can be on our way."

Garn's smile turned brittle, and a muscle jumped in his jaw. Ah. So, he did not like being told what to do. Good to know.

"Don't you want to hear why I'm turning myself in first?" Garn asked.

I shook my head. "That, Senator, is none of my business. I am merely here to ensure that you get to your destination safely. But if you would like to make a statement to us, there will be plenty of time for that during our travels. Now, if you will show us where your bags are, we can be on our way."

Garn nodded and climbed to his feet, coming to stand near me. There was a moment of hesitation, and I saw fear flicker across his face. His voice dropped to a whisper, and the implacable smile evaporated. "I'm sorry. They were going to kill me."

I barely had time to process Garn's words before he was diving out of the way as two gunmen threw back the curtains at the edge of the room. Garn ran from the office. Indara and I reached for our lightsabers before the men could fire a shot.

It should have been predictable the way the blades powered up before blinking once, twice, and then going out. I had just enough time to exchange a glance with Indara before the first blaster bolt whizzed past my cheek. I used the Force to shove Indara sideways before flipping backward out of the way, blaster bolts pelting the area where we'd just been. The sound of the blaster cycling for another barrage was a terrible sign.

The room offered precious little in the way of defense. There were no desks or tables to hide behind, and leaping away from the blasterfire required most of my attention. The men shooting at us—both human—had terrible aim, which was the only reason Indara and I were not yet dead. There was nowhere to take cover.

"The pillows!" I shouted to Indara before hastily reaching out with the Force and using it to throw the nearest cushion at one of the men. It wasn't much, but it was enough to distract him. The pillow exploded in a rain of fragrant feathers, and I grinned. Of course Garn was the type of man to have cushions filled with lonara feathers.

These feathers were highly combustible. The natural oils that gave the feathers their pleasant aroma were volatile, which was why they had been outlawed by the Republic.

Thank goodness for Senator Garn and his disdain for lawful behavior.

I leapt out of the way of another blaster bolt before grabbing as many pillows as I could with the Force and launching them at the shooters, Indara following my lead. There were ridiculous numbers of pillows in the space, and what could have been little more than a distraction turned into an onslaught as the men became inundated with the things. The assassins, annoyance written across their features, aimed for the pillows instead of us.

And that was their final mistake.

"Get down!" I yelled to Indara, and dived away from the feathery mess near the men. There was an audible whoosh as a blaster bolt hit one of the mass of feathers floating around them, the combustion of this single feather creating a chain reaction that in turn created a flaming cloud of disaster. The men screamed, and I ran toward the door, Indara at my heels.

"We have to get Garn," I said. We ran out into the hallway only to see Garn's droid blocking our path, the compartments on her forearms opened to reveal a number of small blasters.

"I'm sorry, but I am going to have to ask you to stay," she said.

Before I could react, the sound of a massive blaster firing echoed from behind the droid, and she fell to the ground, her entire back missing, the edges melted. J-6 stood behind her, her chest compartment open and the oversized weapon contained within still smoking.

"Your droid has a blaster?" Indara asked, eyes wide.

"Several. She takes personal defense quite seriously," I said.

Indara did not seem to appreciate the joke.

"Looks like you were right. It was a double cross," J-6 said. "Ew, gross. Who adds such garish details to a protocol droid? She has to be totally unbalanced."

"Did you see Garn run past you?" I asked J-6.

The droid shook her head. "No. There was no one in the hallway after I exited the lift."

"Garn must have another exit at his disposal," I said, pointing down the hallway in the opposite direction, back toward the receiving room. "Indara, you go left; I'll take the right hallway. Be careful. Garn obviously has nullifier tech at his disposal."

Indara nodded and ran off, and I turned back to J-6 to give her one last instruction. "If the men who tried to kill us are still alive, make sure they stay that way."

"Are you sure?" J-6 asked. A simple question, but not for a droid who was supposed to have been programmed to raise children.

"Yes. I have some questions for them." I was glad that Indara wasn't around to hear J-6's query. Explaining it would have required more information than I was ready to share. I was already pretty sure I was going to have to discuss just why it was that I allowed my droid to have blasters. As though I could stop J-6 once she had her circuits set to a course of action.

And then, with one last look at the destroyed droid, I went looking for Garn.

Chapter Fifteen

For the past week or so, ever since the Council had first tasked Indara with finding Master Rwoh, the Jedi Knight had felt out of her depth. She wasn't used to being shot at, or having to fight at all, much less without her lightsaber. She wasn't used to dealing with Jedi Masters who seemed to dislike the Jedi High Council, and she definitely wasn't used to so much *lecturing*. Indara had never met a Jedi Master who liked the sound of her own voice more than Vernestra Rwoh.

But as she ran full tilt down the thickly carpeted hallway searching for Garn, Indara realized that, of all those things, it was easiest to get used to being shot at. Remarkably easy. And for the first time in quite a while, she felt *capable*. She had confidence in her abilities, and she knew that whatever happened, she would be able to face it without hesitation.

That almost made the getting-shot-at part worth it.

Almost.

The hallway ended in a turbolift that stood open, waiting to receive a passenger. Indara didn't think that Garn had managed to use the lift and get down to the street level in the time they'd had to fight the gunmen, but she figured it was better to take the chance than to turn back and be wrong. If Garn had fled the building, at least she might then find him before he fled the planet.

Indara jumped into the lift. It offered only one destination, represented by a symbol she didn't recognize. Still, she punched the button, harder than she normally would have, and the lift descended. The Force seemed to crackle through her, energizing her and spurring her on. Or perhaps that was just adrenaline. Either way, she was ready to find Garn and drag him back to Coruscant. And not just because he'd tried to have two Jedi murdered. He was not a good man, and Indara would be glad to have him in a senatorial holding cell, unable to spread any more chaos and misery through the galaxy.

When the lift doors opened, blasterfire peppered the space. Indara dived out of the lift, rolling until she found cover behind an ornate landspeeder. She pulled out her lightsaber and attempted to power it up, relieved when the green plasma blade glowed, bright and strong. She hated not being able to use her lightsaber. It felt too much like trying to fight with one hand tied behind her back.

Indara stood up and began walking in the direction of the blasterfire, using the lightsaber to repel the bolts. "Give it up, Garn! This is only going to make things worse."

There was no answer, but the blasterfire stopped. The sound of an engine revving was unmistakable, though, and Indara had just enough time to leap into the air—the Force giving her height far beyond what she could physically achieve—before the landspeeder hit her.

Time seemed to slow as Indara looked down at the driver. She had expected to see Senator Garn's white-blond hair, not ivory fur. A Gigoran missing an eye looked up at her as the vehicle sped underneath her, and Indara felt a moment of recognition before her feet hit the ground once more. She spun around to watch where the landspeeder went, but it careened up a ramp and out of view. Most likely an exit to the street a few levels above.

Indara wasn't certain whether it was the same Gigoran she had seen on Haileap, but it didn't feel like a coincidence. How many Gigorans missing an eye could there be in the galaxy? It felt like the Force pushing her in a specific direction.

Either way, the Gigoran was not her immediate concern. Garn was. There had been only one person in the landspeeder. So where had the senator gotten to?

Indara cautiously searched the remainder of the garage, her heart thumping against her rib cage as she prepared for an attack. But none was forthcoming, and when she found Garn on the ground, head twisted at an unnatural angle, she knew that searching any further would be futile.

Indara powered down her lightsaber as she took in the sight before her, clipping the weapon to her belt with a sigh. Senator Garn was dead. And her mission was a failure.

Indara didn't feel any sadness at seeing the man spread out on the ground. His death was his own doing, the consequence of his many terrible actions. The illegal weapons he'd been accused of sending to conflict-ridden planets had caused far more misery than anything else, and if anything, perhaps his ending had been too swift.

There was a far-off ding as the turbolift returned once more, and Indara backtracked until she could see Vernestra exiting. "Garn's over here. Someone broke his neck."

Indara led the way, Vernestra following her to where Garn's body lay. The Mirialan sighed heavily. "Sad and infuriating all at the same time," she said. "Did you search the body?"

"No, I had just found him when I heard the lift," Indara said.

Vernestra knelt next to Garn, rummaging quickly through his pockets. There were a few credits and Garn's senatorial pass card, which would serve as sufficient credentials to let him travel anywhere, and nothing else but a holo-emitter. "Doesn't seem like he was planning on going very far," Indara said.

Vernestra snorted. "Maybe he figured the combined effect of the two gunmen and their nullifier would buy him some time." She powered up the emitter, and a woman's face appeared. "Odd."

"Hey, I recognize her," Indara said, holding her hand out. Vernestra set the emitter in the Jedi Knight's waiting palm, and Indara studied it a moment before nodding. "Yeah, I saw her on Haileap. Along with the Gigoran."

"Gigoran?" Vernestra asked, eyebrow cocked.

"Yes. There was a Gigoran fleeing in one of the landspeeders when I came to find Garn. He actually tried to hit me, so I had to leap out of the way. But before I saw him here, he was in Port Haileap. Well, I didn't know it was the same Gigoran, but the emitter makes it seem likely."

Indara handed the emitter back, but Vernestra was patiently waiting for her to continue her story. "Anyway, I stopped there on my way to find you. While I was getting a meal at a local tavern, there was a shoot-out: A man was asking this woman to give him something; she refused because she thought he was trying to cheat her. And then the Gigoran came in and tried to shoot the place up. So. Not a coincidence? Maybe this is all related somehow."

Vernestra finished looking over Garn and stood. "I have found that when it comes to illegal activities, the galaxy tends to feel very, very small. We need to alert the local authorities since there's also the matter of the two gunmen up in Garn's offices. After that, we can contact Coruscant. Maybe someone there knows who this woman is."

Indara nodded, and with one last look at Garn, she followed Vernestra back to the turbolift. As she entered, her stomach growled, annoyingly loud. Indara grimaced.

"Hey, do you think they have a noodle shop here on Thelj?"

Thelj did not have a noodle shop within the range of the city, and so they had to settle for dumplings instead. The savory pockets of dough came in a bowl of spicy, aromatic broth that Indara picked up and drank before going after each of the prizes located in the bottom.

Vernestra's bowl steamed, untouched, as she inspected the holo-emitter. Once Indara had finished her food and ordered another serving—she was hungrier than she'd been in years—she gestured at the device with her soup spoon. "What are you doing?"

"There are markings on here. I'm trying to figure out if there's something more than just the image of the woman. Smugglers sometimes hide encrypted messages below a seemingly innocuous message—ha!"

Vernestra put the emitter down, and an image of Garn played. Indara looked around to see if anyone else was paying attention, but they were the only ones in the restaurant, the hour far too early for most dinner customers.

"If you are listening to this, then I am dead," the image of Garn began, "and to be honest I probably deserved it. I have not been a good person. I've hurt many people, and I hope that this one last act can make up for some of the ills I've caused.

"Sigeo nocht rewnat qas bindt lokicgh fro."

Indara frowned as the image of Garn looped back around to the beginning of the message. "I—what language is he speaking?"

"It sounds like Fruscti. It's a dead language. There were some artifacts found bearing the language on Killof as well as Truvi, Loit, and a few other places. No one has been able to ascertain what happened to the people who originally spoke the language, but the artifacts usually occur in places that other cultures have also deemed to be holy sites. We can have Jay-Six see if she can translate it. It might be a bit much for her records, but we can always check with the Temple on Coruscant."

Indara's second bowl of soup arrived, and she devoured it as quickly as she had the first. Vernestra watched her with some amusement, and Indara felt her cheeks heat. "I don't know why I'm so hungry today."

"How often do you use the Force?" Vernestra said, drinking her own broth and daintily eating the dumplings.

Indara sighed, sensing a lecture. "What does that have to do with anything?"

"If you aren't used to using the Force in such a way, it can be taxing, at least until your body adjusts. You know, not everything I say is a criticism. Sometimes I'm just making conversation, trying to get to know who you are as a person and as a Jedi," she said, dropping her spoon back in the bowl. "But your response does make me wonder... was your master critical?" Vernestra asked.

Indara's mouth took on a sour cast. She picked up her cup and drank the rest of her juice. "I'd rather not discuss it," she said, even as she remembered her master berating her, in any number of training sessions, for her inability to parry his strikes. "I'm ready to go if you are."

Vernestra nodded, but not before giving Indara a too-knowing gaze. "Well, regardless, I know you are a capable Jedi, Indara. The Council would not have sent you after me if you were not. But your inexperience can get both of us killed, and as long as we're working together, please know that the things I tell you are merely information, not a judgment of your skills or lack thereof."

Vernestra stood, tossing a few credits on the table as a droid trundled over to remove the bowls and clean the surface.

Indara stood as well and wondered about the shift in Vernestra's tone. Had Indara misjudged the Jedi?

She wasn't sure, but something in what Vernestra had said did make Indara wonder if she had let their initial interaction color her opinions a bit too much.

As she followed Vernestra out of the restaurant, she thought perhaps she should reassess her opinion of the Jedi Master. So much of what she knew about the woman had been informed by her research, and Indara was beginning to realize that perhaps research on its own was not enough. Especially when it came to a certain Mirialan Jedi Master.

Vernestra Rwoh was more complicated than Indara had initially thought.

Chapter Sixteen

It was late when we finally made it back to the *Cantaros*. J-6 was not waiting for us, and a holomessage revealed that she'd gone to see if she could find supplies to replenish the galley. That was the difference between J-6 and many droids: She didn't always need an instruction to complete a task. She was pretty good at picking up what needed doing all on her own.

Her ministrations to the two gunmen in Garn's residence had ended long before the local authorities had arrived. Neither had survived, but the local officials we spoke to were adamant that it was of no concern, as they were overworked and would not be prosecuting the deaths. Both men were well known on the planet as guns for hire—not even bounty hunters, just the kind of cheap muscle that men like Garn would employ for any number of nefarious tasks. It made me feel slightly better that we hadn't accidentally killed an innocent roped into some kind of plot. I wasn't even certain what Garn had thought to gain by trying to kill two Jedi.

Unless he'd had a falling-out with his co-conspirators and the setup had been a last-ditch effort to redeem himself. I considered the idea and found it to be the simplest and most logical explanation. Perhaps that was what his encoded message was about. Once J-6 returned, I would ask her to translate the phrase, but for the moment I had more pressing matters to attend to.

Indara's annoyance radiated from every line in her body as she led the way up the boarding ramp, and a headache had started up behind my eyes. It had been a long time since I had worked with another Jedi, especially one so young and sheltered, and I was handling it poorly. I could sense that. Indara felt like an erstwhile Padawan to me, her inexperience and wonder belonging to someone much younger, but she wasn't. It was difficult to remember that she had not come of age during a conflict. She may have seen local skirmishes, like those on Genetia or Soika, but nothing that compared to the fighting I had done in my youth.

I was concerned that Indara was woefully unprepared for whatever it was we were about to face. And I wanted to help her, to protect her from the danger that was inevitable for a Jedi in the galaxy. Perhaps my own experiences had shifted my perspective of what skills were most beneficial to a Jedi. I had spent my youth in near-constant combat, a far cry from the experiences of most Jedi.

And I had the feeling that what I considered teaching, Indara considered pandering. Our conversations had begun to take on a tone more combative than I liked, and I needed to adjust my tactics so that we could work more effectively together. I sensed that this was only the beginning of what we would have to endure. The Force had brought us together for a reason, and I did not think we had reached the end of the path laid out for us.

Once we were on the ship, I went to the comm unit in the cockpit, Indara following along like a ghost.

I sent a call to Coruscant, using the Temple's most heavily encrypted line. It took a few moments to establish a connection, then another few minutes for the Jedi monitoring the channel to take down a general report for the Council. Once that had been handled, I requested to speak with Master Yaddle. We were, of course, told that the Jedi Master was indisposed, most likely asleep. I left a message for her to reach out at her earliest convenience before I cut the call and turned to Indara.

"We should wait here on Thelj until Yaddle or the Council gets back to us. It's my instinct that we should try to run this matter to ground, since it's clear that someone is manufacturing nullifiers. This is two of them now. Every single other investigation into the device turned up nothing, but I think we might be able to discover something useful. So I plan on pressing them to let us continue digging into the matter. But until then, if you aren't too tired, I'd like to show you something."

Curiosity flitted across Indara's face before she caught hold of her expression and scowled once more. "Sure. Why not."

I nodded. Indara had been brave enough to share a bit of her truth with me. I figured it was long past time I did the same. Perhaps that would thaw a bit of the frostiness that had settled into our exchanges.

She followed me as I led the way to the empty hold where I sometimes stored supplies but most often meditated or practiced my fighting forms. We stopped before a door to a small storage room, and I cleared my throat.

"I'm not sure what you read about me in the archives—because after our discussion about Garn, I have no doubt you researched me before going to Cerifisis—but whatever it is, it's woefully incomplete. Mostly because I've made it a habit to hold back details that I felt were unnecessary and a bit too close to my emotional truth. My pain, my loss, my joy: Those are all mine, and the Order has no claim on them. But without them ... I can only imagine I appear as little more than an icy, Force-wielding machine, and that is not who I am."

Indara opened her mouth to reply, and I raised my hand to forestall whatever she was about to say.

"You don't have to like me. But I would like for you to understand who I am, and how that shapes my view of being a Jedi. If you'll indulge me?"

Indara nodded, and I took a deep breath before letting it out. I shed my robes, hanging them on a hook that I kept for just such a reason, as the space was small and could become overly warm. Indara removed her robes and did the same. I pressed the door button and gestured for her to join me in the storage room, and she did so, her expression curious. It was a tight fit, just the two of us, and I adjusted to allow for the second person. Usually when I came here, it was by myself. I was not used to sharing this secret with anyone.

"I asked you something about your master, and your response makes me think that you do not have pleasant memories of the man who trained you. And I'm sorry to hear that, because I loved my master in a way that I have always hoped was true for all Padawans. The purpose of a Jedi taking an apprentice is to instill and further the ideals and the joy of the Force, of being a Jedi and working for the light. I realize that it doesn't always work out that way, but it should.

"But before I continue, what do you know of Jedi Master Stellan Gios?"

Indara's brows drew together as she thought. "The Fallen Star, a Jedi known for self-sacrifice and a staunch dedication to the Order even to the end. I also know he was your master," Indara said.

I nodded. "Stellan Gios was and still is one of the most loyal, dutiful Jedi I have ever met. Which is why I had this created after his untimely end."

I pressed a button in the wall—one of four—and a life-sized hologram of Stellan appeared within the space before us. He grinned, his eyelids crinkling in the corners, before he began to speak.

"There are a number of things you're going to need to remember, Vernestra, but trust me: You've got this. And just in case you don't, here are the most important things to hold close:

"Always trust in the Force," the hologram of Stellan continued, laughing a little as he too often did. "But more important: Trust in *yourself*. You know what it feels like to be a steward for the light. It means that you give of yourself until there is nothing left. So when you are uncertain, when the way ahead is too dark, ask yourself why. Is it because you are working against the best interests of all those who live here with us in the galaxy? Or is it because you are unsure that you're doing the best thing? Because a little worry is normal. But too much fear can lead us to believe we are working for the good of all when we are only serving ourselves."

The hologram of Stellan continued speaking, just as he had all those decades ago when I'd become a Jedi Knight, but I touched the button to banish the hologram.

I gestured toward the door, and Indara led the way out. Once we stood outside in the hold, I smiled at her. I couldn't quite read her expression, so I didn't try.

"That was . . . thank you for sharing that with me. You're right. I think I made a snap judgment about you based on what I'd read and not who you are or how you've treated me. Although you can be a bit . . . much."

I laughed. "Fair enough. What I just showed you is one of the last messages my master sent me. I had the message loaded to the ship so that when I lost my way, I could listen to it again, have him there by my side just as he was when I was a young Padawan.

"So I apologize if my asking about your master was upsetting, but I still live by the principles mine taught me. I should never forget that not every master-Padawan relationship is as it should be, and I regret the misstep."

"You still watch old holos of your master? Isn't that . . . is that not attachment?" Indara asked, her expression confused.

I shrugged. "I don't think so, because I have never put the people I loved over the will of the Force. People I loved have died, and I have always accepted that this is just the nature of the galaxy. I don't fear losing the people I care for, but I do feel each loss quite keenly." I took a deep breath and let it out. It had been nearly a decade since I'd spoken this openly with anyone.

"But regardless, I shared this with you so you can understand the kind of relationship I had with my master, and how he shaped the kind of Jedi that I am now. The things I tell you, the knowledge I try to impart, comes from what I consider to be the spirit of sharing and connection within the Order. I know you are a perfectly capable Jedi. I have seen you handle yourself admirably. I meant what I said in the restaurant, and I hope that going forward we can be a bit more open with each other. It is simply what Stellan would have done. And what I, as his eager student, now do as well."

Indara nodded, her expression tragic. "My master's last words to me before I became a Jedi Knight were to chastise me for my unkempt robes," she said, her voice little more than a whisper. "So you are correct. I do not have the fond memories of my master that you have of yours."

I took a deep breath and let it out. "His dissatisfaction with you was a direct reflection of his own self-worth. I know I cannot undo the hurt his behavior caused, but you are a good Jedi, Indara. And I'm glad to have you helping me on this mission. I'm sorry if I haven't been the best at expressing that. But I want to offer you Stellan's wisdom as well. I don't have access to the logs of every other Jedi Master, but I have this one here, at your disposal. Feel free to view it at your leisure."

Indara nodded. "Thank you. And, uh, thank you for sharing this with me," she said, gesturing to where the hologram had been. "I know it must be intensely personal."

"Because it isn't in my file?" I asked.

She laughed. "Yes. But even so, I want to apologize as well. I've felt very unbalanced since I left Coruscant to find you—and, well . . ." She trailed off, taking a deep breath and closing her eyes before exhaling and reopening them. "I'm glad you think I'm a good Jedi. Because I don't."

"None of the good Jedi ever do," I said. "A good Jedi will always feel like they are falling short. It was only ever the Sith who felt justified in their actions."

"A Sith? Now you're talking like an archivist."

I laughed. "Why don't we get some rest before Yaddle calls? I have a feeling she isn't going to like what we have to tell her, and I'd like to be well rested before that happens."

Indara concurred, and we made our way back to our quarters. I was feeling a bit conflicted at having shared some of my databank of holos with her, but even if she told the Council, what could they do? Many of the messages I had were also in the archives. It just so happened that for me they were more than a footnote in a file.

They were my touchstone.

I entered my room, stripping off my tunic and leggings and falling back on the bed in just my underthings.

I was awakened what felt like moments later by the gentle ping of an incoming message. I grabbed my tunic from the hook I'd hung it on and shrugged into it before answering the call on the private comm unit in my room. Yaddle was predictably on the other end.

"Vernestra. The Temple guard said your message was urgent."

"Did you read the update I sent to the Council?"

Yaddle nodded. "So Senator Garn is dead."

"Yes. He was killed by someone we believe to be one of his associates. Oh, and he tried to kill me and Indara before he died."

Yaddle's eyebrows rose at that bit of information. "You did not include that in your official report to the Council."

I didn't want to tell Yaddle my honest thoughts on the Council as a whole, so I stuck to what I could diplomatically say out loud. "I wanted to discuss it with you first before I sent along an in-depth report." I gave Yaddle a quick rundown of what had happened in the senator's office before concluding, "I am guessing you are now going to tell me that Indara and I should track down the location of this woman and see what she knows."

"No," Yaddle said, her expression revealing none of her usual mirth. "You have done as the Council requested. You and Indara should return to Coruscant. We have other matters that could use your attention, since this issue has been put to rest."

"Wait, no," I said, feeling suddenly unbalanced. "I have to see this through."

"I appreciate your dedication to the cause, Vernestra, but we have already assigned the investigation into the nullifiers to another Jedi Master. You have no obligation to continue down this path of inquiry."

For a moment I wondered if Yaddle was manipulating me, offering a more desirable option to see how I would react. But then I remembered that the older Jedi Master did not play such games. Yaddle was never coy. She was direct and to the point. It was why we had always gotten on so well.

"I have to," I told Yaddle. "I had a vision."

She was one of the few Jedi who knew of my hyperspace visions. I wasn't even sure that the entirety of the Jedi High Council knew about them, or at least knew about the degree to which they'd been useful in the past.

At the reveal of a vision, Yaddle straightened slightly. "What did you see?"

"Stellan. At first he told me he had something he needed me to find beneath the icy waters, and then he was fishing." I hesitated, because I didn't want to share all the details of the vision, especially when I wasn't quite sure what it was telling me. "I believe he wants me to run this nullifier business to ground. And I think I should."

"And Indara?" Yaddle asked, the holo jerking as the signal waned and waxed again, coming in sharper than before.

"I would like to continue working with her. I can sense when the Force is at work. Even if it's working through a Jedi Master who perhaps knows when the Jedi around her might need a little push in one direction or another," I teased.

Yaddle snorted and waved the comment away. "Bah. I have no idea what you're talking about. But if you want the task, it's yours."

"Great. I'm going to need access to the Jedi Archives. What is the nearest temple to Thelj? Banchii?"

"Banchii is closest, but they are preoccupied with a number of issues, including a planetary outbreak of haver fleas. You should try Hynestia, Vernestra. Their local archives are quite robust and go back centuries. I think you would find it most enlightening. Especially since the last Jedi to have investigated the nullifier is there. You Know Jedi Master Quintana, correct?"

I blinked. I did know Quintana. The two of us had worked together on a handful of missions. But it was not the name of an old acquaintance that gave me pause. The Hynestian temple was where I'd first met Stellan. A warmth ran over my skin before I laughed. It would be too easy to read too much into this. So I didn't.

"Well then, I suppose Indara and I are off to Hynestia."

Chapter Seventeen

Hynestia, like Thelj, was a planet with a cold climate. Hynestia, unlike Thelj, was not cold enough to warrant domes, and so the walk from the *Cantaros* to the temple was a miserable one despite the lined cloak Vernestra had loaned Indara. The Jedi Knight did not like the cold, and being on Hynestia was reminding her why.

When Vernestra had told Indara that they were going to find the missing woman and see what they could learn about the nullifiers, Indara had felt several emotions at once. She was elated that the Jedi Master wanted to continue to work with her but also a bit exasperated that Vernestra had made the decision unilaterally, proving that they were not quite working as a team, even if it seemed they were getting along better by the day.

Mostly Indara was worried that this was quickly becoming a much more important—and dangerous—mission than they'd originally set out on. She hoped they would figure out who had killed Garn and stop them. Every time Indara closed her eyes, she saw Garn's twisted body. The man needed justice, even if Indara wasn't quite sure he deserved it.

After Vernestra had shared the holo of her master, Indara had returned to the storage closet in the cargo hold to watch the rest of the message. She was reluctant at first, but Vernestra had offered and Indara thought perhaps some inspiring words were exactly what she needed.

There were other clips as well, even though she did not watch those: a tall, broad-shouldered middle-aged human whom Indara was pretty certain was Imri Cantaros, a prominent Jedi philosopher who had once been Vernestra's Padawan and had died a number of years ago; an elderly brown-skinned woman who was some sort of scientist; and several other Jedi, including Rowan Urr and Keeve Trennis, one of the Lost, those Jedi Masters who had left the Order by their own choice. Indara was planning on asking if she could view the others once the opportunity arose. She had the feeling Vernestra would not mind.

But Stellan's advice had been exactly what Indara needed, and she watched his holo twice through. His words filled Indara with hope and pride, and she could hear Vernestra assuring her that a master was supposed to help their Padawan become a good and confident Jedi, not tear them down and leave them faltering. And it was in that moment that Indara had realized the grave disservice her master had done her.

More than that, she began to think about the many ways in which she had undermined herself over the past year. She had brushed aside the praise from her fellow archivists and pretended that every kind word directed at her was pity, not a real compliment. She needed to be kinder to herself. Because Vernestra was right.

She was a good Jedi. Now she just had to work on becoming a *better* Jedi.

So as they walked through the drifted snow to the Jedi temple, Indara tried to remind herself that she was on the path she needed to walk, that of building her skill set, steps that led to greatness—even if the snow that occasionally made its way under her hood and down the back of her collar when the wind picked up made her feel more like a petulant child. She tried using the Force to hold on to heat, pushing the cold away, the inverse of the technique Vernestra had taught her on

Cerifisis. While she did feel a measure of relief from the cold, she was still far from comfortable.

Vernestra for her part did not seem to mind the cold at all. She wore the same set of robes as always, her only concession to the drop in temperature covering her bald head with the hood of her robes. She moved sure-footed through the snow, her robes swirling around her, and residents of the planet cleared out of her way with murmurs and head nods of respect. She was a Jedi Master through and through. The Vernestra Rwoh whom Indara had read about truly was a pale imitation of the reality. The woman was much more complex than she'd thought. She had the ability to be exactly who she needed to be in every single situation, and Indara wondered which one of them—if not all—was the true Vernestra.

The trip from the *Cantaros* to the temple was mercifully short, and the large ornate doors to the building opened on their own as they approached. When they entered, the doors closed just as quickly behind them, the warmth of the foyer a shock after the frigid temperatures outside. Neither Vernestra nor Indara bothered removing their outer layers, though. The overall temperature was still a bit cooler than Indara would've preferred.

Vernestra strode to the center of the temple, which was curiously empty. Braziers burned at odd intervals, casting a warm glow, far more soothing than the chemical lanterns Indara would have expected. While Vernestra searched for the Jedi who maintained the temple, Indara took the opportunity to look over the space, which was made of a lovely pale brick, windows placed high in the walls but letting in very little light. It was larger than Indara had been expecting.

"Is this your first time on Hynestia?" Vernestra asked.

Indara nodded. "Yes. The workmanship reminds me a bit of the temple on Astrali. This is nice."

"Jedi temples are not *nice*. They are statements, monuments to the greatness of the Order," said a voice from off to the right. Indara and Vernestra both turned toward the sound. An older Devaronian Jedi

Master emerged from a side corridor, her face covered with downy gray fur. The woman walked with her head held high and her spine straight, as though she were a queen entering her throne room. Indara had the absurd thought that she and Vernestra could have a competition to see whose posture was better, as each of them stood so confidently tall— even if Vernestra was on the shorter side.

"You were supposed to be here a week ago," the Jedi continued. "What have you been about? The Order may have gotten lax about the individual responsibilities of a Jedi, but I have not."

Indara frowned just as Vernestra began to chuckle and pulled back her hood, amusement crinkling the parallel rows of diamonds outside of her eyes. "Quintana! Unless you've been blessed with premonitions in your old age, I do believe you have us confused for someone else."

The woman let loose a bark of surprised laughter and slapped her knee. "Vernestra Rwoh! What a lovely surprise to see you, old friend. Have you taken a Padawan again after all?"

Indara reached up to pull back her hood, and Quintana inclined her head in apology. "My mistake. You are no Padawan. Let me try this again." She cleared her throat and held out her arms. "Welcome, fellow Jedi, to the Hynestian temple."

Vernestra snorted and shook her head. "Too late, you've scandalized us both. Indara, this is Jedi Master Quintana. Quintana, Indara and I are working on a sensitive matter, and we were wondering if we could use your terminal to connect to the Jedi Archives."

Quintana nodded. "Let me take you both to the terminal."

The Jedi Masters led the way, and Indara was happy to follow behind. The foyer led to a hallway that opened onto a training area, a small kitchen visible off to one side. As they walked, Vernestra and Quintana chatted, giving Indara the impression that the two were old friends.

"I cannot tell you how surprised I am to see you here," Vernestra said. "I sent a message to you on Kryger a few months ago, but I suppose you did not receive it. I ran into your former Padawan, Princho. He sends his regards, for whatever that is worth so many months later."

Quintana sighed. "Thank you for letting me know. There unfortunately was no message forwarding because there is no terminal there. The temple of Kryger was abandoned last year. A mudslide after an unprecedented rainy season. The entire planet is in the midst of environmental collapse, and so I helped evacuate those who were eager to leave before being assigned here. I was thinking you were my new Jedi support staff, since everyone keeps getting routed to the burgeoning conflict on Genetia, but alas, you are not."

"No, and I'm sorry that you've been placed in such a spot. How long have you been waiting?" Vernestra asked.

Quintana sighed again. "The Council has been promising me replacements for months, but it turns out that there are any number of taskings that are far more important than a small temple such as ours. So far, I have had more Jedi than I can count get reassigned before they even arrive. I've managed to keep things going on my own, thanks to a few droids, but I have the feeling that it is only a matter of time before this temple is shuttered. The Council seems much more focused on the larger temples in the Inner Rim," Quintana said. "Here we are."

The terminal was an older model and sat in a small room, a simple table and chairs and a comm unit the only other things in the space. Lanterns high in the walls provided the only light, and while the rest of the temple evoked austerity combined with grace, the terminal room was far more utilitarian.

"Do you need any assistance?" Quintana asked.

"Actually . . . yes. Can you tell us what you know about the four-seven nullifier? Especially things that may not have made it into the official record. Yaddle told me you had been one of the many Jedi to investigate the matter over the years."

Quintana crossed her arms and leaned back a bit. "Four-seven nullifier? Friend, that was a long time ago."

"Yet the past is ever present," Vernestra said with a grim expression. She quickly filled Quintana in on the most recent developments with Garn, and Quintana tapped her lips with a forefinger as she listened.

"Interesting. Here's what I know, mostly from research: The device itself was quite effective but highly unstable. It used recainium as its power source, which is why Senator Tia Toon refused to even consider adding the device to the arsenal of the Republic, since not only is recainium illegal, but it is also highly unstable. There was a girl who had designed the prototype, a Kuranu girl, but I cannot recall her name."

"Klerin Chekkat," Indara helpfully supplied. "I don't suppose you discovered what happened to her? I couldn't find any hint of her after the events on Valo."

Quintana shook her head. "I am afraid not. You have to understand, I was assigned to investigate the matter nearly twenty years ago, after a device was rumored to have been used on Soika. But I was never able to validate the report. I spent months running down leads and found nothing verifiable in the end. My case files are accessible if you would like to read them for yourselves. I submitted a copy of my personal files to the local archives when I arrived on Hynestia."

"Recainium," Vernestra said, still considering Quintana's earlier words. "Is that why the Order didn't think finding the prototype was a priority? No one but the most well-connected smuggler would have access to recainium."

Quintana shrugged. "No idea. But I'm not surprised that it has become an issue now. There is nothing the criminals of this galaxy would like more than having a leg up on the Jedi, and even a rumor can be worth something in the right hands. Anything else? Our terminal here is a bit older and has its share of quirks. Do you know how to use it?"

Vernestra looked to Indara, the older Jedi's raised eyebrows making it clear the question was better answered by her.

"Oh, ah, yes, I'm familiar with this model. We have a few on Coruscant," Indara said.

Quintana smiled. "Excellent. I'll have the droids prepare the midday meal. Join me in the solarium when you're ready. I'd love to hear what else you've been up to," she said, squeezing Vernestra's arm affectionately before she departed.

Once she was gone, Vernestra gestured for Indara to sit at the terminal. "I figure you probably have far more experience with this than I do."

Indara nodded and sat. "So, any idea what I should look for? We know what the woman looks like. What else?"

"Hmmm, before we do that, let's try running the phrase that Garn spoke in his last testament through the Temple's archives." Vernestra pulled the holo-emitter from within a pocket hidden in her robes and played the audio so that the terminal could pick up the sound. But after a few minutes, it was clear that there was no result within the local Jedi Archives.

"Maybe his pronunciation is off?" Indara offered.

Vernestra sighed. "That could be. Let's focus on the woman instead. I'm guessing she must be somehow important to replicating the nullifier. Perhaps figuring out a different power source, since recainium would be nearly impossible to find. You said she had something they wanted, right?"

Indara thought back to the scene she had witnessed on Haileap. "Yeah, she said that she knew what she had, which sounds like she was familiar with the device as a whole. So maybe a scientist of some sort? I can search the catalog of recent scientific articles, focusing in on disciplines related to power generation on a small scale. Perhaps we can find her that way."

Vernestra nodded. "Brilliant idea."

Indara quickly accessed the records available within the temple. The search went slowly even with Indara's knowledge of the system. Each query returned a number of results that were stored in a nearby room that then had to be analyzed one by one. The task could have gone more quickly with a droid, but Indara preferred to do the work herself. There was something calming about the simple act of research. It was a good way to let ideas bubble up, and as Indara discarded yet another article about new energy technology, a thought occurred to her.

"You know," Indara said, "maybe Garn was killed because he'd already shared the location of the woman? He's a senator, so it would make sense for someone to ask him to find her, since he'd have access to just about every record, public and classified. If that's the case, maybe she's been reported missing over the past couple of days. Or has even turned up dead."

It was a dark line of thinking, but Vernestra nodded. "It would make sense, especially since they killed him so publicly. That definitely sounds like an organization cleaning up loose ends. I cannot imagine they would be any more clandestine about killing her if she also double-crossed them. Good thinking."

Indara added the new factors to her query, including any dispatches sent out for missing scientists, and the machine beeped quite quickly. There were twenty results returned, and the fifth one was their scientist: Florinda Jackard. Indara easily found the datafile and loaded it into the terminal, scrolling through the information. She was wanted for questioning after an incident on Ruathi. According to the classified governmental dispatch that had been sent to the Temple, her last known employment was as a grant recipient on Seswenna. She was also listed as a former member of something called the Collective. "This is weird. What is the Collective? There doesn't seem to be any location given."

When the information came up on the screen, Vernestra spun on her heel and leaned over Indara's shoulder, peering at the display. Indara was startled by the sudden movement of the Jedi Master, and when she turned to her, there was a look of recognition on her face. Did she know the woman? "Is everything okay?"

"Yes." Vernestra blinked, visibly working to reestablish her usual calm demeanor. "I know where we need to go. Pull up whatever information you can about the woman from the archives. I'll tell Quintana that we do not have time to stay for a meal. We need to be on our way."

Vernestra left the room without another word, and Indara pulled all the details she could find onto a new data disk. She had a strange feeling that she'd missed something important. But she wasn't quite certain what it was.

Still, she now knew Vernestra well enough to trust that the older Jedi would share in due time whatever it was that had provoked the sudden reaction. They were clearly working together now, a real partnership. Vernestra had even let her take the lead on searching the database. Even if Indara wanted to balk, she had absolutely no reason to.

And so she grabbed the data disk and followed Vernestra to the next step of their investigation.

Chapter Eighteen

Spira was supposed to be a paradise. Sun, sand, beaches as far as the eye could see. Beautiful beings of all species. "And quality spice," Grizela had promised.

But so far all Nilsson had found was a sunburn and mediocre spice, and the companions he'd paid to keep him company had been less than stellar, as boring as having tea with his grandmother. And now the meeting with the investors he'd approached about his latest business venture had gone long, so he wouldn't have a chance to get out to any of the bars and clubs. In fact, Nilsson was finding himself a man without patience, and bad things happened when he lost his temper.

"Look. Do you want in or not?" Nilsson finally said, interrupting the human man who had been going on at length about the possible risks and rewards of the plan. He'd paid out of his own pocket to secure the luxury suite in a highly coveted beachside resort, and he'd been disappointed that so few of his invitations had been accepted by any of the real power players. Instead, the assembled group was a ragtag lot, not the usual quality investors Nilsson dealt with. Part of that was because the meeting had been postponed so he could make a quick stop on Thelj for Hinra to clear up a few loose ends. But it was mostly because Nilsson had to rely on his own shoddy network for this deal, since he had finally cut Garn out once and for all, the traitor.

He still couldn't believe he'd had to have his best friend killed. Well, not really his best friend. There were no such things as *friends* in the weapons-smuggling business. There were associates and obstacles, and when the former became the latter, it made sense to remove them from the board. Garn had been about to sing to the Senate, and for what? Immunity? A nice letter from the Republic and house arrest in a luxury apartment on Thelj? That icy dung heap? Please. Garn had lost his nerve. He got old and scared, and Nilsson had done him a favor having Hinra put him out of his misery.

But the loss of Garn's connections hurt. Badly. And Nilsson refused to listen to one more underworld accountant dissect his offer.

Nilsson looked to the doorway to see Hinra make a subtle hand signal: *Time to go.* It was dangerous to stay in one place for too long, and the Gigoran was in constant communication with Grizela, her voice in his ear keeping tabs on whether there might be trouble. Nilsson was relieved to have a reason to escape.

The meeting had gone from boring to tedious, and there was spice to be smoked.

"Look. Friends," Nilsson said, taking in the gathering. Along with the human, who had been brought by the Twi'lek representative for the Hutts, there were two lower-level officials from Genetia, a trio of bickering scientists from the Techno Union, and a representative from the Bounty Hunters' Guild who wore a hooded robe to conceal their features and had not said a word. This was usually the kind of nonsense that Garn handled, glad-handing the marks, and Nilsson wondered if he was out of his depth. But that had never stopped him from succeeding in the past.

Well, his father's limitless bank accounts had helped.

"You all have struggled because of the interference of the Jedi. What I am offering you is a way to level the playing field. Without lightsabers, the Jedi have nothing but parlor tricks. My nullifier not only disrupts their weapons but also allows you to use your blaster of choice, something no other nullifier has done in the past."

"What is the power source?" one of the Techno Union scientists asked, the human woman tapping her chin.

"A synthetic crystal known as kinver, one that my associates are eager to produce once they have the credits they need. A fuel source you will need to purchase through me. You cannot think I'd be so foolish as to power the device with something easily attainable. You will have reverse engineered a version of my nullifier within a few weeks. And since kinver is entirely synthetic, I have a guarantee it will take a few years before you can find a new energy source, since crystals aren't so easily reverse engineered. This ensures that my efforts are rewarded."

Nilsson stood, feeling annoyed and restless at the endless questions. He was handing them a gift, a way forward without the constant fear of the Jedi disrupting trade deals or handing business partners over to the Republic for justice. And instead of saying thank you and pledging funds, they wanted schematics. He was not a detail-oriented person, and anyone with half a brain would recognize that. Instead, they tried to baffle him with bantha fodder.

As though he hadn't already rehearsed every single sentence of this conversation before the meeting was even planned. These fools thought they were subtle. He could see right through them. He almost pitied them.

Nilsson gave the assemblage a bow. "I think that is about all the conversation I'm willing to entertain on this matter. If you're in, feel free to transmit the credits through the usual channels. Anyone who has not responded in twenty-four hours is out, and I will move on to my next potential customers. No exceptions."

Nilsson was almost to the door—Hinra waiting not so patiently—when he heard someone clear their throat behind him. He turned, slowly, a twitch starting up above his left eye at the sound. "Yes?"

"Where is Senator Garn? We usually deal with Garn," one of the officials from Genetia said, looking around the room as he spoke, as though he was seeking additional buy-in. No one else was silly enough to agree with him, and Nilsson forced a smile as he addressed the whey-faced human.

"You want to talk to Garn? Sure, happy to help you out." Nilsson pulled out his blaster and shot the man twice in the chest. Smoke billowed up from the wound, acrid and meaty smelling, and the other Genetian official sighed but said nothing.

"Garn is dead," he said, addressing the rest of the gathering. No one else had moved, and the representatives from the Hutts looked impressed at the sudden murder. "He was a liability. I'm going to say this once, and only once: I do not care where your loyalties lie. I do not care why you hate the Jedi or what you can possibly gain by having a weapon like the nullifier in your arsenal. What I care about is credits, in my pocket. I am not here to get reelected or to prop up my failing planet with your bribes." He gazed at each remaining member of the group. "I am here to sell you weapons. Weapons that will now be cheaper since Garn isn't gouging you for his cut. If you have a problem with that, find another dealer. But I promise you, none of them have what I have."

Nilsson holstered his blaster once more, nodded to the assembled gathering, and left, followed by Hinra. The nice thing about having a Gigoran on his payroll was that few people were willing to challenge him directly. Genetia might send him a strongly worded message given that he'd just killed one of their officials, but that was easily solved by a conciliatory gesture like a new pulse cannon. People tended to overlook a little death if it led to a better deal.

Once they were outside the hotel suite where they'd held the meeting, Nilsson took the turbolift to the roof. A shuttle was waiting to take them back to his ship, left in orbit so that they could make a quick departure. They'd no sooner exited onto the roof than Grizela stepped out of the shuttle, holding a datapad and tapping on it furiously.

"There you are. How was the—never mind," she said as she looked up at Nilsson and saw his expression. "The bounty hunter I hired is here. I figured you could chat with her before we depart. I also got you this."

Grizela produced a small, clear bag of spice, shimmery and silver in the daylight. Nilsson took it with a critical eye. "What is this?"

"Lozen's Choice. Mined from a secret place on Jedha. They say you can see the Force if you smoke enough."

Nilsson nodded. "Nice." He took a deep breath and let it out. Bounty hunters. He really hated them. They were always so incredibly smelly, as though they weren't clear what a bathroom was. He vastly preferred handling things in-house, but he was currently strapped for employees—he'd had to clean house after the disaster at the labs on Ruathi. One could never be too careful when it came to traitors. But with a reduced workforce now, he had to contract out quite a bit of work. He didn't have the time to murder everyone who needed it all by himself. "Yeah, let's talk to this bounty hunter and get this over with."

Grizela stepped aside to let Hinra enter the shuttle first so that he could secure the area, Nilsson following. His attention was all on the small parcel he held in his hand. He hoped it was something halfway decent. It had been a rough day.

Once inside the shuttle, Nilsson was pleasantly surprised to see that the bounty hunter he was supposed to meet was a woman, and an attractive one at that. She wasn't human, but something else, with pale-green skin and an impressive crest of rainbow feathers. The silver lines working their way across her face highlighted the exquisiteness of her bone structure. The skintight red bodysuit she wore left little to the imagination, and Nilsson almost wondered if perhaps Grizela had gotten confused. As far as Nilsson was concerned, Pantorans were known for being pretty, not smart. Two of his father's wives had been Pantoran.

"If you don't quit staring at me like that, I will pluck out your eyeballs before moving on to your tongue," the woman said. Nilsson inclined his head in embarrassment.

"I apologize. My last few interactions with bounty hunters have been . . . underwhelming."

"Yes, well, I assume that's why the guild sent me. Look, I just need an image and last known location of your target and I'll be on my way. You know my price?"

Nilsson looked to Grizela, who nodded. "Her record is spotless. She's well worth every credit."

Nilsson sat on a couch piled high with pillows, gesturing to his number two. "If Grizela says you're worth it, then you are worth it. Anything else?"

"Any difficulties I should know about?" the woman said as she took the holo-emitter from Grizela.

Nilsson looked to Hinra, who was wearing his vocalizer. "Jedi," the Gigoran said. "One was on Thelj. They will most likely be looking for the woman as well."

"Jedi?" the bounty hunter said with a sigh. "That is a problem."

Nilsson scowled. "You're refusing the job because of a Jedi?"

"No. I said Jedi are a *problem,* not a *deal-breaker.* If you want me to handle the Jedi as well, it's going to be triple. And I get the full fee up front."

Nilsson looked to Grizela, and she nodded, indicating that he should agree. "And what if you can't kill them?"

The bounty hunter smiled, revealing a terrifyingly serrated line of teeth. "I have yet to meet the creature I can't kill. And if that should come to pass, there will be a good chance I will be dead, so you'll have to take it up with the guild."

"Fair enough," Nilsson said, licking his lips. The engines to the shuttle started up, and the bounty hunter turned to go. "I didn't catch your name . . ."

"Because I didn't offer it. Good luck with your little venture, and enjoy your spice."

The woman took her leave, Grizela escorting her out. Nilsson couldn't think of anything to convince the bounty hunter to stay, and he was a little disappointed to see her go. He was willing to bet she would have been fun. At least worth breaking his personal rule of never seducing the help.

Once she was gone, he gestured to Hinra. "Why didn't you tell me there were Jedi on Thelj?"

Hinra stared at him, the white-furred man's black eyes barely visible through the hair on his face. "I did. You were smoking Star's Disaster at the time."

Nilsson narrowed his eyes as he reached into a compartment on the couch, pulling forth a travel pipe for his spice. "Hinra. I think I would have remembered you mentioning Jedi."

The Gigoran said nothing, but when Grizela returned to the room, he turned to her. "Did I tell Nilsson about the Jedi?"

She wrinkled her nose, so that the gold tattoos on her face folded. "Of course. Why? Did you have questions?"

"How many were there?" Nilsson asked, dumping a measure of the spice into the bowl of his pipe and enjoying how the silver and white granules tumbled over each other.

"Just the one. Hinra said it was the same one as in Port Haileap." Grizela stopped whatever she was about to say next. "Sir, would you maybe like a spa appointment before we head to Ruathi to see how things are going? You seem . . . tense."

"Yeah. Yeah, okay."

She nodded and began to type on her datapad. "Okay, I'll make sure to schedule that in for you."

"Great. Now everyone sod off. I want to enjoy this without yet another problem being brought to my attention."

Grizela and Hinra left the cabin, heading up to one of the cramped jump seats in the shuttle. Nilsson didn't think they were lying to him, but he certainly didn't remember hearing about the Jedi. That was definitely something he would remember. No one ever forgot a Jedi, not even a spicehead like him.

But then he was lighting the bowl and drawing deep on the narcotic smoke, and most everything fled from his mind.

He didn't see the Force, but he did feel pretty damn good.

Chapter Nineteen

As soon as I heard the name Florinda, I knew I needed to get back to the *Cantaros*. I couldn't remember everything from the last vision I'd had of Stellan, but I definitely remembered the bouquet of flowers. In the vision they had just been flowers, nothing remarkable. But now I realized they must be related to the florinda, a weird purple and yellow flower that grew in only one place I knew of: Ingae. I'd been there a number of times, and I disliked how close, how personal this was beginning to feel.

But there was no mistaking the name, or the vision, or the fact that our mystery woman was from such a place. After all, the Collective, a group of academics who had fled the more populous parts of the galaxy, was on Ingae. And what better place for a wayward, rogue scientist to hide than among other scientists?

I found Quintana in her office, muttering at figures on a datapad. She looked up as I walked in. "Hungry already? I'm not sure if there's anything ready just yet, but I suppose we can make do."

"Indara and I cannot stay. There's something we have to see to, but I thank you again for your help."

"You're leaving so soon?" Quintana asked.

"Yes, I'm afraid so. We didn't think we'd be able to find the woman we're looking for so quickly, but we did, and now we want to make sure we can get to her before anybody else."

Quintana nodded. "You know, you were asking about the four-seven nullifier, and I remembered something: Ty Yorrick was working as a bodyguard for the girl and her mother who said they'd designed the device. She might know something more that she can share, if she's even still alive. She'd be ancient by now. I spoke to her briefly when I was investigating, but she was not exactly helpful."

I coughed a bit and gave Quintana a rueful smile. "Ahh. I knew Ty once. She and I didn't part on the best of terms before she retired from the Order. I wonder if she still has the same message exchange as she did a decade ago. And if she'll even respond if I reach out to her."

Quintana laughed and leaned back in her chair. "Oh, this is a story I haven't heard—Vernestra Rwoh making someone angry. How ever did that happen?"

I rolled my eyes at Quintana's sarcasm. "Please. It's more interesting when I haven't somehow rubbed someone the wrong way."

Quintana grinned. "Well, if it's any help, the last I heard, she was somewhere in the Hetzal system, living on a farm."

I nodded. I didn't have time for a side trip before going to Ingae, but if I had I would have tried to find Ty. I truly did owe her an apology, and I was ashamed I hadn't made more of an effort to speak with her in the past. And now it was probably too late.

I said my goodbyes to Quintana, met Indara in the foyer, and made my way back to the *Cantaros*.

I needed to revisit the notes I'd made after my most recent vision. I had to see what else I might have missed.

J-6 didn't need much urging to leave Hynestia. We were barely outside of the planet's mass shadow before she jumped to hyperspace. "Please tell me that the next planet we go to is going to have a temperate climate. The cold is bad for my circuits."

"I couldn't agree more," Indara said, plopping into one of the jump seats in the cockpit. "I've forgotten how much I don't like the cold. There are never enough layers."

"Indara. Could you meet me in the galley?" Since I'd put the bit of information together in the temple—and now knew my most recent vision truly was pointing me toward solving the mystery of the nullifiers—I'd wrestled with whether to tell Indara about my visions or not. During the walk back to the ship, I'd realized that trying to keep my ability a secret around her would inevitably lead to disaster. I was just beginning to earn the younger Jedi's trust, and it had been far too long since that had happened. I didn't want to break our fragile peace by withholding something like my hyperspace visions.

But I still felt conflicted about telling her. It felt a bit too much like sharing a very intimate detail, and I disliked talking about the visions. Yet I knew that honesty was my best course of action. I had barely made it to my quarters before the last vision had overtaken me. Who was to say that the next time, Indara wouldn't witness it happening for herself? It was far better to share the information now rather than in the aftermath, when I was still feeling slightly addled.

Indara gave me a curious look at my request but nodded. I made a brief stop by my quarters to grab my datapad before meeting her in the galley. She'd already heated up water for tea and held up two of the canisters I kept on hand.

"Is tea appropriate, or should I opt for something stronger?" There was a tightness around her eyes, and I realized she must think that I was about to share something awful with her. I tried to give her a reassuring smile.

"Tea is all we'll need. This conversation is about me, but you're welcome to indulge if you'd like."

She nodded and brought over the perna, a subtle, smoky herbal tea that was actually my favorite. I sat and let her prepare two cups, appreciative of the time to gather my thoughts.

When she'd settled in, I took a deep breath and let it out. "I have something I want to tell you, something that few Jedi know about me, yet another thing you would not find in my file, at least not the part that is available to most Jedi. I'm telling you this because I need you to have a framework for what I'm going to share with you.

"You asked me last time we spoke why I didn't care for hyperspace. The reason is simple: I have visions while in hyperspace."

I took a sip of my tea—which was perfect—and gave Indara a moment to ponder what I had just said. I could see the range of emotions as they flitted across her face: surprise, curiosity, and then, finally, wariness, which I had come to realize was Indara's default expression.

"You have questions, and I am happy to answer them," I finally said when I felt the silence had gone on long enough.

"What are they like, your visions?" Indara asked.

"They are . . . unsettling. I have no control over when I am pulled into them, and they have gotten stronger and more abrupt as I have grown older. I am a terrible pilot, but that has nothing to do with the visions," I added with a smile. "When I left to become a Wayseeker, my visions got to the point where I felt I could no longer fly safely on my own, which is why I have Jay-Six. Sometimes the visions leave me a bit . . . incapacitated afterward. They are taxing, and I have never felt steady flying in their aftermath. In the past, I have given the task over to whoever I was working with or even my Padawan at times. But as a Wayseeker, I needed a permanent assistant. Someone who could fly without question and someone I trusted implicitly, because when I am consumed by a vision, I am completely helpless. One of my former Padawans once remarked that it was like I wasn't there when a vision struck, and I would say that is probably the most apt description of what they feel like. It feels like I leave my body and travel to the vision. Whether that is the cosmic Force, the living Force, or some interstitial place created by my brain, I don't know. But I do know that when the visions are useful, they tend to be uncanny in what they show me. Which is why I've shared this with you in the first place."

I opened up the file on my datapad where I'd made a rough sketch of the items I'd seen in my most recent vision and pushed the tablet forward so that Indara could see it.

"Shortly before we reached Thelj, I had another vision. I made a note of it because it stuck with me long after I returned to my senses, which is not always the case. In the vision, Stellan was fishing and had pulled up a dead, bloated fish that contained several items in its belly: a nullifier like we found on Cerifisis, a bunch of flowers, some crystals, and a spice pipe. I, of course, knew that the dream must be in reference to the original four-seven nullifier, which was first discovered when Stellan was on Valo."

"By Elzar Mann and Bell Zettifar," Indara said.

I nodded. "Yes. I wasn't sure what the rest of this was in reference to, but then when we saw the information for Florinda, I knew what the flowers were. The florinda is a specific species of flower that grows on a planet called Ingae. The Collective is a group of scientists who started a commune there more than seventy-five years ago. I would guess that our missing woman, Florinda, was born there, or that her parents spent time in the Collective. As for what the crystals and the spice pipe represent, I'm not sure. But I know we need to make a trip to Ingae. It's the best lead we have. Hopefully someone there knows this woman or can tell us where she might be."

Indara looked at the datapad for another moment before sliding it back across the table to me. "This is incredible," she finally said after another lengthy pause. "The Force speaks directly through you."

I laughed. "I do not know about that. I've spoken with many Jedi far wiser than me on this matter, and there are any number of theories for why this happens. But I will say this: I have far more visions that I've never been able to make sense of than I have helpful ones. This just seems to be a case where the strange things that happen to my brain in hyperspace are useful. It would be folly to read anything more into it than that."

We sat in companionable silence for a moment before Indara cleared her throat. "When I was trapped in the mines, I thought I saw someone. A Kessurian male wearing temple robes. He stood over me, and when I turned toward him, he knelt next to me. He didn't say anything, just knelt and rested a hand on my forehead. I remember feeling such a sense of . . . not peace, but a calm that felt restorative. Like someone tucking you into bed when you're sick. There may have been something else, I'm not quite sure now, but I definitely remember the way he looked down at me.

"When I woke from the bacta, I asked about him, asked if he'd gotten out okay. They told me there hadn't been any Kessurians in the rescue operations. In fact, there weren't even any Kessurians working in the mines. But I know what I saw. And more important, I know what I *felt*."

Indara sipped her tea thoughtfully, and I held my breath as she contemplated her next words. "I didn't bring it up again, because I could see the way people's expressions changed when I did. I think some of them thought I'd been delirious. I'm not entirely sure I wasn't. All that is to say, I understand. Not only how . . . unnerving such a thing can be, but also how uncomfortable it can be to share it. So, thank you for trusting me, again."

I stood, grabbing the tea and my datapad. "And thank you for trusting me as well. It's a long way to Ingae. The planet is on the edge of Wild Space, and the way is . . . fraught. Luckily, Jay-Six knows the navigation well. She'll alert us when it's time to strap in."

Indara frowned. "Strap in . . . wait, what does that mean?"

I grinned. I couldn't help it. Indara was about to be in for a wild ride. "You'll see. Try to get some rest. Meditate, enjoy the downtime until we get there. Because I promise you: Once we arrive, we will not stay long. The sooner we find this missing woman, the better."

And with that I took my leave, eager to find some peace and quiet of my own.

Chapter Twenty

Indara was in the middle of a dream about too many cakes when she was woken by a series of alarms screaming from every corner of the *Cantaros*.

She fell out of her bunk, her robes twisting around her body haphazardly, before she gained her footing and rushed headlong to the cockpit. Vernestra followed behind her, less agitated, yawning widely.

"What's happening? Did we hit something?" Indara asked as she realized the sounds were the proximity alarms coupled with the stabilizers all screaming an alert.

"No. We are on the initial approach to Ingae," J-6 said. "Time to sit down and fasten your restraining belt, because it is going to be a bumpy ride."

Indara plopped into the jump seat, fastened her belt, and peered past J-6 through the viewscreen. "I'm sorry, is that an asteroid belt?"

"Asteroids as well as a few deep-space mines. The Collective takes their privacy very seriously," Vernestra said dryly.

"But what if someone tries to go through the asteroid belt by accident? Isn't that dangerous?" Indara asked.

Vernestra shrugged. "Jay-Six, can you put the incoming comms on speaker for Indara?" she asked. The droid complied, and immediately there was a cacophony of voices in various languages. Vernestra sighed. "Jay, can you please limit it to just the Republic's official navigation channel? We can't listen to every single channel at the same time."

"That's because your brains don't have the power of my processors," the droid said, sounding a bit smug. But she did as she was asked, and immediately the broadcast changed to a single message.

"You are about to enter a highly restricted area. Trespassing is forbidden. For your own safety, please turn back. There will be no other warnings but this. Message set to repeat in three, two, one."

The message began to repeat, and Vernestra gestured toward the viewscreen. "If the sight of that isn't enough to deter a ship, the alert should be. It's broadcast across every single channel in this area, so there is little chance of accidentally flying through the space. Oh, and I hope you don't get flight sick. Because the path is . . . a bit much."

"And Jay-Six knows the path to get to Ingae?" Indara asked. Already the ship was dipping and diving in an alarming way as it navigated through the space, and the droid made a sound like laughter, a strange crackle of her vocabulator. It was unnerving. Indara did not think a droid was supposed to be able to laugh.

"Of course I know the way through the asteroids. Ingae is my home. Now hold on. It's about to get fun."

The ship suddenly dipped and lurched hard to the right, and Indara grabbed hold of the restraints across her chest. She had no sooner done so than the ship began to invert itself, diving at the same time. It rattled at a far-off explosion.

Indara looked at Vernestra, her eyes wide with alarm. "What was that?"

"Proximity mine," Vernestra said, unbothered. "We'll probably hit a couple as we make our way through. Part of the Collective's very stringent security measures. They sometimes drift due to the solar flares."

Indara closed her eyes and reached for the Force, the familiar crackle of energy calming her enough that her brain could leave its panicked train of thought. This was a bad idea, but neither Vernestra nor J-6 seemed alarmed, and J-6 had even said that this was the way home. Which meant they must have made this trip before. Indara just couldn't understand what was on the other side. Was a group of scientists really that protective of their privacy?

Indara wasn't sure how long it took to get to Ingae—the swooping, diving, and shimmying from the explosions seemed to go on for over an hour. But eventually it all fell silent, and when Indara opened her eyes—still a bit nauseous from the trip—it was to see a beautiful blue-green sky and wide-open fields full of yellow and purple flowers.

"Those flowers are florinda," Vernestra explained, with a gesture toward the viewport. "Welcome to Ingae."

Indara might have spent the last year of her life in the Jedi Archives by choice, but she had traveled before that. She had seen the many-splendored falls of Dalna and the Lake Country of Naboo. She had marveled at the endless shifting sands on Leonit and gasped at the massive tree cows on Holpern. But nothing prepared her for the beauty of Ingae.

It was, quite simply, stunning.

The purple and yellow flowers, florinda, bloomed in riotous abundance in the deep-green meadows, their massive heads bowing endlessly in the gentle breezes. J-6 flew past fields and over snowcapped purple mountains before turning sharply through a pass and following a silver ribbon of river through a verdant green forest filled with some species of conifer.

And then the mountains opened up, revealing a wide green valley and a serene mirror of a lake. Fields of crops began to appear, and on the far edge of the lake was a city. It was small, nothing like the levels of habitation and commerce that made up Coruscant, but it was modern and clean. By the time they landed in the dockyards, a fleet of droids rolling up with chirps and beeps, Indara was fully in awe.

"This place is amazing," she said as she and Vernestra walked down the boarding ramp, J-6 clomping along behind.

"Yes, which is why the Collective defends its peace so arduously. In the aftermath of the Nihil conflict, quite a few of the scientists who had worked for either side in one capacity or another found themselves pursued for their knowledge and expertise. It became unsafe for a few of the experts, and they decided to start a colony out here, a place where scientists could pursue their experiments for the good of the galaxy, away from those who would like to profit off their breakthroughs. Thus, the Collective was born.

"This way. The council house is in the center of town."

They stepped their way down a crushed-stone path toward a knot of buildings, taller than the rest but not more than four stories high. It could have been a newer town in any of the more populous Outer Rim planets. Indara could barely believe she was on the edge of Wild Space. "How have I never heard of this place?" she asked, taking in the people making their way through the streets, a few of them watching the passage of the Jedi with hooded, wary eyes.

"The secrecy is the point. Ingae only appears on a few maps, and then as a gaseous giant that is highly uninhabitable. Those who join the Collective are recruited or may apply for asylum, but few who leave are allowed to return. Entire families are raised here, children educated, and when they come of age, they must make the decision whether to stay or go. Living here, devoting one's life to science . . . it isn't an easy path. But it is somewhat like becoming a Jedi: a calling that is not for everyone. Here, this is our destination."

Vernestra had stopped before a magistrate's office, the building painted in shades of blue. The doors slid open effortlessly, and she led the way inside. Indara turned and realized J-6 had disappeared at some point, off on her own business. Vernestra did not seem too concerned about her missing droid, so Indara was not worried, either.

Inside the office, a young Kage woman with pale skin and white hair sat at a terminal, typing furiously. She glanced up at them, her golden gaze landing on them briefly before she returned to her work. "Jedi. That is a new one. Are you applying for asylum or visiting?"

"Visiting. We are here to speak with Felix Sunvale," Vernestra said.

That got the young woman's attention, and she stopped what she was doing to really study the Jedi standing before her. "Stars. You're Vernestra Rwoh."

She sprang to her feet and came around the front of the desk, holding her hand out and grabbing Vernestra's forearm in the greeting of the frontier. "It is an honor to meet you, Master Rwoh. I'm Kilare Qwet, and my grandmother was on the initial expedition you escorted here to Ingae. Here, why don't the two of you follow me? You can sit in the receiving room while I get Magistrate Sunvale."

Kilare led them to a simply appointed sitting room, and they'd no sooner settled in the chairs than an older human, his skin a deep brown and his head completely bald, entered. His eyes crinkled with affection when he saw Vernestra.

"Aunt Vern! This is a surprise. Did you send a missive?" he asked. Indara tried to hide her shock but failed, because the man turned to her next. "Ah, and who is your friend from the Order? Not another of your Jedi scientists looking for escape?"

Vernestra smiled tightly. "Felix. You talk too much before thinking. No, Indara is a Jedi Knight helping me investigate the small matter of a nullifier. A powerful one that can even interfere with lightsabers. We're looking for a scientist who may be involved, and I think she may be one of yours. Florinda Jackard. You know the woman?"

Felix laughed. "Know her? We grew up living next to each other. She's about twenty years younger than me, but yes, I know her. She studied under Mom for a number of years before deciding that she wanted to be out in the galaxy. She left a few years ago. I doubt anyone has heard from her since. Her parents found their rest shortly after Mom, and I haven't seen any incoming messages from her or about her. Actually, I haven't had any incoming messages at all in a while. We even thought maybe one of the comm satellites had gone down, but we still get the latest holos on the relay just fine."

Vernestra smiled. "I told your mother that people would forget about this place with enough time. Either way, what can you tell us about Florinda?"

Felix gestured for the Jedi to follow him. As they walked, Felix taking them down a winding hallway, Vernestra looked over her shoulder at Indara. "You have questions. I have answers."

"He called you Aunt Vern," Indara began.

"When I was younger, my closest friends called me Vern. A needling joke that became a real mark of affection. One of those people was Felix's mother, Avon Sunvale. She was one of the founders of the Collective. We were close until she died."

Indara thought about the holo she'd found, the elderly dark-skinned human. "You considered her family."

"Jedi do not have family, they only have the Order," Vernestra said, but there was something in her tone that made Indara think she was mocking the quote. "*Aunt* is a term of endearment. Do not worry about me, Indara. Attachment is no threat to me. I understand the difference between affection and obsession."

"The Jedi scientists? You helped them flee the Order."

"'Flee'? Hardly. You do know that not every Padawan rises to Jedi Knight, and there are any number of younglings who never manage to find their place in the Order. If those members happen to have a scientific calling, they have an open invitation to come here and find a measure of peace. And yes, the Council knows of the existence of this place. They are one of the few groups who do. So keep that in mind."

"I'm sorry, this just feels . . . surprising," Indara admitted.

"If you have never considered leaving the Order, then these are not discussions anyone would have had with you," Vernestra said.

Indara followed along, deep in her thoughts. It was only when they entered a room full of terminals behind Felix that Indara realized Vernestra sounded as though she was speaking from experience.

Had the Jedi Master once considered leaving the Order? It seemed preposterous, and yet there was something about Vernestra that felt part of the Order while also completely and entirely separate from it.

The room they entered bore a number of terminals and large databanks the likes of which Indara had never seen.

"Welcome to our library. Let me pull up Florinda's file," Felix said.

He sat at a terminal and began to type furiously. After a few moments, he leaned back. "So it looks as though her parents had family on Seswenna, and that was where she went after leaving here. Our agents out in the galaxy did their required one-year and two-year check-ins with her, and she stood by her decision. She did not answer requests for a three-year check-in."

"You said she worked with your mother while she was still alive. Was it on crystal theory?"

"Yes, in fact," Felix said. He pulled a datastick from the terminal and held it out to Vernestra, who took it and deposited it somewhere within the folds of her cloak. "She was developing an alternative source of oscillating energy, something that could replace more volatile substances."

"Like recainium?" Vernestra asked.

Felix grinned, delighted. "How did you know?"

Vernestra pursed her lips and blew out an annoyed breath. "Because sometimes the Force whispers, but lately it's been yelling."

Chapter Twenty-One

After we got the information from Felix, we did not stay on Ingae, as much as I would have liked to accept the invitation he extended. There was no time to enjoy a respite. Someone was hunting a scientist, and we had to hopefully find her before they did.

J-6 was already back at the ship when it was time to leave, and she'd unloaded a few of our supplies, trading them out for local rarities like xuacan tea and pickled freening, delicacies we could not get elsewhere. I half wondered if J-6 was homesick. It was fully possible she wanted to return to her job of doing supply hauls for the magistrate, which was what she was doing when my friend Avon had asked her to accompany me on my travels as a Wayseeker. But I didn't want to broach the very tricky subject of feelings—what, if any, the droid might experience—in front of Indara. That felt like J-6's personal business, and I would respect her privacy.

It seemed a shame that we were leaving so quickly after arriving, but I had a feeling we needed to find Florinda as soon as possible. It wasn't quite an instinct, but I definitely sensed an urgency, as though she was the key to unraveling the entire nullifier business.

"Will it take long to get to Seswenna?" I asked J-6 as she got settled into the cockpit.

"Not too long. Plenty of time to read the messages that came in before we landed on Ingae."

I blinked. "We had messages? Why didn't you tell me?"

"I was occupied with safely traversing the way to Ingae. Remember the asteroids and mines? I've sent them to your personal comm unit," J-6 said, then turned away. I had the feeling I had insulted her somehow, but I decided to leave it be for the moment.

Once I'd entered my quarters, I began to pull the messages down. They had all come in shortly before we reached Ingae, but none of them were flagged as urgent.

The first was from Yaddle. "Jedi Master Vernestra Rwoh, please reach out on a secure channel at your earliest convenience. I have an investigator here from the Senate who would like to speak to you and Jedi Knight Indara." That was the entirety of the message. It lacked the warmth that I was used to from Yaddle, and I had a feeling that she hadn't been alone when the message was recorded. I deleted it immediately. I would send a status update when I was good and ready. Which was most likely going to be right before we headed back to Coruscant.

I always found it better to ask for forgiveness rather than permission. And the last thing I wanted right now was the complication of trying to work with someone from the Republic.

The next message was a bit more surprising.

A Tholothian woman peered out from the hologram, scowling as though she wasn't used to sending such messages. "Jedi Master Vernestra Rwoh. It's been a while. A Jedi Master named Quintana told me you've recently run afoul of the four-seven nullifier, and asked me to reach out to you. You aren't the first Jedi, nor will you be the last. I'm on Ruathi, and I have a few things I can tell you, but not over holo. Come find me at the Dented Droid, near the dockyards."

I played the message once more, but I wasn't imagining it. Ty Yorrick had decided to reach out to me after all. I wondered what Quintana had said to thaw her frosty feelings toward me. Whatever it was, I owed the older Jedi a gift. Perhaps a nice set of teas.

I listened again to Ty's message; the time stamp indicated that it had been sent a few hours after we'd left Hynestia. Ty's quick response was good. I had a feeling it meant she was just as keen to find out who was manufacturing the nullifiers as I was.

Once I had saved the message for future replay, I stood and headed toward the cockpit to tell Indara the news. But we made the jump to hyperspace, and I began to fall . . .

I landed on a windswept hill overlooking a smoldering ruin. Stellan stood beside me in his temple robes, his tanned skin smeared with soot, his lightsaber powered up and ready for battle.

I had been ripped from reality and thrown into yet another hyperspace vision. This time with no chance to even acknowledge the transition.

"We waited too long," Stellan said. Right as his lightsaber sputtered out.

I didn't recognize the planet we were on or what was happening.

The question was whether this was something that had *already* happened or *would* happen in the future. And since I didn't recognize the landscape, I had to believe it was the future.

Down in the valley below—a rocky, craggy landscape rendered in shades of black and gray—other Jedi fought. Blue, green, and yellow lightsabers repelled blaster bolts, the only color in the landscape, before suddenly sputtering and going dark. The figures moved through haze and smoke, shadows in a grim tableau. There was no way to know who was winning and who was losing, but the screams that filtered up to me made it clear that it did not matter.

People were dying.

Stellan began to stalk determinedly down the hill toward the raging battle below, and I ran to catch up with him, my movements slow and bogged down the way they sometimes are in dreams. As I hurried forward, I saw dozens of dead people of all species, their bodies littered across the landscape in a gruesome display.

No matter how I tried to keep up with Stellan, he pulled farther and farther away, leaving me behind in the macabre garden of death, my only companions the endless parade of corpses. Jedi and people of all species, a galaxy's worth of corpses. There was usually no scent in my visions—only sight and sound—but this time it was different: The scents of overheated blasters and iron-rich blood assaulted my senses, the smoke wafting around smelling of burning flowers and cooking meat. The odors created a miasma that made me raise my arm over my mouth to avoid the awful stink.

Where was I? And what was so significant about this place?

Not all of the dead were Jedi, so this was not entirely about the nullifier as far as I could tell. I could not understand the significance of what I was seeing. Every single person seemed to have died of blaster-fire, which was not unusual, and a few of them had strange marks on their faces, as though they had clawed at their skin before they died.

I stopped and knelt next to one of the bodies, and I could see it wore a nullifier. I realized that this was the common link among the people here: They were all wearing nullifiers. Even the Jedi.

I came out of the vision with a gasp, disoriented for a moment as I regained my bearings. I was on the floor of my quarters, and I crawled over to the nearest chair, using it to lift myself off the floor.

It took a long moment before I could reach for my datapad to record what I remembered of the vision, and a few moments past that before I could make notes without my hands shaking. It was rare that I had visions so . . . visceral. I hadn't returned to myself that shaken in a long while.

There was a gentle knock at my door. "Yes, Indara?" I called, not bothering to move from where I sat.

The door slid open and she stepped inside, her expression puzzled. "How did you know it was me?"

"Jay-Six rarely bothers to knock. Did you find something?"

Indara nodded and held out her datapad. "I was looking through the information Felix gave us and cross-referenced it with what we had from the temple. Then I took everything we know about Florinda

Jackard and ran it through to see if there were any alerts that might give us an idea where she's been over the past few years. I found an old presentation she did on Seswenna about alternative energy sources, but it seems like that was from more than two years ago."

A headache was beginning behind my eyes, and I nodded to show that I was listening. "So it seems like she's on Seswenna after all."

"Maybe not. I found a more recent request for a person of interest related to a factory disaster on Ruathi. It may be where she was last seen. I thought you might be interested in looking at what I found."

Indara handed me the datapad. I took it, the tremor in my hands nearly imperceptible. At least, that was what I thought. Indara gave me an assessing look, and I sighed.

"I had another vision," I said, answering the question she hadn't yet asked. "This one was much more... violent. I don't quite understand what it meant, but I have the feeling that the nullifier could have consequences beyond what we imagined." I added, "And this is excellent analysis, Indara. I think there's something worth looking into here."

"Should I ask Jay-Six to reroute us to Ruathi?"

I nodded. "Yes. Because I also had a response from an old friend, Ty Yorrick. It seems she's on Ruathi as well. She knew the family who invented the original prototype for the Republic, and I'm hoping maybe she knows something about what happened to the nullifier in the aftermath of the disaster on Valo. So it certainly does seem like we may learn more on Ruathi."

Indara nodded. "I'll go speak with Jay-Six." She turned to leave, then paused in the doorway. "Are you sure you're feeling all right?"

I forced a smile. "I'm fine. But thank you."

It was a lie. I still felt shaken from what I'd seen. I just hoped that whatever waited for us on Ruathi would provide some much-needed clarity.

Because according to my visions we were running out of time.

Chapter Twenty-Two

When the ship touched down on Ruathi, Indara was the first person down the boarding ramp. She waited at the bottom for Vernestra, who had been a bit withdrawn since her most recent vision. Indara didn't know what was on her mind or even what the elder Jedi had seen, but there was something in her expression—a tightening around the eyes and a near-constant pursing of the lips—that made Indara think the vision was somehow worse than Vernestra's usual, even if Indara had no idea what "usual" might be.

Now, walking along the dockyard offerings on Ruathi—there were at least three noodle shops that she could see, and a number of intriguing-looking grill stands that smelled delicious after too many shipboard rations—Indara found herself looking to the elder Jedi more and more, trying to understand what about her vision had left her so preoccupied.

"We need to find a tavern called the Dented Droid. I'm guessing it isn't too far from here," Vernestra said. She seemed like she was waking from a long dream, and she scrubbed a hand over her face. "Hopefully they'll serve food as well."

"I know I keep asking this, but are you doing okay?" Indara asked. She didn't want to pry. She'd learned by now that Vernestra was not one to share her feelings lightly, nor was she one to bog down the conversation with idle chat, preferring instead to enjoy the silence. But Indara could sense that this was more than an ill mood. Something had rattled Vernestra deeply, and if the elder Jedi was willing to share, perhaps she could lighten the load. They were, after all, a team.

But Vernestra just gave Indara a tired smile. "My visions are too much with me these days. I see battlefields filled with smoke and hear the screams of the dead and dying. Usually when my visions end, so do their impacts. But now . . . let's just say that I think our mission may have greater importance than either of us knew."

Indara nodded, and a blinking sign on a building in the distance caught her attention, a stooped and decommissioned serving droid located outside the door. "I think that's our tavern right there."

The Dented Droid was not the nicest dockside tavern, nor was it the worst. As they entered, Indara's boots stuck to the floor, but for the most part the place looked clean and well maintained, the furnishings on the newer side. The clientele looked to be mostly humans with a few Twi'leks rounding out the crowd. So an ancient Tholothian woman with a steely gaze, sitting at a back table, was more obvious than she would have been in another establishment. Vernestra took a deep breath and let it out next to Indara before heading right for the woman.

"Hope you haven't been waiting long," Vernestra said, pulling out a chair next to the Tholothian woman, leaving Indara to sit in the chair that was just a bit too close to her boots. The strange woman gave Indara a smirk before dropping her feet to the floor and leaning forward slowly.

"Long enough. Who's your sidekick?" There was a pile of unshelled pomo nuts in a bowl on the table, and the woman reached forward, cracking one open and tossing it into her mouth as she spoke. She appeared old, her movements slow and deliberate, but there was a youthfulness to her, despite her age.

Vernestra sighed before forcing a tight smile. "Indara, meet Ty Yorrick. Ty, this is Jedi Knight Indara. She's helping me investigate the reappearance of the four-seven nullifier."

"Seems like the Order is always cleaning up its various messes. Lucky you," she said, her expression defiant as she looked to Vernestra.

Indara had the feeling that the older women had history. She knew Ty Yorrick's name from various treatises she had read, but there was nothing about why she'd left the Order or when she'd rejoined it in the aftermath of the Nihil conflict. There were definitely some grievances here, most from Ty toward Vernestra, and while Indara was curious about them, she was far more interested in a good meal.

"Nice to meet you, Ty. If you'll excuse me, I'm going to see if I can order at the bar. It seems like the serving droids might be otherwise occupied," Indara said.

Ty nodded. "It's fight day, pretty much the busiest day of the week. If you want anything, the bar is definitely the best place to order. Especially since most places will be closing down before the fights and won't reopen until later tonight after they let out."

Indara looked from Ty to Vernestra and realized that whatever needed to be said wouldn't be uttered in her presence, so she forced an overly bright smile. "Well, I'd love an ale. Can I get either of you anything?"

Both women shook their heads, so Indara escaped to the bar to see if the tavern served ale. The table that Ty had chosen was deep in the back of the establishment, and as Indara approached the bar, the bartender turned toward her. "Ale and whatever your daily special is," she said, and the man nodded.

Indara leaned against the bar as she waited for her order, turned toward the door so that she had a clear view of the street outside. She was only half paying attention to the foot traffic when a Gigoran walked past with a human woman, the two deep in conversation.

Indara felt a spark of recognition. She headed toward the door and peered out. At first, she thought it couldn't possibly be the Gigoran from Thelj, but then he turned slightly and she saw the scar where his eye should have been. How many one-eyed Gigorans could there be in the galaxy?

She looked over her shoulder toward the table with Vernestra and Ty, debating whether or not she should tell them. The animation in Ty's hands as she spoke and Vernestra's exhausted slump in her chair convinced Indara that she would be better off just following the Gigoran on her own. After all, if she didn't, he would be out of sight before too long.

Indara began to walk, weaving through the crowd and staying far back enough that the Gigoran would not notice her. He towered over most of the people around him, and so she was able to find him quite quickly, stepping lightly until she was only a few meters behind. She could just hear the conversation happening before her, the human woman keeping up a constant stream of chatter that the Gigoran only responded to in grunts and chirps, the vocalizer he wore either broken or not turned on, since there was no translated speech on his end.

"Yeah, so as far as I can tell, she hired three people, all of them the bottomest of feeders. No one will miss them. Which is great, since Spicy wants no witnesses left. Loose ends and all. You still got them addresses?"

Another series of chirps from the Gigoran. The pale-skinned human woman nodded.

"Good. You need anything, me and the boys can help. We've got a few pens cleared out if you want to have some fun. You just let me know."

The woman walked away, turning left down a very narrow alley while the Gigoran continued ahead. Indara debated whether to follow the woman, but the phrase *loose ends* made Indara think that the Gigoran was by far the greater threat.

So when he turned into a park, she followed him without hesitation. The Gigoran headed right for a residential building, the squat houses crowded close together. Indara followed, weaving this way and that to avoid the kids playing in the street. No one paid her any mind as she passed—except one small child who snapped his head around, his eyes meeting Indara's. She gave the boy a smile before continuing on her way.

The Gigoran ducked into a housing tower, the kind often frequented by those with few credits and a lack of concern for their safety. The stink of spice emanated from within, and Indara took a deep breath and followed where the Gigoran had gone. She stood just inside the threshold, waiting for her eyes to adjust to the sudden gloom. The hallway full of refuse and prone bodies—spiceheads obliterated on the drug—was expected.

The fist that came flying toward her face was not.

Indara managed to duck, avoiding the punch only through the speed her connection to the Force lent her. Before she could straighten, the Gigoran was charging toward her, and she held her hand up, using the Force to push him back and pin him against the wall.

"I have some questions for you," she said.

Indara had barely uttered the words before she felt a sharp, stinging sensation in her neck. One moment she was holding the Gigoran in place, and the next she was lying on the floor of the apartment building, her vision blurry. She reached for the Force, but it was distant, like a lightning storm on a far horizon.

"Don't worry, little Jedi. We'll take good care of you," a feminine voice said.

And then the world went dark.

Chapter Twenty-Three

I have been a Jedi for a long time. I have helped some people and brought others to justice. I have learned and forgotten more than many of my peers. But no matter how long I lived, I would always and forever regret the way my friendship with Ty Yorrick—forged in the aftermath of our fight with the Nihil—had ended.

And judging from her attitude, she was not going to let me forget my role in the fight.

Indara had scurried off, most likely sensing the tension when we sat down, and Ty watched me from across the table, her arch look leaving no doubt that if I wanted the information she had, I was going to have to work for it. But that was okay. I knew how to apologize.

Unfortunately, I was pretty sure that what Ty wanted was for me to grovel.

"I owe you an apology," I said, getting straight to the point. There was no reason to be anything but straightforward. "I was wrong. And in the heat of the moment, I spent more time defending the Order than trying to understand your position."

For most of the day, the remnants of my Force vision had cluttered my thoughts, the screams of an imagined battlefield reigning supreme.

But now, sitting across from Ty, her gaze direct, I was transported back to the night more than a decade before, when she had first told me she was considering retirement from the Order.

We'd been on Fracni, a small, out-of-the-way planet near the Juinkwy Triangle, a convergence of hyperspace lanes that was often used by smugglers to hide their passage, since it was possible to switch direction suddenly within the juncture. Ty and I had just tracked down a group of pirates smuggling bootleg bacta, a scheme that involved charging small planets like Fracni a king's ransom and then giving them nothing but spice-tainted grain water. The effect was that patients immediately felt better but never *got* better. It was a brilliant scam, definitely one of the better ones I've seen in my lifetime. By the time people realized they'd been duped—it took a few hours before anyone registered that while they felt better, they weren't healing—the pirates were long gone.

Ty and I had been able to handle the pirates and reclaim most of the credits of those who had been defrauded on Fracni, and we were about to go on our way. I had just marked another anniversary of the loss of my Padawan and was still struggling to accept my failures and mistakes that had led to his death. Ty had been a Wayseeker for a number of years; Fracni was her latest stop. We had met by chance. I had just returned to Wayseeking, and the fact that we had both ended up in the same part of the galaxy to work together for a good purpose seemed like more than a happy coincidence. It felt like the Force at work.

Ty did not agree.

"You should have left the Order," she said. "After what happened. Why are you pretending like you'll one day want to go back to Coruscant?"

We'd been sitting in a restaurant in the city center, a small, drab place mostly frequented by locals and catering to a very diverse crowd. Ty had a local ale in her hand while I was sipping at my tea, a plate of half-eaten dumplings on the table between us.

"I will go back, though. I always do," I said. "How else can we push the Order to change, to remain independent, if we aren't working from the inside? Change will begin on Coruscant. It always does."

Ty had snorted. "You don't have to be a Jedi to spread the light, Vernestra. You can be your own woman. What will you do next time they want you to escort a senator to an event like a sword-wielding child-minder? And you cannot believe they'll let you be a Wayseeker forever. Not as a Jedi Master. There aren't as many of us as there were a century ago. Stars, there aren't even as many of us as there were a decade ago. And the reports! How many of us have offices now? Do you *like* filing after-action reports? Every day, the Republic and the Order get closer and closer to being the same thing, and then where will the Jedi be? No, the only way to remain autonomous is to strike out on your own, under your own flag. Without any oversight from the Order. Not even that provided to a Wayseeker."

Ty's words had chilled me. If I were honest, they had *terrified* me. The Order was all I had ever known, and even if I didn't agree with it all the time, I did believe in it. But what Ty was saying, leaving the Order behind . . . it felt like heresy.

And I had lashed out with what I thought at the time was cool pragmatism, but now I recognized it had been the truth mixed with a bit of cruelty. I was a Jedi, but I was not perfect.

None of us were.

"The things I said to you back then," I began, the past clinging like spiderwebs, sticky and unpleasant as we sat in the Dented Droid, "were unfair and unkind. And I am sorry for that."

"You told me that I was better at quitting than any other Jedi you'd ever met," Ty said, a flash of pain twisting the dark skin of her face before she regained control of her emotions. "You went straight for the killing blow."

"Yes," I nodded. "I did. It wasn't my best moment, there is no doubt of that. Retirement isn't quitting. Which is why I'm willing to admit as much now. I should have sought you out long before now to apologize.

But whether you accept it or not doesn't change the fact that I need your help."

Ty dropped a handful of shells on the table, brushing her palms together to clear the rest of the crumbs. "Why so much interest in the device now?"

"Because we found one on Cerifisis and another on Thelj. What we've found so far indicates that someone is looking to produce the device on a larger scale, this time with a fuel source other than recainium. I just keep thinking that this has something to do with Klerin Chekkat, but there are no records for the woman after Valo. She just . . . disappears from the galaxy."

"So, you think someone is trying to sell the device?"

I shrugged. "I don't know. But Garn was killed for a reason, and it's hard not to think about the amount of money something like the nullifier could make an unscrupulous person. I will add that I have had visions around the matter, but as you know, there's never any real way to determine what in my visions is real, and what is just a really complex metaphor," I said. Ty knew about my visions from when we had teamed up to work on a few missions back when I was still a young Jedi Knight. It had been a good partnership: I was a stickler for detail and Ty was more likely to make decisions based on her gut. We complemented each other in that way.

And even if our paths had diverged, I still had to believe there was a reason the Force had led me to Ty Yorrick once again. Sure, she may not like me very much, but she still had a strong code of ethics, and she would be no happier than the average Jedi about pirates and other criminals having access to a weapon that could disrupt a lightsaber.

Ty leaned back briefly, her joints cracking audibly as she did so, even though she did not seem pained at the movement. "I can tell you this: You're closer to the source of the most recent batch of nullifiers than you think. They were refined right here on Ruathi."

I frowned. "Wait, how do you know that?"

"I took a job a few months back. Don't look so surprised, even an old woman has to eat. The government here on Ruathi is very unstable. The previous party in power made the planet sort of a safe haven for pirates and other lawbreakers. They refused to let Republic officials arrest anyone on the planet and even turned away the Order quite a few times. Then the people of the planet led a grassroots campaign to eject that ruling party and instill a sense of law and order here on Ruathi. One of their goals was to petition to join the Republic. A few weeks ago, a couple of nights before the pivotal elections, someone planted the seeds for a riot. The people's party won, thankfully, and when they began to investigate the cause of the riot and the fire that burned through a good portion of the city, they were able to trace it back to a factory. Which is where they found this."

Ty reached into a knapsack next to her and threw a partially damaged bangle on the table. I picked it up and frowned.

"This looks almost like the nullifier I found on Cerifisis."

"It's an older model. The empty chamber right there is where the recainium was stored," Ty said.

I gave her an arch look. "There is recainium in here?"

She grinned. Even I could hear the annoyance in my voice. "Relax, Jedi. It doesn't work. The recainium is long gone. From the testing an official did, several other power devices were used to try to amplify the signal of the crystal matrix within."

"So someone was experimenting here on Ruathi to see if they could find a safer way to power this," I said with a sigh, setting the partially damaged device back on the table. It was nice to know my hunch had been correct, but it was also unsettling. "Do you know who?"

"Not yet. We're looking for a scientist who came here and worked in the labs, but while I have a description, I don't have a name. It would be nice if I did. My final payment from the government rests on providing them with a potential suspect. Several people died because of the riots, and the damage from the fire intentionally set at the test facility destroyed several neighborhoods before it was doused."

"I can help you out with that. Florinda Jackard," I said, pulling the holo-emitter I carried from within my robes and powering it up so that the woman's likeness was illuminated in the center of the table. "She is a scientist who is known for creating experimental crystal power matrices. Like the kind that might be necessary to replace a highly unstable mineral before a device can be produced en masse."

Ty's lips pursed, and then she looked around the tavern. "Hey, where did your sidekick go? Marlip is a slow bartender, but he isn't that slow."

I frowned, because I hadn't even noticed that Indara had been gone far longer than was necessary to get something to drink. I looked toward the bar, but I didn't see her anywhere in the tavern. "Hmmm. Perhaps she went to get food. She's a Jedi. She'll be fine."

Ty laughed and climbed slowly to her feet, stretching once she was standing. "Always so secure in the Order. Vernestra, most of the people on Ruathi don't like the Jedi. Remember when I said that for decades this planet catered to criminals? There are still far too many people who would happily trade information on a Jedi for a few credits. For all you know, that poor Jedi Knight could have been ransomed back to Coruscant by now. Let me grab my repulsor chair, and we'll go find her."

I wanted to argue with Ty, but the reality was that even the savviest Jedi could fall victim to an unexpected attack. And Ty obviously knew the planet better than I did. "I'll speak with the bartender," I said, but I needn't have bothered. Ty was already sitting in a hovering repulsor chair she'd parked near the table, navigating it ahead of me toward the bar and calling out to the Besalisk bartender in a language I didn't understand. He laughed and gestured toward the door, and Ty turned back to me. She didn't bother trying to keep the concern from her face.

"Marlip said she went outside a few minutes ago. He said something seemed to catch her eye, but he couldn't tell what."

I took a deep breath and let it out. If Indara was going to go chasing food, the least she could have done was let me know. She wasn't the only one sick of rations.

"Well then, let's go find an errant Jedi."

Chapter Twenty-Four

When Indara woke, the first thing she noticed was that her hands were bound behind her. The bindings were incredibly tight, and a surge of panic rushed through Indara, the memory of being pinned in the mines long ago too similar to her current predicament.

But she quickly gained control of herself, reaching for the Force and the calming reassurance she always felt at sensing the crackle and spark of life within the galaxy. Once she was certain that her initial sense of panic was far away, she began to take in her surroundings. She was on a stone floor, dampness and cold seeping in through the thickness of her robes. Her lightsaber was gone, of course, but other than that it seemed like she was mostly unharmed. There was an aching pounding in her head, most likely from whatever had been used to knock her out, and her mouth was incredibly dry. Her feet weren't bound, and as Indara sat up, her vision began to swim and the dim lights illuminating her cell swayed sickeningly.

"Ayyy, you go moving about like that you'll be no good in the bout. You jest rest up there, jest rest up."

The voice that spoke was heavily accented, and Indara turned toward the sound at a glacial pace. In the cell next to her was a

Chadra-Fan, the man's fur greasy and matted, a large chunk missing from one of his ears.

"I... where am I?"

"You're in the fight pits, Jedi. Bad place to be. You must have some gigantico gambling debts," he said with a hoarse laugh. "Good night to fight, though. It's beast night. You won't have to face down the champion. You have a much better chance of survival against a gheriol than one of Moigh's gladiators."

"What's a gheriol?" Indara asked, just as the scraping sound of metal against stone drew her attention. A scrawny, pale-skinned blond human woman and a massive Houk male, his broad shoulders and muscular arms the only features more distinctive than the orange ridges across the top of his skull, walked the pathway directly outside the cells. The woman wore a dress that may have once been grand but had fallen into disrepair even though she carried herself like a queen. There was something vaguely familiar about the woman, but Indara could not place what.

"Well, look at this, Var," she said, peering in at Indara. "Hinra truly did bring us a human Jedi! Oh, what fun. Can we use her first? The Chadra-Fan is boring and old."

Var crossed his arms, his biceps bulging. "People like to see Chadra-Fans get chewed," he said, his Galactic Basic faltering.

The human woman slipped into another language that sounded to Indara like Houkese—making Indara think her previous announcement was for her ears only—and the two argued until the woman stomped her foot and crossed her arms, the beginnings of a pout twisting her lips.

Var threw up his hands in annoyance. "Fine. Fine, Kliva! As you wish. If profits are low, it is the fault of you."

Var walked away, and the woman, Kliva, bent down to grin at Indara. Her natural teeth had been replaced by sharpened metal pieces, and Indara realized why the woman looked familiar: She was Kliva of Arnt, a famous pirate who had been pardoned by Garn during his early years as senator. Indara had seen the woman's face in the datafiles she'd pulled on Garn.

She'd also just seen the woman talking to the Gigoran she'd followed before she'd been knocked out. It seemed logical that the two of them were working together. But why?

It was a break in the investigation, and Indara refused to let the opportunity pass without exploiting it. "Who is Hinra? Is he the Gigoran I was following?"

Surprise lifted Kliva's eyebrows. "What a curious little Jedi you are. I'm surprised you can talk after the dose of lointy venom we shot you with."

Indara ignored the woman's attempt at misdirection. "Who does Hinra work for? And why did they kill Garn?"

Kliva laughed and walked away, Indara watching her go. "I tell you what. If anything is left of you to talk to after you face the gheriol, then I will happily answer your questions."

There was another scraping noise before the cells fell silent again, the only sound the wheezing in the cell next to Indara's.

"What's a gheriol?" she asked again, falling back onto the stone floor, the surge of adrenaline that had powered her fading and leaving her exhausted. She wanted to stay awake, but she had a feeling her best course of action was to get as much rest as she could until they came for her. So when unconsciousness started to claim her, she didn't fight it as hard as she would have liked to.

"It's certain death, is what it is," the Chadra-Fan next to her said as her vision began to swim. "But at least you will die quick. Mercy, but small."

Indara closed her eyes, but before she drifted off once more, she had a surprisingly optimistic thought: They could find out who had killed Garn and why.

All she had to do was fight a deadly beast while half drugged and with her hands tied behind her back.

Wasn't that exactly the kind of thing a Jedi Knight was supposed to do?

Chapter Twenty-Five

Nilsson looked at the workers in his private lab on Septra and tried to remind himself that it was not their fault that they were incompetent. Of course they did not fully understand the purpose or conceptual engineering of the nullifier. He'd kept everyone in the labs isolated in their work tasks for a reason. If no one had access to the full design, then it would be impossible for them to steal his prototype the way Florinda had.

What he had not counted on, though, was that everyone he had hired since her could be so useless.

There were three teams. One was supposed to manufacture the housing for the device, creating a bangle that was in essence two separate pieces that could be snapped together around the nullification matrix. The second team was supposed to create a way for the nullification matrix to be produced faster, cutting the time of production down from a week to a matter of hours. And the last team, the one that had very little to do because Florinda had not fully shared her crystal matrix, was supposed to be growing the crystals that would power the device, crystals that would eventually burn out and need to be replaced, creating an endless stream of revenue that Nilsson could use to fund the development of his other projects, like the large-scale—and highly illegal—disruptor cannons that rebels on Genetia had been requesting for nearly three years.

Instead, what Nilsson was getting was a laundry list of excuses, most of them being variations on a theme: Without plans, how would they know what the device was supposed to look like?

The head scientist for each team—a trio of Cereans who had not come cheap—had been sending nonstop holos requesting an in-person meeting, and Nilsson had refused until Grizela had recommended that he stop by Septra to speak with them. He'd wanted to refuse again, but then Grizela had revealed that they were far behind on their work, and that despite many promises and assertions made before these scientists had been hired, they seemed utterly confounded on just what was required of them.

Nilsson didn't care for Cereans, and being in the same room as the scientists made him deeply uncomfortable. The female of the group wore a hat to cover her incredibly long skull, but neither of the males did, and Nilsson found their elongated heads distracting. Not in an alluring way, but in a way that turned his stomach thinking about what it would look like if he were to put a blaster bolt in one of their heads. Messy, most definitely. They did have two brains, after all.

His thoughts could have been driven by the massive amount of spice he'd smoked before the meeting, but he didn't think so. He was pretty sure his revulsion was just because Cereans were grotesque. Smart and hardworking, but terrible to look at.

"I need you to explain to me once more why your teams seem to be having so much trouble accomplishing their tasks. Not yours," he said, pointing to the lone female of the group before she could start yammering on again. "I know you don't have a design for the power source. I swear if you bring it up one more time, I will find you a one-way ticket to the center of an active volcano. Trust that I'm working on it,"

Nilsson added. Well, his bounty hunter was working on finding the plans. And as soon as she found Florinda Jackard, that problem would be solved. But without a housing or a nullification matrix, none of it would matter.

And yet the brilliant minds in front of him wanted to argue that their way was better.

"You have both designs and plenty of examples for what I asked of you. I even gave you the last two prototypes I had. So why, exactly, am I here? And tell me without using the word *difficulties*," Nilsson said, his patience fraying. How was it that everyone he worked with was a fool, even those who were highly intelligent? *That* was a phenomenon worthy of study.

The eldest of the trio, a snowy-haired man who liked to speak as if he bore the authority on the project—even though each of the scientists had been hired on their own merit—stood. "Nilsson, you are not listening to us. Without any kind of integration, we keep creating new prototypes that do not interact well. You asked us to take a process that normally requires months and pare it down to a matter of days. We can do that. But we need to collaborate."

Nilsson groaned. He had no more patience for the conversation, nor for the Cereans. So he was going to handle both of his problems at once. "Look. One week. You have one week from today to come up with a final prototype, something simple enough that it could be assembled by Gamorreans. If you do not, every single week that passes after that, one of you will be killed. Do you understand?"

The old man began to sputter. "We cannot possibly finish the work in one week. Two, perhaps . . ."

The older man had barely finished speaking before Nilsson stood and pulled out his blaster, shooting the man in the head. He fell to the ground, blood pooling around him as the other two scientists remained where they were, frozen in surprise. Nilsson leaned over the table to check out the mess below. Surprisingly neat. Nothing like he'd been expecting.

"Huh. Human heads splatter much more disastrously," he murmured to himself before turning back to the remaining scientists. "Your colleague very generously bought you an additional week. Two weeks. And then one of you dies. Good luck."

Nilsson turned and left. Grizela was waiting for him in the doorway with the yellow-skinned Twi'lek who oversaw the operation, Erial. Nilsson had never much cared for the man, but he usually produced results.

"I want daily updates. And do not let them out of your sight. I cannot afford a repeat of Ruathi at this point in the process. I have orders coming in, and I need to start shipping the device by the end of the month. Understood?"

Erial nodded, his smile flashing sharpened teeth. "Any preference on how I kill them?"

"No. But save the woman for last. She's the most important. I can hire any scientist for process improvement. I need someone specialized in crystal matrices for the power issue, and those specialists are hard to find. Speaking of which," Nilsson continued, turning to Grizela, "please tell me the bounty hunter has found something."

"She sent an update a few hours ago. The status was still inconclusive. She found the ship Florinda used to flee Ruathi, which was the same ship she had on Haileap when she tried to broker the deal. The bounty hunter thinks she may be able to find her based on the ship data. Apparently, the woman stole the ship from a hauling company that has a locator on their vessels."

Nilsson laughed in delight. "Finally, some good news."

Grizela gave him a tight smile. "I have better news. Hinra confronted our mysterious Jedi on Ruathi. He got the drop on her right before I left to come here. He had to travel to Nar Shaddaa to get one of the loose ends, but he said he left the Jedi with Kliva."

Nilsson felt his good mood sour just as quickly as it had arrived. "Kliva is a reckless fool. There is no rational reason she should be placed in charge of keeping a Jedi secure. We need to get to Ruathi right away. I need to know why this Jedi is following Hinra. It seems odd that she keeps turning up wherever we are. Unless... has there been any sign from your contacts that the Republic is investigating Garn?"

Grizela shook her head. "No. None at all. Once he died, so did most of the inquiries."

"Hmmm. Either way, it's probably safer just to see that she dies. I need to make sure there is nothing linking me to Garn, and the Jedi are always trouble."

Grizela nodded. "The ship is ready to leave whenever you are. It should not take too long to get to Ruathi."

Nilsson nodded. "Good. And send a message to Kliva. Tell her if the Jedi isn't in one piece when we arrive, it will be *her* head."

Chapter Twenty-Six

Ty and I investigated all of the food establishments near the tavern, searching for Indara, starting with the noodle places. It was a bittersweet reminder of my first Padawan, and I wondered what Imri would have thought of Indara. They weren't very much alike, but I liked to imagine they might have gotten along, bonding over a shared love of food.

None of the proprietors of the shops in the dockyard had seen a human Jedi, and a call back to J-6 on the ship revealed that she had not returned to the *Cantaros*. I tried calling her directly on her comlink, and there was no answer. Whether she had traveled beyond the range of the small device or had run into trouble, I didn't know, but I did know that it was unlike Indara to be gone for so long without any kind of notice.

"Any ideas where she might have gone?" Ty asked. I did not expect the former Jedi to help me look for my missing partner, but Ty had offered her assistance and I was willing to take any help I could get, even if it was given begrudgingly.

I shook my head. "I have no idea why she would have even left. You said the bartender thought something had caught her attention?"

Ty nodded. "It seems odd to me. What could have been that remarkable?"

I stood in the middle of the road and turned slowly, taking in the dockside offerings. There was nothing worth noticing in the space. Just the usual food stalls and gambling dens with a constant flow of people as travelers made their way on and off ships . . .

It clicked into place as I looked around, watching the crowd ebb and flow. "She was following someone," I said to Ty.

Ty nodded. "That seems the most likely conclusion, but it leaves the larger questions of who she was following and where they were going."

"Yes, it does," I said. I gazed at the route back to where the *Cantaros* waited and then in the opposite direction, deeper into the city proper. "I think she went that way, into the housing areas. If her quarry had been heading toward a ship, she would've wanted my help to stop them before they managed to leave the planet."

Ty raised an eyebrow in my direction. "That's a big jump in logic. She could have gone the other way just as easily."

Ty was right, but I hated not having any idea of what to do. "Let's just head this way a bit and speak with the shopkeepers. Perhaps someone noticed her passage."

We began to make our way down the market stalls, asking people if they'd seen a Jedi. For the most part, the sellers just gave me a flat stare, neither answering nor ignoring me, and it was clear that there was no love for the Jedi on Ruathi.

I was beginning to get frustrated at the lack of any kind of acknowledgment when I saw a small human boy with night-dark skin staring at me, wide-eyed. Something, some instinct, pulled me toward him. I waved and he waved back, but the way he stared at me made me think I was not the first Jedi he had seen.

I walked over to the child, Ty grumbling in her chair behind me, but not following. The boy was dirty and unkempt, and he had a box, a spray bottle, and a rag, ostensibly to clean the boots of those who stopped. I knelt so that I was at his level. "Do you know what I am?"

He shook his head. I held my hand out and levitated the box between us. He watched for a moment before giving me a gap-toothed grin. And then held his hand out and did the same.

Ty chose that moment to move her chair closer to better hear our conversation. "Why are you . . . oh," she said.

"He's attuned to the Force," I said.

"Too young to know that he's doing the impossible and too old to join the Order," Ty said, a note of bitterness in her voice. But she was right. Once, that would have made me pity the boy. Now I was not sure whether such a fact was a blessing or a curse.

The boy didn't seem to speak, whether by choice or because he couldn't, I wasn't sure. But he understood me just fine. "I'm a Jedi. Have you seen someone else dressed like me today?" Since he could feel the Force, he may have noted Indara's passing.

He nodded and pointed toward the street that led past a park and back to the housing areas of the city. I smiled and pulled out a ten-credit chip from my pocket, holding it out to him. He grabbed the money and ran off, disappearing quickly into the crowd.

"Well, you've made someone's day," Ty said.

I stood and looked in the direction the boy had indicated. "You should think about seeing if he's here later. He can't join the Order, but he could use some monitoring," I said.

Ty scowled. "I don't make it a habit to adopt every street kid I meet."

"You could," I said with a smile. "After all, wasn't that one of the reasons you gave for leaving the Order? 'Maybe it would be better if there was more than one option for those strong in the Force to learn to use it,' I remember you saying. And I didn't disagree."

Ty laughed. "Be careful there, Vernestra Rwoh. That doesn't sound very much like the talk of a Jedi Master."

I snorted. "If the people of Ruathi don't like Jedi, maybe we can use that to our advantage. But before we do, I think I need a costume change."

After a quick stop at the *Cantaros* to switch out my Jedi robes for the shirts and trousers of a hauler—I'd been to enough planets where the Jedi weren't very popular that I kept a host of other clothing options—Ty and I headed in the direction the street kid had indicated. He wasn't back in his spot with the box, but I saw Ty noticing and perhaps even looking for him a bit. Ty seemed to think she was better off alone, but it was impossible not to sense the loneliness that emanated from her. She'd always felt that way to me, as though once she'd lost her original connection to the Order when she was a Padawan—through no fault of her own, and a tragic tale to be sure—she'd also lost a bit of her ability to connect with others. But she still cared about people. The fact that she was on Ruathi trying to help stabilize the government for the good of the people illustrated that she wasn't a misanthrope. I'd always felt that she just needed a little push to realize that she liked people more than she let on.

We headed away from the dockyards through neighborhoods of tall buildings, the living compartments stacked on top of one another like crates waiting to be loaded onto a hauler. Ruathi was not a rich planet, and it showed in the housing units, which looked like they had been installed centuries ago during the era of hyperspace expansion. Ruathi had been settled slightly after a node was located nearby on a route from Corellia to Erdo, a mining planet that had once been prosperous but whose mines had shut down a few decades ago. It seemed that as the fortunes of the people on Erdo shifted, so, too, did those on Ruathi. Many of the apartments had balconies with plants, but just as many looked to be vacant, people choosing to leave Ruathi rather than stay and fight a corrupt government over dwindling prosperity.

As we traveled, I looked for people to talk to, hoping that now that I no longer looked like a Jedi, the citizenry would be more willing to talk to me. But I saw no one, a fact that I found odd. The city had been much more crowded not more than an hour ago.

"Where is everyone? It seems very odd that the streets are so empty around here this time of day."

"It's fight day. One day a week, the gambling halls host bouts in their arenas. It used to happen every day, but it was so detrimental to what little economy is left here on Ruathi that the government changed it to a once-weekly event by law."

"Wait, you're telling me that these fights are so well liked that people were just not going to work?"

Ty nodded. "Worse than that, people weren't even operating their businesses. Government employees were neglecting their duties; the entire city of Aradonia basically ceased to function. It's because of the gheriol. It's a local creature, clever, and with the ability to hypnotize its prey. People challenge the creature thinking it will be easy to defeat because it cannot charm you if you have your eyes closed. Either way, it doesn't matter who wins, the practice is barbaric. But very, very popular."

Ty pointed toward a side street. "Why don't we check out the gambling district. If Indara was following someone, that would be their logical destination today. No one misses the fights. Maybe we'll overhear something there about a Jedi. I do a lot of my best work eavesdropping in the gaming halls, so it's worth a shot."

I nodded. I had no other clues to find Indara. Wherever she was, I just hoped she was all right. I was beginning to worry that she had come to real harm.

And I did not think I could handle losing another Jedi on my watch.

Chapter Twenty-Seven

A bucket of fetid water woke Indara, and she sat up choking and sputtering and then gagging when the stink of the water hit her. It smelled like pond scum mixed with sewage. She wiped it off her face as best she could, burying her face in her shoulders since her hands were still bound behind her back. She didn't bother doing much else. It didn't quite seem worth the effort.

A man grinned down at her, his expression maniacal. "Up and at 'em, hero. Your big moment is almost here."

Indara climbed to her feet, still unsteady but better than she'd felt the first time she'd woken. Her cellmate was gone, the Chadra-Fan having been taken away for some other purpose. Indara hoped he was okay. Gambling debts seemed like a very stupid reason to die.

The man with the bucket opened the cell and beckoned Indara forward. He pushed her ahead of him, Indara stumbling from the aftereffects of the poison they'd dosed her with, and they began to shuffle slowly toward an open door that had not been visible from Indara's cell.

"Don't try any of those mind tricks on me. I know what you Jedi are like. You were the ones who hauled my pappy in for stealing credits from a banking ship. He'd probably still be alive today if you hadn't sent him to rot in a prison ship orbiting Tulpi. He died playing farmer."

"I'm sorry about your loss," Indara said, although she only half meant it. The man grunted in response, perhaps sensing the insincerity.

"What is it exactly that I'm fighting?" Indara asked, but the man didn't acknowledge her question. The sound of a crowd stomping its feet got louder the closer they got to wherever they were going. The hallway they traveled down reminded Indara of the tunnels under the archives, and for a single moment she fervently wished she hadn't been dragged along with Vernestra Rwoh on her mission to right the wrongs of the past.

Indara banished the thought and steadied herself. She was a Jedi. All she needed was to figure out a way through the moment. She could do it.

The narrow hallway opened up to reveal a large dirt ring, and Indara blinked as overhead chemlights blinded her for a moment, her escort shoving her forward violently. She didn't fall, but it was a near thing—her hands being bound behind her back made her incredibly unsteady. There was a collective hush over the crowd for a second as her eyes adjusted, and when she could see again, she realized that she was in an arena of sorts, a barrier of twisted metal pieces separating the spectators from where she stood within the ring. She couldn't see the crowd because of the brightness of the overhead chemlights, but she could sense them: a large number of people, all of them watching her.

"Tonight we have a most special challenger for you," came a voice through a loudspeaker system. "*A Jedi!*"

The roar of the crowd was deafening, the sound of their excitement and fury reverberating through Indara's chest. From the way they sounded, she did not think they were going to be cheering for her.

There was a scraping metal sound as the door she'd entered was pushed closed behind her. Indara tried to take the measure of the ring, but she was too woozy. It was also hard for her to move with her hands bound behind her, and the strange dark spots that had been left in the dirt of the arena did not inspire a lot of confidence that she would be able to escape this encounter.

A high keening sound echoed from the doorway across the arena, and the audience echoed the sound back, as though they were calling the creature to them. The strange little Chadra-Fan had called the creature a gheriol, and Indara tried to think if she had ever heard of it. She hadn't, and when the door opened, she braced herself for something large and threatening.

What she was not expecting was a creature that looked like a cross between a tooka cat and a sun snake. The animal had a long sinuous body with six legs placed equidistant from one another in the middle third of the body; the neck and a long tail made up the remainder of its length. It was heavily furred, and a ripple of rainbow-colored light played across the black pelt as the creature moved, some kind of bioluminescence. Indara was so busy staring at the thing approach that she almost did not realize it was lunging toward her with an open maw, teeth dripping with viscous fluid, until it was mere centimeters away.

Indara leapt backward, the Force giving her more height and distance than she would normally have but not nearly as much as she'd hoped. Her connection to the Force was shaky, and she had to attribute it to the poison in her system. The audience's disappointment was audible, and Indara tried to shake off the moment. She had to think. There was no help coming for her. Vernestra probably didn't even know where she was.

So what would the Jedi Master do?

She would improvise. Indara looked at the creature once more, and this time she realized that what she thought were eyes were just a very detailed pattern on the top of the skull. A pattern that rippled down and became one with the undulating light. Yet again she was entranced by the pattern of the fur. She watched it ripple, unable to look away. So many colors. What did it all mean? There was something worthwhile there, an answer to a question that hadn't been asked ...

Indara leapt high as a set of jaws snapped at her legs, the teeth catching her robes instead. This jump was better than the previous one, her connection to the Force getting better as she moved and sweated out the remnants of the poison.

The crowd groaned in disappointment and began to boo. "Bite the Jedi, you kriffing beast!" someone yelled. Yep, they definitely were not rooting for her.

Indara noticed that there was something interesting about the fur. Somehow the pattern kept distracting her, the dancing light hypnotizing her. The gheriol must have some way to charm its prey before attacking. Indara thought that she could use that to her advantage.

She turned her back to the creature. The color patterns on the fur, which had started up again as the creature stalked closer, had been responsible for her momentary lack of attention. If she could avoid looking at the thing, perhaps she could take some time to get her hands free ...

It suddenly occurred to Indara that she didn't need her hands free. What she needed was to turn the creature's attack back on it. She thought of the histories she had read about Ty Yorrick and other Jedi who seemed to have an affinity for beasts. Perhaps that was the solution here. Not direct action, but a sort of connection. Indara closed her eyes and opened herself to the Force as fully as she could. And then she reached for the gheriol. She could do it. She could bond with the creature. She didn't have many other options.

The stomp of approaching footfalls was the only warning that Indara got to move out of the way, but as she did she felt snapping teeth near the side of her face. She opened her eyes to see the gheriol running past her, circling back toward her with its mouth wide open and the teeth snapping. There was no color display this time, and Indara had to throw herself to the side to escape the attack, landing hard on her shoulder. The creature had seemed to realize that she wasn't charmed by its display and sped up its attacks, launching them faster than before. Indara rolled over onto her stomach, scrambling awkwardly to her feet just to have to leap into the air as the gheriol charged once more. It seemed as though as soon as her feet touched the dirt of the arena, the animal was on her again.

She used the Force to slow her descent as she reached for the creature through the Force. She could sense the animal, but she could not make the last bit of connection to convince the creature she was neither food nor a threat.

The gheriol had not yet charged again, its sides moving as its breath heaved. It tried another display of colors, but Indara turned away before she could be enraptured by the dancing light. She reached out with the Force once more, insistent, and this time whatever tenuous connection may have been there slammed shut, like a door. Indara swore under her breath. Time for a new plan. She'd pressed the attempt to bond too far.

The gheriol charged again, but this time it seemed more half-hearted than before. Indara was again able to dodge the assault, but she could feel the weakness in the move. The remnants of the poison still made her legs shaky and her head pound. Her mouth was dry and tacky, and all she wanted was to lie in the dirt and sleep. She had to figure a way out of the ring. Dodging gheriol attacks for the next hour wasn't feasible. She needed to wrap up the fight sooner rather than later.

"Well, it seems our Jedi has lasted longer than our last challenger," the announcer said. The crowd booed and yelled, mostly insults that Indara could only half hear. But there was no need to understand the words to get the sentiment: Jedi were not loved on Ruathi.

"Let's make this interesting!" the voice added as another door began to scrape open. Indara had just enough time to see another gheriol released into the ring—this one easily twice the size of the first—before she realized that things were about to get much worse.

She *really* had to get her hands free.

Her heart pounded. If she didn't act quickly, she was going to be completely out of options. Her vision was beginning to go blurry, whether from the poison or the effort, she wasn't quite sure. So she took a deep breath and did the only thing she could think of. Something she would never normally do.

She ran directly toward the creatures.

Indara had once read that the best way to make certain animals flee was to make them think you were the threat. The gheriols didn't seem to have eyes, but they had no problem detecting Indara's movements. One of the nice things about the robes that Indara wore was that they made her look bigger than her actual size. So she began to yell, as loudly as she could. As she yelled, she hopped up and down, hoping they sensed her and would think her large and menacing, a bigger threat to them than they were to her.

It was a simple idea, but Indara wasn't sure if it was smart or foolish. The gheriols seemed to freeze, uncertain what to do. The two creatures might have been used to fighting people thanks to the arena, but they didn't seem to anticipate being attacked so directly. Indara took their momentary hesitation to flip herself into the air over their heads, landing behind the creatures, her back to the rudimentary metal fencing that separated the audience from the ring. She then leapt up as quickly and quietly as possible, using the Force to keep herself tethered to the fence. She held her breath and remained completely still.

She waited a beat hoping it had been enough, and as the gheriols began to pace around the space where she'd been—clearly confused as to where she'd gone—she allowed herself a small moment to celebrate her victory.

She had been close enough to the creatures to realize they had no eyes, at least none that Indara could see. They were all teeth and bioluminescence and fur. To Indara, this seemed to indicate that they were primarily underground, cave-dwelling creatures. Ruathi had an extensive series of limestone caves, one of the many reasons the planet was beloved by smugglers. If Indara's hunch was correct, the creatures relied on their other senses to track and attack. They might be able to scent her out, but there had been no indication that they were doing any such thing, and every time she'd landed after launching herself into the air, they were there to attack. Which led Indara to the belief that the creatures tracked their prey via vibrations through the dirt.

If she wasn't in the ring, there was no way for the creatures to track her. At least, that was what she was hoping.

As she clung to the rusty metal of the barrier, the creatures began to paw and snort, turning their heads this way and that. They stalked around the ring, but neither of them seemed to be able to figure out just where Indara was.

Which did not make the audience very happy, for obvious reasons.

"Booo! It looks like our Jedi is no fun," the announcer said. The audience began to stomp their feet in anger, and members of the crowd slammed into Indara from behind, trying to dislodge her from the barrier. The assault picked up strength, but Indara held fast, the Force keeping her in place even as her heart raced and a fine sheen of sweat broke out on her body. She would not be moved. Not without a monumental effort. Her hands were still bound behind her, and as the audience slammed into her, she had to unlace her fingers from the fencing. The spectators did not seem to be above breaking her fingers just for the fun of it.

"Let me through! I'll get that kriffing Jedi down," said a voice from behind Indara. Someone slammed into the fencing with enough force that Indara's teeth seemed to rattle in her head. Again and again came the battering against the fence, until an odd crack sounded as the protective fencing began to come loose.

But it was only the panel that Indara clung to that broke free, and only on the sides. Indara swallowed a shriek of alarm as she began to fall forward, headfirst, as the metal panel pivoted downward. She still held fast, and it was a long moment before the enraged crowd behind her realized that while they had managed to dislodge the fence, they had just opened up the arena to the creatures stalking around angrily in the dirt ring.

No longer able to cling to the protective fencing upside down, Indara fell awkwardly, striking her hip hard on the dirt. The fencing landed on top of her, the bottom still attached to the low wall of the ring. She rolled over just in time to see the two gheriols launching their way into the crowd over her, the broken piece of fencing a perfect ramp up and out of the ring and into the audience.

The cheering and jeering of the crowd immediately gave way to screaming, and the sounds of the creatures' teeth rending flesh were terrible. Chaos quickly reigned, and the sound over the speaker of a microphone being dropped and the announcer running away was all that was louder than the screams of hunting animals and fearful attendees.

Indara lay in the dirt, her sides heaving, her hands still bound behind her. She felt like she should help, but she was exhausted. The fencing that had given the gheriols a clear path to the spectators had her trapped in the dirt, a cage of safety. There was nothing she could do even if she wanted to. The bitter laugh that erupted from her was swallowed by the screams of fear coming from the gallery.

She just hoped there weren't too many deaths.

Chapter Twenty-Eight

Ty and I were navigating through the less savory end of the gambling district when we heard the screams.

We both immediately turned toward the sound, down a narrow alley to where people were fleeing one of the arena entrances. I led the way while Ty steered her chair along behind me at a slower pace. I caught the arm of a human woman, her face twisted in fear. "What's going on?" I asked.

"There was a Jedi fighting tonight, but then the barrier came down and the animals escaped. They're tearing into people inside. We had to get out. I have to go! It's not safe."

The woman pulled free of me and rejoined the crowd, and I looked down at Ty. "Have you ever wrangled a gheriol?"

"No. But there's a first time for everything."

We pushed past the people escaping and entered the hall. The place smelled of mold and bodies, the metallic scent of spilled blood emanating from deeper within. The crowd lessened as we got closer to the arena, and when we stepped inside, I was not quite prepared for the sight that greeted us.

The space was dominated in the center by a dirt ring surrounded by metal fencing. Behind the barrier, rows of benches rose up to a couple of meters from the ceiling. It was a standard arena, even if the space was well worn and a bit run-down. What was not normal was the bodies. Limbs from several species were strewn about, and bodies were draped across benches in their death throes. What had been a fun day out had turned bloody and violent, and I despaired at the senseless loss of life from the awful practice. What kind of people happily pay money to watch other people fight animals? And more than that, why was such a monstrous practice legal? It had led to nothing but misery on all sides.

There was a clicking sound to my left, and I drew my lightsaber and powered it up as a long black creature stalked near, its fur flickering a mesmerizing display of color. I could feel myself being pulled into the charm the flickering lights cast, and I looked away. "You said these things hypnotize their prey, right?"

"Yes," Ty said from behind me. She had left her chair behind and was slowly making her way to where I was, one hand on a bench to guide her cautious steps. "Don't look at them directly."

I looked away from the creature, watching the movement from the corner of my eye. It seemed wary of my lightsaber. "Can you handle this?"

"Of course. I'm old, not dead. Find Indara."

I moved slowly toward the ring, wary of moving too quickly and drawing the gheriol's attention. I crept toward the place in the fencing where the barrier had come down, and there, pinned under the loose piece of fence, was Indara, her hands bound behind her.

"Indara! Are you okay?" I called, my voice pitched low. A quick glance over my shoulder revealed Ty concentrating as she tried to connect to the gheriol through the Force.

"Yes! Thank the stars you're here. Did you get the gheriols?"

I blinked. "Ty is communicating with it right now. She's quite good at taming beasts."

"No, Vernestra, there are two of them. That isn't the only one!"

Something slammed into me from behind, and I tumbled forward. I reached for the Force and used it to correct my path, flipping forward and landing feetfirst in the dirt ring. I slid back a bit and looked up to see another gheriol, this one at least twice as large as the one Ty was engaged with.

I was no good at communicating with animals through the Force. That was Ty's specialty. Instead, I lifted my hand and used the Force to raise the piece of fencing that leaned down over Indara, lifting it cleanly from the space and wrapping it around the gheriol. The creature screamed out in displeasure, and I saw the gheriol near Ty jerk as well.

"Ty!" I shouted, but my warning came too late. The smaller gheriol lunged toward Ty, and I reached for it with the Force, lifting the creature into the air so that it couldn't claw Ty to death. She looked at me with an expression somewhere between annoyance and relief.

"I could have handled it myself," she said as the creature snapped and snarled at her from where it hung suspended in midair.

"I know. But we both have enough scars." I released my hold on the creature as Ty took hold of the creature herself, using her own abilities to lift free another piece of broken barrier fence to wrap around and restrain the smaller gheriol just as I had with the larger beast. A few people who had been hiding ran out of the arena once the creatures were subdued, but my attention was on Indara, who was looking at me with a mixture of embarrassment and relief.

"So, you got yourself kidnapped?" I teased.

She groaned. "I'm just glad you found me. I saw the Gigoran who killed Senator Garn walk past the tavern, and I followed him. I think he was here to kill someone, but I'm not sure why."

She turned around, and I used my lightsaber to cut through her bonds. She rubbed her wrists in relief. "We need to find Kliva of Arnt. She runs this place alongside a Houk. She was also talking to the Gigoran when I saw him. She's the one lead we have."

I turned toward Ty. "We're going to find the owners. Got this?" I asked, gesturing toward the two snarling creatures, who were getting calmer and more docile by the moment.

"By the time you return, I'm going to have a couple of brand-new friends. Go. I'll meet up with you later."

I pointed toward a booth at the top of the arena. "I'm willing to bet a year of rations they're up there."

I tucked my lightsaber into my belt and ran toward where a set of rickety steps led up to an observation booth high above the arena, Indara's footfalls behind me. But when I burst into the room, it was completely empty. Good thing no one had taken my wager.

Indara entered behind me and pointed to a hatch across the room with a ladder that descended. "When they brought me in, it was from a place someone called the pits. I think there has to be an exit from down there as well."

I nodded. "Do you want me to go first?"

"If you don't mind. They poisoned me with something. That's how they got the drop on me. I'm not sure what it was, but I'm still not feeling great."

"Don't worry, we'll get you some noodles when this is all over," I teased.

Indara sighed. "Noodles sound amazing. Well, that and clean robes. But also noodles," she said.

"I'm glad you're safe," I said, a small acknowledgment of the overwhelming relief I felt.

Indara nodded, and I touched the ladder to center myself before jumping into the hatch. It was a long fall, passing down through the spectator area and then farther down into the bowels of the facility. Without the Force to soften my landing, I would have broken an ankle or worse.

I moved out of the way so that Indara had space to follow, and she landed next to me with a soft thud. We stood in a tunnel lit with hanging lanterns, the sickly yellow glow leaving deep shadows in between the lights. The walls appeared to be natural limestone, and the far-off sound of water dripping echoed back to us. "Do you recognize this place?" I asked, keeping my voice low so the sound wouldn't carry.

Indara shook her head. "I think this is a different area than where I was kept."

There was only one way to go, so we walked ahead, quickly and quietly. We had gone about a dozen meters when the sounds of voices raised in anger filtered back to us. Ahead, a far-off light filtered under a door, and I powered up my lightsaber.

"I'll take the lead. Follow at your own pace."

I sprinted down the hallway toward the door, the Force lending me speed and keeping my steps quiet. The closer I got, the easier it was to hear the voices raised in argument, a man and a woman. Hopefully, they were our quarry.

I sliced up and across the metal door once and then again, my lightsaber making quick work of the barrier. As the pieces fell away, I used the Force to clear the debris from the doorway. As I entered the room, a blaster bolt fired toward me, but a flick of my wrist and the bolt was reflected back right at the Houk who had fired. He crumpled to the ground, and I turned toward the human woman who stood with her arms crossed.

"I won't talk. You can try all you want, but I'd rather die than turn traitor."

Indara entered the room, taking in the dead Houk before turning to the human woman. "Kliva. Garn is dead. He was killed. And you know who did it."

I gestured with my lightsaber toward Kliva, my gaze on Indara. "You seem like you've had time to consider your line of questioning. So, I leave it to you."

Indara nodded, her spine straightening as she realized what I was asking of her. She walked up to Kliva and waved her hand across her face.

"Tell me who killed Garn."

There was a moment where Kliva tried to fight Indara's will, but it was a short struggle. Her gaze went far away.

"Nilsson. Weapons broker, big fish, spicehead. Very, very dangerous."

A chill ran down my arms as I remembered the vision with Stellan: the putrid fish, the crystals, the pipe. Things were beginning to fall into place.

"Does he employ a Gigoran?" Indara asked.

Kliva slowly nodded. "Hinra. Scary but not the most dangerous person on Nilsson's crew. You gotta watch out for Grizela. She's the one pulling the strings, making them dance."

"What about Florinda Jackard?" I asked. "Does she work for Nilsson?"

"Used to," Kliva said. "Stole from him. Lotta credits if you can find that one."

"Where can we find Nilsson and his crew?" Indara asked.

Sweat had begun to appear on Kliva's brow, and she frowned as well. "Nilsson? You won't find him. He's a ghost."

A blaster shot rang out, a burn appearing in Kliva's middle before she fell to the floor. I spun to see the Houk sitting up on his elbow. He grunted before falling back to the ground, either unconscious or dead.

I powered down my lightsaber. I spotted Indara's on a nearby desk and flipped it to her. She caught it in midair and clipped it to her belt. "Let's get out of here. We've gotten all we're going to get." I couldn't help but give Kliva and her companion one last look. More wasted lives. It was exhausting.

Indara nodded. "Wait, there were other prisoners, in the cages."

I followed her down another narrow stone hallway to a room with a number of cells, but every single one was empty, with stains settling into the ground that pointed to unfortunate ends. Indara looked stricken, and I tried to summon up a platitude that would make the situation less bleak, but I had nothing.

Sometimes the cruelty of the galaxy defies explanation.

Indara seemed even paler than before, and I managed to catch her just before she collapsed. I used the Force to lighten her a bit before tossing her over my shoulder and turning back the way we had come. Already I could hear the shouts of the local authorities as they entered the building. They would see to the injured better than I could.

We had a name. Now the goal was to find out just who this Nilsson was. Easier said than done. But I knew someone who would have the information, even if the visit would be awkward.

Perhaps for the first time since leaving Thelj, we were finally on the right path.

Chapter Twenty-Nine

When Indara woke, she was back on the *Cantaros,* lying in the quarters that Vernestra had assigned to her. J-6 stood nearby and turned toward the bed once she noticed Indara was awake.

"Finally! Wait one second while I remove the medline from your arm."

Indara sat up and watched as J-6 very quickly—and gently—removed the medline, spraying the spot with an absorbent adhesive before leaving the room.

Indara sat on the edge of her bed for a moment until there was a knock on the door.

"Come in," she called, and the door opened again to reveal Vernestra standing on the other side. She'd changed back into her tunic and trousers, no longer dressed as a regular civilian and looking once more like a Jedi.

"How are you feeling?" she asked.

"Better. I take it we've left Ruathi?"

Vernestra nodded. "We're going to see a friend of mine. Well, 'friend' might be a stretch. An acquaintance, a bounty hunter I know from the old days. The woman in the arena said that Florinda had a price on her head, and that makes me think Nilsson probably hired a bounty hunter to handle the matter. And now that we know names, Deva should be able to get us some more information. The kind of answers that queries to the Jedi Temple won't produce." There was a lot of missing subtext in what Vernestra was saying, and Indara got the sense that perhaps the information the acquaintance of Vernestra had access to wasn't all aboveboard.

There was a scrabbling sound in the hallway, and Indara froze as a gheriol poked its head in the room. "Um, do we have a stowaway?"

Vernestra looked down at the creature, scratched its head idly, and turned back to Indara as the animal wandered off. "We're dropping the gheriols off at a refuge on Hetzal for Ty. She decided to come with us since she needs to find Florinda Jackard for the Ruathi government. The woman apparently started a riot to cover her escape." Vernestra quickly filled Indara in on what she had missed while she was out and about on her own adventure. It wasn't much, hardly worth the visit, and Indara tensed for whatever Vernestra was about to say next.

"Is this the part where you tell me that I was a fool for going off by myself?" Indara asked, unable to keep the bitterness from her voice.

Vernestra's brows rose in surprise. "No, this is the part where I tell you we bought food for you before we left. I visited three different noodle carts since I wasn't sure what kind you preferred. The food is in the warmer in the galley."

Indara tilted her head and studied the older Jedi. "You aren't going to give me a lecture?"

"No. I'm not a hypocrite. You saw an opportunity and took it. I most likely would have done the same." Vernestra's gaze went distant, and she laughed a little. "Actually, I definitely would have done the same thing. Also, we're in this together. Why would I lecture you about being a Jedi? I think we're past that."

Indara nodded, feeling not exactly relieved but something between that and being proud of herself. The doubts that had plagued her in the aftermath of the mine collapse on Seswenna for once felt silly. Of course she was capable. She was a Jedi. Why had she ever doubted that?

Vernestra grinned and continued. "Besides, things worked out for the best. If you hadn't followed Hinra, we wouldn't have the information we need to move our investigation forward."

Indara didn't quite know what to do with what sounded suspiciously like praise, so she just nodded. "Wait, that reminds me: Was Jay-Six able to do anything with the phrase Garn uttered in his holo? We came up empty in the archives, but if she has a robust translation program, she may be able to run it down."

"The phrase in Fruscti? *Sigeo nocht rewnat qas bindt lokicgh fro.* No. At this point, I'm hoping Deva will be able to help us out with it. She has a very unique knowledge base, and I have to believe it's important. Garn did not strike me as a man who would let his death be in vain. If he made a point to include that phrase, it must give us some vital piece of the puzzle."

Indara nodded. "Okay, I have to confess that I'm curious: How do you know this friend? Did you meet her while being a Wayseeker?"

"Associate," Vernestra corrected. "Deva Lompop. She's no one's friend. And no. I met her long before I became a Wayseeker. She's Shani, and they live longer lives than even Mirialans. She's a former Nihil I worked with a long time ago, and we've crossed paths many times since. I don't fully trust her—she follows her own whims more than anything else—but she's extremely useful. Either way, I am sure you will find her . . . fascinating."

The trip to the animal refuge was quick, and Ty seemed loath to send the gheriols away. Indara found herself sad to see the animals go as well, even though she would remember the feeling of them hunting her for a long while. Still, it wasn't their fault they'd been put in such a predicament, and Indara was not one to hold a grudge.

During their trip, Ty had explained how the animals had almost been hunted to extinction on their native Ruathi, the caves taken over decades ago by smugglers. In the refuge on Hetzal, the pair that had been in the arena would have a chance at a decent life; they might even return to their native habitat if the government was ever able to push environmental reforms through. Either way, though, they were much safer on Hetzal. That seemed to Indara the best possible outcome. It had to be better to live a pampered life far from home than to be starved and released weekly into an arena to kill people who had the misfortune of falling into debt.

Indara wished they could spend a bit more time on Hetzal. There were a number of historical sites she wished to visit. Still, her disappointment was short-lived once they flew to the asteroid that Deva Lompop called home.

They exited hyperspace somewhere between Dalna and Wild Space, a location that J-6 seemed to have input manually. Indara decided to sit in the cockpit with the droid as they approached. Ty and Vernestra were sharing a cup of tea in the galley, and ever since the droid had tended to her, Indara had found herself even more curious about her. J-6, for her part, did not seem to mind the company.

"Jay-Six," Indara began hesitantly. They had left the hyperlane and were making the haul through realspace. There was nothing but inky darkness through the viewport; even the stars seemed to have abandoned the sector they were in. "I want to thank you for taking care of me when I was ill."

"There is no thanks necessary. I was by far the most qualified," the droid answered, the vocabulator tone mild. "Standard medical care is part of my programming."

"Wait, does that mean you have other programming in addition to child care?" Indara asked.

J-6's head turned to her slowly. "Of course I do. Who can exist on only their primary functions? We should all grow and change as we exist. Ah, looks like we're in range of Deva's asteroid."

Indara wanted to ask the droid more about this "growing," but she knew a change of subject when she heard one.

J-6 flew the ship straight into a hangar bay that contained only a couple of decrepit-looking ships. It seemed that such a place should have a far more impressive fleet of vehicles; there was plenty of room for more. As they touched down, no one came to greet them, and that struck Indara as odd as well. But she was pretty much just along for the ride, so she said nothing and went to find Vernestra and Ty once J-6 had lowered the boarding ramp.

Neither of the women was on the ship. Instead they waited for her at the foot of the boarding ramp, Ty sitting in her repulsor chair. "We need to hurry," Vernestra said. "We have about two minutes before Deva's defenses are triggered."

"Doesn't she know we're here?" Indara asked. She had no sooner stepped off the boarding ramp than it was retracting behind her, as though J-6 wanted to make sure she was not even remotely involved in whatever nonsense was about to occur.

"No. If I'd told her, we never would've even gotten inside the hangar. On the initial approach, I used an old trick to jam the security protocols, beaming several conflicting codes. This allowed us to enter the hangar. Deva's security has always been a bit old-fashioned, and it's just our good luck that she hasn't updated it. I hope you can run. Because we need to move."

Vernestra took off running, and Indara looked to Ty, who shrugged before taking off as well, her chair fast enough to pass Vernestra and leave the Jedi behind. Indara followed, using the Force to lend her speed, but she was only halfway to the lone doorway out of the hangar when alarms started to blare.

"It seems as though your friend reset her alarm system," Ty called over her shoulder as they hurried to the exit.

"Acquaintance!" Vernestra yelled back. She had barely finished uttering the word when a hail of blasterfire rained down from proximity guns placed around the ceiling of the hangar. Indara dived behind some nearby shipping crates. The blaster bolts landed harmlessly, the crates providing ample cover, even though Indara could smell burning material. She inspected her robes and found another blaster burn. She was glad the bolt had missed her, but this was becoming a troublesome pattern.

"State your name and your business, Jedi, before I gas you and eject your corpse out into the black," called a woman's voice.

"Deva, it's me, Vernestra Rwoh," came the answer from nearby. Indara peeked up and over the crates to see where Vernestra had ducked into a maintenance chute to avoid the blasterfire. Ty was nearby, the repulsor chair behind another pile of crates, although hers looked far less sturdy than the ones Indara had chosen.

"Vernestra Rwoh. I thought I told you to forget my name after Avon's funeral."

"I know, but I need your help. We're looking for a missing scientist. There's a contract on her, and we need to find her before a weapons smuggler by the name of Nilsson does."

There was a snort of derision. "You came here to convince me not to cash in my bounty?"

Vernestra popped out from the maintenance shaft, her lightsaber powered up as she stood out in the open. "You have that bounty?"

"Yes. Real pain, too. Woman is harder to find than a white wing flying through a snowstorm. She may not be very good at choosing business partners, but she's been able to go to ground. I haven't found her. But if you're looking for her, you must be the Jedi my client added to the contract. So if I kill you, that makes my job easier."

Vernestra laughed, taking the statement as a joke, even though Indara did not think the woman had been kidding.

There was a whirring sound, and a wide overhead door that hadn't existed before began to rise nearby. "Come inside," Deva called. "It seems like we have some things to talk about."

Indara stood hesitantly, still half expecting to be shot, but it seemed Deva was no longer angry, just curious. Indara fell in behind Ty and Vernestra as they led the way deeper into the asteroid. The place was a marvel of modern engineering. Indara could only imagine what the bills on such a place must be like. She knew bounty hunting could be lucrative, but she had no idea it was quite this profitable.

The hallway from the hangar ended in a large foyer, where a woman wearing a skintight red bodysuit greeted them coolly. She was tall and thin, with green skin and silver lines running across her face. That, along with the crest of rainbow feathers on her head, marked her as a Shani. Indara had seen references to the secretive species but had never met one. The stories held that their homeworld was in Wild Space, and that the original Shani had been travelers who ended up working with the Hutts long ago. But there were also conflicting reports that the Shani homeworld had been destroyed by some forgotten species, forcing them into the Outer Rim. Indara had even read histories positing that the Shani had once run afoul of the Sith, which was why there were so few in the galaxy. Either way, there was no definitive truth about the Shani, and Indara had never thought she'd meet one in her lifetime. She had a number of questions, but she doubted that she would get any answers given the distrustful way the woman was watching them.

"You do understand that the location of my home is supposed to be a secret. The only reason you even know where I live is because Avon trusted you, and I trusted her. Do you know how many people would like the chance to kill me? And here you are bringing strangers—Jedi, no less." Deva took in Ty and Indara with an expression somewhere between annoyance and exhaustion.

"Ty Yorrick. No longer a Jedi," Ty said, her tone mild. "Just old and tired."

Deva looked toward Indara, who raised her hands in surrender. "Jedi Knight Indara. Guilty as charged. But I am glad to meet you."

Vernestra sighed heavily. "Deva. Jay-Six flew us here. Your secret remains safe."

Her expression changed immediately. "Jay is here? Why didn't she come in?"

"Because I was waiting for the shooting to be done. I just got replated," said a voice from behind Indara. She turned to see the droid clomping along, her steps leisurely. "Do you know how hard it is to find someone to do rose gold these days? Everything is platinum or yellow gold."

"That's because you're out of style," Deva teased.

J-6 made a sound like a snort. "I am always in fashion," she replied. It was impossible not to notice how the droid's arrival had thawed Deva's chilly countenance by quite a bit.

But even a springtime lake could still have ice. "Well, as glad as I am to see Jay-Six, I cannot say the same for the rest of you," Deva said.

"What if I told you I brought you lompop liqueur," Vernestra said, producing a bottle from her robes with a grin.

Deva laughed. "I would say I apparently need to improve my security, since you didn't even drop it. Fine, let's meet in the solarium. I just had it landscaped, and I daresay I'm quite proud of it."

Deva led the way through her home, even though the word didn't quite convey the magnitude of the space. Indara noticed what looked to be a control room full of monitors and a hallway that led to a suite of rooms before they exited into what could only be described as an indoor garden. They passed through it, ending up in a smaller room with sunken seating.

"I will make tea since you still cannot afford to hire help," J-6 said, walking away as everyone else settled into a seat.

"She's not wrong," Deva said, leaping down into a seat. "I got this place at an auction. It was confiscated from one of the Grafs after their fall from grace." She grinned. "Nothing better than a liquidation sale."

Deva sobered and gave Vernestra an arch look. "Of course, now that you have your hand in my pocket, it's going to take longer to be able to hire help."

Vernestra leaned forward. "So you've met with the man?"

Deva nodded. "Spicehead, not a human, though. Near-human? Brown hair, pupil-less green eyes. Striking, even if he reeked. But I met him on a shuttle. I don't think he's the kind of person who stays still, if you get my drift. What do you want with him?"

Vernestra's brows drew together as she considered Deva's words. "He hired a scientist named Florinda Jackard—who worked with Avon, by the way—to improve upon an existing design for a nullifier that could disable not only blasters but also lightsabers."

"Oh no! A device that can incapacitate your fancy plasma swords. That would be a problem," Deva said, sarcasm thick in her words. She seemed to relish the thought, and Indara couldn't help but wonder how she and Vernestra knew each other. She definitely did not seem enamored with the Jedi. "It seems strange he would want her dead, but I also did not get the impression that the man put a lot of thought into anything but getting his way. He gave me the impression that he came from an affluent family. His Galactic Basic had an educated accent."

"I am looking for Jackard because she started a riot on Ruathi that led to a number of fatalities. The government is very interested in holding her accountable," Ty said. "I am no longer with the Order, and the nullifier is no concern of mine. And if you are disinclined to work with the Jedi, I am sure we can negotiate something. Ruathi is a poor planet but one that remembers its friends."

Vernestra's expression went stony at that bit of information, and Deva grinned, showing serrated teeth.

"Now we're talking," she said.

Deva looked to Indara, who raised her hands. "I'm just here with Vernestra. I have no favors to offer. But I am an archivist interested in the history of your people if you'd ever like to discuss such a thing."

"Interesting, but I'd rather pull out my feathers one by one," Deva said, her smile positively feral.

J-6 returned with a teapot and several cups, her arrival dissipating some of the tension. "Here. I'm going to organize your foodstuffs. Your pantry is a mess." The droid dropped off the tray before leaving once more.

Indara leaned forward and poured tea for the group, since it was something to do.

Vernestra continued talking. "So back to your contact for the job . . . you were saying you met Nilsson on board a shuttle?"

"I did. He rode in a hopper that was worth more than most people on Coruscant make in a year. I don't think that was strictly because of the weapons trading, though. Like I said, he moved like someone who has always had money. Well spoken, confident, short-tempered. The last of those could be from the spice, because even his ship reeked of it, but I don't think so. I think he is someone with money who found their way into a very lucrative—if reprehensible—line of work."

"Did you notice a Gigoran named Hinra with him?" Indara asked as she filled her own cup and settled back into her seat.

"Yes, seemed to be his enforcer of sorts. I'm sure you already know this, but the real problem you're going to have is his agent, the one who seems to be running things for him. Pantoran by the name of Grizela. She's smart, and I have the feeling that she's the real brains. Either way, that's all I know. Not much more than what you have."

Indara sipped her tea and looked around the room. Ty seemed unbothered, but Vernestra was clearly frustrated. From the conversation Indara had with the Jedi Master on the *Cantaros,* Vernestra had obviously thought that Deva would have more information to share. In fact, Indara wondered if they wouldn't have been better off returning to Coruscant and petitioning the Republic for help. Surely there was information about this Nilsson somewhere in the archives.

"Do you know any Fruscti?" Indara asked, impulsively. Deva Lompop turned toward her, and Indara had the sudden realization that the woman was a predator. Her cool gaze felt somehow dangerous, as though with a single insult Indara could end up her next meal.

"I do . . ." she said, clearly surprised by the question. "Why do you ask?"

Indara swallowed down her sudden nervousness. "There was a phrase from Senator Garn. We believe Nilsson was working with him and had him assassinated. Garn left a last testament, and within it he said—" She looked to Vernestra, who sat up and cleared her throat.

"It was something to the effect of *Sigeo nocht rewnat qas bindt lokicgh fro.*"

Deva's eyes widened. "'The son of the brightest king casts the darkest light.' Well, there you go. There's your answer right there. Which makes sense because I did have an associate tell me that Florinda Jackard had once been on Pinara, but it seemed like outdated information. It is possible she ran there, right under the nose of the man who is looking for her."

Indara looked to Vernestra and then Ty, not quite understanding the reference. But it was clear that the older Jedi did.

"Can someone fill me in on what that means?" Indara finally asked when it didn't seem like anyone else was of a mind to state what—to them—was obvious.

"'Bright King' is the nickname of the president of Pinara. Kolin Summach," Vernestra said, her expression pensive. "They called him that because he managed to overhaul the power grid in the aftermath of an economic disaster that nearly destroyed the planet, a series of groundquakes followed by floods. Pinara was nearly lost, but Summach managed to force through enough reforms that the environment was stabilized, at great cost to the people. The sector has a moon where spice is mined, and Summach annexed the moon and declared the spice trade legal, using the proceeds to fund improvements to the planet."

"And fill his own coffers," Ty added, sipping her tea.

"He made a lot of promises to the people of Pinara, but they were promises he kept," Deva said. "There were rumors that he had rebuilt the planet by using his own corporations, the true ownership buried under a massive amount of bureaucracy. And that he had an equal stake in the spice trade he legitimized. The Republic tried to sanction him but could never get anything to stick. From your quote, it seems as though Garn knew that Nilsson is Kolin Summach's son. Nilsson Summach."

"Like father, like son, it seems," Vernestra said. "I wonder if he's managed to use his father's prestige to hide his own dealings."

"It would explain why he's never been discovered," Ty said. "It seems unlikely that Florinda would return to a place where he has such clear connections, but I don't think we have any other leads. I'm heading back to the ship. I'm going to reach out to some contacts on Pinara to see if she possibly went to ground there. Maybe she truly is hiding somewhere familiar." She turned toward Deva and inclined her head in a nod of respect. "It was lovely to meet you. If you ever have need of a monster hunter, call me." Then she turned her chair and headed back to the ship.

Vernestra stood as well, and Indara climbed to her feet, even though she was loath to leave Deva's beautiful solarium. But she felt like there was something she was missing.

"Deva, thank you. I owe you one," Vernestra said.

"You owing me one isn't enough. Do you know how many credits I'm losing by letting you and your crew take in Jackard instead of delivering her to Nilsson?" Deva said.

Vernestra raised a single brow in her direction. "So she is on Pinara? Do you know where?"

"Of course I do. I've already sent the information to your ship. But I hope you know I expect to be compensated."

Vernestra inclined her head. "I do. Which is why I have this for you." She reached into her robes and drew forth a stone the size of her fist, one that glowed with a strange inner light. "I was gifted this by the Keepers of Dytrew after I helped them with a particularly vicious creature devouring their villages. You know what it is?"

Deva leaned forward, eyes glimmering, an expression of avarice lighting up her face. "Is that truly a sunstone?"

Indara gaped. The sunstones of Dytrew were a highly prized commodity, not just as jewelry but also for their ability to focus and strengthen energy. The stone Vernestra held was worth far more than any bounty.

Vernestra tossed it to Deva, who caught it in midair. As she held it, her eyes closed. "Oh. Yes. This will do. Consider us even."

Vernestra smiled. "Good. I wouldn't want to feel indebted to you."

There was a momentary pause, the silence awkward, and then Deva cleared her throat. "Well, it was nice of you to stop by," she said, not moving from where she sat with her cup of tea, her tone completely insincere. "Make sure to send my regrets to Nilsson. I'm really going to miss spending his credits. But fair is fair."

Vernestra didn't say anything, but as they were leaving, Indara could not help but notice that the woman seemed happier than she should have after paying too much for the information they'd gotten. She wanted to ask her why that was, but Vernestra gave her a look that seemed to say, *Not now,* and so Indara said nothing.

As she and Vernestra climbed aboard the *Cantaros,* Indara was surprised to see J-6 was already in the cockpit, firing up the engines. Ty sat in one of the jump seats, her chair already stowed away in the cargo area. Indara said, "Any problems, Jay-Six?"

"No, it was just as you said it would be. If she doesn't send a message to her contact for the Florinda Jackard contract in four hours, mine will send instead. Either way, Nilsson and his people will know we are en route. But I do not think you have much to worry about. Deva Lompop would not turn down a payday. She is—at heart—a pirate."

As the ship left the hangar, Indara was thoroughly confused. "I've clearly missed something."

"I'm sorry, I should've explained. I knew Deva wouldn't give me any real information, not without protecting her own interests," Vernestra said as they left the hangar. "So Jay-Six did a little sleuthing for us while we were having tea."

The droid swiveled in her seat. "Just in case you did not know, I am not just a pretty face."

"Wait, so this was all a setup for Deva?" Indara asked, feeling a bit silly.

"Of a sort. I figured that she had already found our missing scientist but was sitting on the information until the time was right. Deva is smarter than she lets on, and her network is vast. I knew that she would try to set us up if she could, and I just needed her to point me in a direction. I think she was being honest about translating Garn's warning, but I doubt the address she gave us is correct. We have to assume that she will tell Nilsson where we and Florinda Jackard both are in an attempt to keep her hands clean and get paid all the same. Either we take care of him, or he takes care of us. Win-win for her. But if she doesn't, if she somehow keeps her word, then Jay-Six has reached out to the arms dealer anyway, and there is still a good chance he will come after us. Jedi are very bad for business."

Indara felt a bit like perhaps she'd been played for a fool, but then Ty nodded. "Smart. And because Indara and I had no idea, we came across as genuine."

"You didn't know, either?" Indara asked.

Ty shook her head. "No. Sometimes the execution of a good plan requires conviction."

"I'm still annoyed that you tried to offer Deva a favor and undercut me," Vernestra said, even though there was no heat to her words.

Ty snorted. "I cannot believe you gave that woman a sunstone. I heard you as I was leaving, you know."

Vernestra shrugged. "It's just a pretty rock. There's a flaw in the crystal that renders it valueless. I only took it from the Keepers of Dytrew because they assured me it was worthless."

Ty stretched. "Well done. Regardless, I am excited to find Florinda Jackard. That woman needs to pay for what she did."

"Agreed," Vernestra said, leaning back in her seat, "and the sooner we can stop this Nilsson, the better off the galaxy will be."

Indara couldn't help but agree, even if she was beginning to feel like she would never truly understand Vernestra Rwoh. Every single time she thought she had the true measure of the Jedi Master, she did something surprising. Indara hated to admit it, but it made her like the woman more.

Manipulating Deva Lompop seemed distinctly unlike a Jedi, but Indara couldn't argue that it hadn't been effective, especially if it led them to their quarry. Vernestra Rwoh seemed to understand more about the galaxy than most Jedi whom Indara had met in her time in the Order, and she was beginning to think there truly was more merit to becoming a Wayseeker than she had thought.

It made Indara wonder once more if perhaps it was a path she might like to walk herself.

Chapter Thirty

Nilsson knew as soon as they landed on Ruathi that he was going to have a very bad day. Especially when he saw the local authorities lingering around outside Kliva's arena. There was nothing good about police.

"I'm going to have a drink. Find out what happened," he told Grizela as they both ducked into a nearby tavern. Nilsson ordered himself an ale from the serving droid and watched as his number two chatted with the bartender, her smile infectious and her body language interested enough that the human couldn't pull his eyes from her. Grizela's beauty was as lethal as her mind, and Nilsson waited for her to return with far more information than he would have gotten under the same circumstances.

Grizela slipped into the chair across from him the same moment the serving droid arrived with his ale. He gestured at the drink, and when she shook her head, he drained the glass and then put it on the droid's tray before it could move away. "Another," he said. The droid trundled off, and Nilsson pushed his hair out of his face and turned back to Grizela. "What'd he say?"

"There was apparently a fight there a few days ago. The usual gheriol fighting, only this time one of the challengers was a Jedi, a human woman. She managed to escape the creature, and somehow she brought the barrier down—or maybe the crowd did, he's not sure. Either way, it was a complete and utter bloodbath."

"Did the Jedi die?" Nilsson asked. If she had, that was at least one less problem on his plate. He still had to find Florinda, but the Jedi was a difficulty he couldn't easily overcome, especially now that Garn was no longer around to provide cover. It was better all around if the woman was gone.

But Grizela shook her head. "No, unfortunately. But the owners did. Kliva and Char."

The droid returned with another ale, and Nilsson took it from the tray before the droid could give it to him, his hand gripping the cup hard enough to nearly crack the thing. "So. The Jedi is lost, and the people responsible are dead. Tell me Hinra was at least able to get rid of the remaining loose ends on this backwater rock. I don't want anyone from the labs left alive."

Grizela nodded. "He tracked two of them down. They're handled. Once Florinda has been put down, we'll just have the lab on Septra. Speaking of, according to Erial, your little visit has paid off. They've got a finalized, repeatable design. Now they just need the power center, and we'll be ready to start shipping out the promised units to Genetia. The scientists have already programmed two droid assembly lines. We just need Florinda."

Grizela slid her datapad across the table toward Nilsson. "And we have that. I just got this from the bounty hunter I hired. It's the location of Florinda. She's back on Pinara, the last place we would've looked. And according to the bounty hunter, the Jedi are tracking her as well, because of the riots she caused here on Ruathi."

"So I can eliminate all my problems in one fell swoop. Finally, some good news." Nilsson drank his ale and stood, throwing a handful of credits on the table. "Let's go. The sooner I can finish this, the better.

Send a transmission to Hinra to meet us on Pinara. We'll take care of the Jedi and then make our way to Septra with Florinda in tow. She once called me a monster. Let's demonstrate to her that her hypothesis was correct."

Chapter Thirty-One

I had never been to Pinara, but as we landed I couldn't help but think it was a beautiful place. The majority of the planet was dominated by mountains, with the capital city of Gloche located in a wide river valley. As J-6 landed the *Cantaros,* the buildings came into view, and as we made our way to the spaceport, everything appeared newer and well kept, a far cry from many of the places I had visited in my life.

Most of that was driven by the president, who had done a very good job of making certain the wealth had been shared, even if he was possibly corrupt. And in fact, as Indara, Ty, and I left the spaceport and headed into the city proper, we saw none of the usual signs of poverty: There were no beggars or graffiti, the streets were free of trash, and everyone looked generally healthy and well fed, regardless of their species. Despite the rumors of corruption that swirled around Kolin Summach, his policies had truly helped his planet to recover in the decades since the Nihil conflict.

We'd only gone a few steps into the city center when Ty stopped her chair, pointing toward an administrative building. "I'm going to need to check in with the local government. Since I'm working as an agent for Ruathi, I need to let them know I'm here on official business. I'm also going to need their help to make sure Florinda gets back to face punishment for her role in the riots."

I frowned. "Are you sure that's wise? We don't know how involved the president is with what his son has been doing. For all we know, the entire government of Pinara could be quietly involved in illegal weapons smuggling."

Ty shrugged, holding her hands up as she did so. "That's not my problem. In fact, it sounds like Jedi business. I'm here to collect a suspect, and if that's a problem, they can contact Ruathi themselves."

"And what if we find her first?" I asked Ty.

She laughed. "Do what you need to do, Jedi." There was no heat to her words, but I had the feeling this was where our paths diverged. An unexpected sadness welled up. We would never again be the friends we had been, and I wished things could have been different.

But Ty was correct. She had turned her back on the Order. And me? That was something I would never do, no matter how much I disagreed with the Jedi High Council.

Ty headed into the building, and I sighed, unable to fully contain my frustration. Indara looked from me to where Ty had gone. "Do we wait for her?"

"No. Ty is liable to frighten Florinda, and we need to figure out what she knows about the nullifier and this Nilsson character before Ty can give her that scowl of hers." I tapped my foot as I weighed my options. "I think we have to find her first. If we do, we can offer her safe passage to Coruscant in exchange for information."

"What about Ty?" Indara asked.

I shrugged in imitation of the retired Jedi. "You heard her. She's just a humble representative of the Ruathi government. They can petition the Republic to have Jackard extradited. Come on, let's go see if we can find her before Ty can."

We made our way to the first address Deva had given us. I took in our surroundings as we walked, a well-maintained neighborhood with buildings made of a deep-gray stone. The buildings did not follow any kind of pattern that I could see, just the haphazard addition of new stories whenever the occupants outgrew their space. There were no children playing outside, but I could see people gaze out at us as we passed their windows. Storefronts were tucked in and around the residential units, and down one side street I could hear the sounds of a market, shopkeepers calling out to potential customers. But for the most part it was a very quiet, very peaceful place.

I could not help but think it was an odd place to hide out from a bounty hunter. Which was probably why it was perfect.

We were heading down the block toward the address Deva had given us when Indara gripped me by my robes and pulled me sideways into an alley. Her eyes were wide. "That's her. The woman I saw on Haileap. Florinda Jackard."

I looked to where Indara was pointing, and sure enough there was Florinda entering the building, a crate of foodstuffs in her arms.

"So, what now?" Indara asked.

I smoothed my robes and stood up straight. "Now we have a little chat—" I was interrupted by Florinda Jackard running out of the building, a looming, one-eyed Gigoran chasing behind her. Hinra. I wasn't sure whether or not Deva had sold us out, but either way we were out of time.

"After them," I cried, taking off running, Indara's footfalls echoing behind me. With the Force lending me speed, I caught up with Hinra quite quickly, and he stopped suddenly to turn around and swipe at me. I held my hand up and used the Force to throw him to the side.

"I'll deal with him! You get Jackard," Indara called. I nodded and renewed my efforts to chase down the woman we'd been searching the galaxy for.

Florinda Jackard rounded a corner into a narrow alley, and I followed after her, then skidded to a stop as I almost ran into the woman herself. Only a few meters away, a man and a Pantoran woman stood before us behind a line of toughs with blasters pointed at us. They looked as surprised to see Florinda and me as we were to see them.

It took me a long moment to realize the armed line of toughs all wore uniforms. I wasn't sure who they represented, but there was no doubt that they were somehow affiliated with the government. The crest on their uniforms was the same as had been on the door of the government building Ty had entered when we parted ways.

"Florinda. Good to see you again," the man said, his voice carrying the dreamy intonations of someone high on spice. He had brown, ropy locs of hair, and his eyes were a striking green and completely lacking pupils. His clothing was expensive, but it was far from the only thing about him that hinted at his wealth. His voice bore the accent of the affluent, and there was a haughtiness to his demeanor that made me think he was used to telling people what to do. He gestured languidly toward me. "And you even brought us a Jedi. Fun."

I didn't wait for him to say anything else. I held my hands up and shoved, buying myself enough time to leap in front of Florinda before the men and women holding blasters could start firing. They fell backward, and as I landed before Florinda, the sound of her retreating footsteps echoed behind me. I had lost my prize.

And now I had bigger problems.

I drew my lightsaber and powered it up. The toughs had climbed to their feet, and as I stood there, the man—who I was guessing was Nilsson—held up his wrist to reveal a familiar bangle. "My grandmother was a genius. And she hated Jedi almost as much as she loved tinkering." He tapped the bangle, and predictably my lightsaber sputtered and then went completely out.

I quickly clipped it to my belt as the men and women with blasters jumped to their feet, taking aim.

I ran forward, reaching with the Force to yank the blaster out of the grip of the Nautolan man before me. The blaster went flying across the alley, and I kicked the man in the face, using the momentum to flip backward behind him where he could serve as a momentary shield. It was an unsavory tactic, but I did not have a lot of options.

Blasterfire pelted the man behind me, and I used the respite to vault off the ground and up the side of the building, then pushed off the edge to another building and up and out of the alley. There was no reason to stay and engage with Nilsson and his enforcers. I needed Florinda Jackard. I couldn't let Nilsson get to her before I did.

Blaster bolts pelted the walls in my wake, but then I was running across the roof and far out of range of the shooters below. From my vantage, I could track Florinda's progress. Unsurprisingly, she was headed right toward the spaceport.

I leapt from building to building, running across rooftops until I was nearly ahead of Florinda. Then, with a deep breath, I vaulted off the side, using the Force to ease my landing, falling into a crouch before the rogue scientist. Florinda reeled backward when she saw me.

"Wait! I'm a Jedi. I'm here to help," I said. "If you don't come with me, you're dead."

"Not likely! I talk to you and I'm dead," she said. "Did you see those people back there shooting at us? Those are the presidential guard! They work for Nilsson. If I go with him, he'll just want me to go to his lab on Septra to finish the nullifier design. I work with you, and he's sure to have someone kill me before I can stop him. Don't you get it? He's *untouchable*."

"No one is beyond the reach of justice," I said, even though the words sounded hollow to my own ears. "Not forever," I added.

She stared at me like I had lost my mind, and perhaps I had. Because she was right. The man had the military working for him. Prosecuting someone as well connected as Nilsson would be nearly impossible, especially since his own father seemed to be able to escape every single accusation lobbed at him. It would require the work of not just the Order but also the Senate and the Republic. And who knew if the Republic would even follow through with prosecution. They could just as easily offer a deal instead.

"I can keep you safe," I said, changing my tactic to focus on the thing I actually believed. "But you only have a moment to choose."

Florinda looked at me and then back where she'd come from, Nilsson's people running our way. She nodded. "Yeah. I choose me."

The blaster bolt caught me by surprise, hitting my left shoulder. I fell to my knees and saw that Florinda held a bee sting, a small pocket blaster. Not usually lethal, but it definitely hurt.

"Sorry. I'll take my chances with the path I know," she said. She dropped the tiny blaster, the single shot expended, and raised her hands, heading back the way we had come.

My one chance to take her in safely was gone.

I scrambled to my feet and ducked into an alley, my shoulder screaming in agony. J-6 was going to give me an earful for my foolishness, and as I ran down the alley away from my failure, I fervently hoped Indara was doing better than I was.

Chapter Thirty-Two

Indara gazed at the Gigoran before her and realized that she was looking forward to the fight. It probably was not a thought becoming of a Jedi, but she was still smarting from the way he'd bested her the last time they'd met. Poison darts definitely did not count as fair play.

"I am going to crush you, little Jedi," he said, stepping forward as he cracked his knuckles. The vocalizer must have been repaired at some point, because each word he uttered was accompanied by a burst of static from the tiny speaker.

"Not likely," Indara said. "If you come with me peacefully, you have some hope for the future."

A deep rumble like laughter echoed through the Gigoran, his fur vibrating with his mirth. "So small. So foolish."

Hinra held up his wrist to flash Indara a bangle, this one easily three times the size of the previous ones they'd found and most likely specially made for him. Indara didn't bother drawing her lightsaber. Instead she shrugged before raising her hand and using the Force to pick up the man and throw him sideways into the nearest building.

The impact left a spiderwebbing of cracks that rippled outward. Hinra began to climb to his feet. Indara lifted him and repeated the attack, this time tossing him into another building on the opposite side of the street. Her footsteps as she approached were steady, measured. And when he stood, a blaster in hand, Indara raised her own hand and reached for the bangle on his arm, using the Force to break the device in half before finally drawing her weapon, powering it up, and standing ready for the attack. The nullifier was truly only a threat to a Jedi when it was a surprise.

Any other time, Indara would have been loath to engage in such a public display. But there was no one else on the street. She would take her time and handle things right.

"I'm not going to kill you," Indara said, waiting. "You killed Garn, and I know you work for Nilsson. Once you can no longer fight, I'm going to take you to Coruscant to face justice for your crimes. They may be lenient if you work with them." Indara wasn't quite certain about that last part—killing a senator *was* a pretty violent offense—but she would say whatever she had to in order to avoid any more violence.

What she was not expecting was for a single shot to ring out. A blaster burn appeared in the white fur on Hinra's chest, and then he fell to the ground in a heap. Indara spun around, lightsaber ready to reflect the next attack, but none came. She scanned the nearby rooftops, looking for the source of the attack, but there was no one to be found. Indara was completely alone, and the street was once more quiet.

The sniper had done what they'd come to do: kill Hinra.

Indara turned back around, shock leaving her limbs chilled. The Gigoran lay spread out, his life gone, and Indara felt empty. It was just such an utter waste.

Indara didn't know how long she stood there in dismay, staring at the dead man, before Vernestra came jogging down the road toward her. People had begun to gather, wondering in a mixture of languages why a Jedi was standing over a dead man and holding a lightsaber. When Vernestra took the weapon from Indara's hand, she let her.

"What happened?" Vernestra asked, gently turning Indara away from the crowd and back the way they'd come.

"I told him that I wasn't going to kill him, that he needed to face justice for his crimes. And someone killed him. A sniper."

Vernestra looked over her shoulder at Hinra's corpse and sighed. "Yeah, I had a similar conversation. Florinda Jackard is with Nilsson. She'll be dead once he has what he needs. I think it's time we return to Coruscant. This is bigger than us and the Order now. We're going to need some help."

"What about Ty?" Indara asked. Her brain felt like it was working at half speed, as though she wasn't quite sure how to put the pieces of the world together to make sense. What kind of man was this Nilsson? Everyone was afraid of him, and people who helped him ended up dead. How could they return to Coruscant when such a man was still out and about spreading misery in the galaxy?

"We'll let her know what we found, but I'm willing to bet she'll agree with us. At least on Coruscant she can plead her case. I have the feeling that if we don't clear out of Pinara quickly, we may not get a chance to leave at all. Come on, we'll hire a landspeeder to get back."

Indara nodded, but all she could think was that there had to be a way to hold people accountable for the terrible things they did.

When they reached the *Cantaros*, Ty Yorrick was already there, the boarding ramp down. She leaned heavily against the doorway to the ship, her agitation clear. "Where have you been?"

"We found Florinda Jackard, but we need to go. Now," Vernestra said. "She decided to go her own way. She's with the weapons smuggler, and he has government backing."

Vernestra walked past Ty without another word, and the woman turned toward Indara, her expression one of surprise and annoyance. "You should've waited for me."

Indara didn't bother to keep the annoyance from her voice. "We are trying to stop a man who is apparently so terrifying that the people who work for him would rather die than testify against him. The people who are loyal to him end up murdered in broad daylight if there is even the slightest chance they are captured. Oh, and the man just happens to be the son of Pinara's president. Vernestra thinks our best bet is to return to Coruscant and plead our case. We're going to need the Republic to get involved to stop him."

Ty took an unsteady step backward, shaking her head. "No way. I'm not going back there."

Vernestra appeared in the doorway to the boarding ramp. "Then we will happily drop you somewhere else. But I suggest you come inside so we can get going. I have no desire to rot in a jail cell until the Order can broker my release."

A strange look came over Ty's face, and she crossed her arms. "And what if the Republic refuses to help?"

"Then we will go to Septra and handle the problem ourselves," Vernestra said, her voice flat. "But there is nothing we can do here on Pinara that will help. Not as long as the government is backing our arms dealer. Florinda may be your quarry, but as long as this Nilsson character can manufacture nullifiers, no one in the galaxy will be safe. Can you imagine the escalation in violence? The ensuing arms race as people try to discover more and better ways to kill one another? The addition of a nullifier is not something the Order can risk."

Ty nodded. "Okay. Fine," she said, the fight going out of her suddenly.

"Great. Now both of you get aboard so Jay-Six can get us out of here."

Indara scrambled up the boarding ramp, Ty entering once Indara walked past. She settled into the jump seat where she usually sat while Vernestra took the copilot's seat. J-6 operated the controls, and Ty stood in the entrance to the cockpit for a long moment before making a sound of annoyance.

"I need a drink. I'll be in the galley if you need me." Her slow footfalls echoed away from the cockpit toward the galley, and Indara was secretly glad that some of the edginess between Vernestra and Ty could be avoided for the moment.

As they lifted off, some of the tension began to drain from Vernestra's face. Once they had left Pinara's atmosphere, she finally relaxed.

"That happened to you before, didn't it?" Indara said softly, and Vernestra turned in surprise. "Being thrown in jail until the Order could broker your release."

"Yes," Vernestra said without hesitation. "Long before I was a Wayseeker, but the risk is always there. Being a Jedi is an honor, but it's also dangerous. Not everyone in the galaxy loves us—you've experienced that firsthand. It seems to be something the Order likes to forget. There are many who fear the Jedi, and even more who would like to exploit our power for their own purposes." Vernestra closed her eyes. "But that's enough about me. You watched a man die today, and that is no small tragedy. One of my former Padawans was Imri Cantaros, and he told me once that every effort, every life matters, as each one contributes to the overall brightness of the Force. He maintained that it was normal and right to grieve the loss of each life, no matter how great or awful, because each death reminded us that there could be darkness, that the loss of any light was worth notice."

Vernestra smiled and shook her head. "I'm not as eloquent as Imri was. If you want to hear him speak in his own words, you're more than welcome to watch the holos I have of him. When I find myself lost, I return to his words more than you know. He knew that the true measure of a good Jedi is not to feel nothing, but to feel everything and let it guide how we move through the galaxy."

Indara was about to ask Vernestra more about Imri Cantaros—she'd long been a fan of his writings but had never met him before he died—when the ship jumped to hyperspace, the black of the nearby viewport turning blue. Vernestra stiffened for a moment, and then a small, surprised "Oh" emanated from her lips.

And the next thing Indara knew the Jedi Master was slumped forward over the controls.

"Vernestra?" Indara called, alarmed.

J-6 leaned over and pushed Vernestra backward so that she was slumped against the back of the seat.

"Hyperspace vision. Help me get her to her quarters. She gets cranky when she wakes up anywhere uncomfortable," J-6 said.

Indara complied, and as they carried Vernestra through the ship, she hoped that whatever Vernestra saw could help them stop Nilsson.

No one else should die because of the man.

Chapter Thirty-Three

The vision came upon me quickly, almost violently. One moment I was talking to Indara, the memory of seeing death up close shadowing her expression, and the next I was standing with Stellan on that awful battlefield, watching people kill and be killed in an endless tableau.

"Can we do this somewhere else?" I asked, and the vision of Stellan shrugged, the scene shifting so that we were once more in the small boat, the waves rocking us to and fro.

"Thank you," I said, sighing. "I'm trying, you know. I've tracked down your flowers and the smoker of spice. I have names, I know what's at stake. But I can only do so much."

"Four days," he said. "That's how long you have until it all begins. Or ends, as the case may be."

"What would you have me do?" I asked. Even in the vision, my frustration was more than I could handle. "I am a Jedi. I cannot be anything but what I am."

Boat Stellan nodded. "Very true. But have you truly used the resources at your disposal? You are not an island unto yourself, you know."

I scowled. "Those weren't even Stellan's words. That was something Imri once said."

The image of Stellan grinned. "And he wasn't wrong."

And then the boat capsized, sending me into the water.

I sat up with a gasp. I was no longer in the cockpit. I was instead in my quarters. Ty slumped in the chair next to my bed, snoring loudly. She startled awake at my movement.

"Indara needed my help to get you in here. Apparently, Jay-Six is bossy but not exactly flexible. I may be old, but I can still use the Force."

I nodded before resting my pounding head in my hands. The scent of whiskey emanated from Ty. I was pretty sure she was drunk. "You found my stash of Longrin whiskey."

"Guilty as charged. You have good taste, Vernestra Rwoh," she said, sighing. "I hate failure. I always have. And I hate that you gave up on finding Florinda so easily."

Vision Stellan's words echoed back to me, and I rubbed my temples. "I just had a vision, and in it I was urged to use all the tools at my disposal, not just the Order. So my question to you is this: Know anyone on Septra? Because that's apparently where Nilsson has his manufacturing facility and where Florinda thought he was taking her."

Ty shook her head. "No. But what are you thinking?"

My vision said I had four days. That wasn't enough time to get to Coruscant and then to Septra, which was on the edge of the Outer Rim. "I'm thinking we need a plan."

We all met in the galley. Ty was mostly sober, Indara looked haunted, the new shadows beneath her eyes making her appear older, and J-6 was, as always, shiny.

"I had another vision, as you all know," I said. "In it, I was told to use all my resources. Right now, that consists of all of you and whatever message we can send back to the Temple on Coruscant. But I don't think the Order and the Republic will be able to work quickly enough to stop Nilsson before he begins manufacturing the nullifiers. And I fully believe that is what's happening right now. So I want to go to Septra and try to stop him. And I want all of you to come with me. Thoughts?"

Ty shrugged. "Is there a plan?"

"Not yet," I said, looking to Indara.

She scrubbed a hand across her face. "I've always thought it was better to ask for forgiveness than for permission, so I think we should go."

I agreed wholeheartedly, but I said nothing and looked to J-6. The droid held her hands up in supplication. "I go where you go, Vernestra Rwoh. Until you tell me otherwise."

I nodded and rubbed my temples as I thought. "We know that Nilsson hired Florinda Jackard to help find a better power solution, and from my brief conversation with her it seemed like she was successful. She mentioned he has facilities on Septra. The planet is very small, so it seems like an operation like that would be easy to find. So how do we do that?"

Indara frowned. "Septra? That's a farming planet. Why would he manufacture anything there?"

"Septra is known for having abundant mineral deposits, including hynaxium and alercite," J-6 supplied. When we all looked at her in surprise, she shrugged. "I do have extensive databanks full of semi-useless knowledge. I was partially programmed by a child genius who loved information. I am a menace at cantina trivia."

"She really is," I said, before shifting back to the subject at hand. "Okay, hynaxium was one of the minerals Avon was using to build artificial crystal matrices. Felix Sunvale said Florinda studied under his mother, so it makes sense that she would have used that as the basis of her design."

"So you think Nilsson located his facility on Septra to take advantage of the mineral deposits there?" Ty said.

"The mines," Indara said. "If you want to build an illegal manufacturing operation, there is no better location than an abandoned mine. It's dangerous so most people will avoid it, and it's underground so he'd be able to escape detection."

I tapped my chin as I thought. "I think we should ask the Order to send us locations of any inactive mines on Septra that may have been bought by one of Kolin Summach's many holding companies. Because I'm willing to bet we'll find Nilsson there."

"You think we'll be able to just walk in and grab Nilsson and Florinda?" Ty asked. "How?"

"Simple: Septra is not part of the Republic. But they want to be. I'm willing to bet membership is a big enough lure that with a request from the Order, they will be happy to cooperate."

J-6 turned toward the door to the galley. "Well, I suppose I should change our route. Septra, here we come," she said, and left.

Indara frowned. "So let's say we find this weapons smuggler and his nullifier factory. How are the three of us going to get inside? He's certain to have very tight security, and he'll be expecting us."

"Plus have nullifiers," Ty said, pointing at Indara. "This won't be easy."

"No, it won't," I said. "But I have a plan for that, courtesy of a conversation I once had with an old Padawan." Neither Ty nor Indara was going to like what I had in mind, and judging by the way they were scowling at me when I finished explaining it, I was right.

Indara looked from me to Ty. "Do we really think this will work?"

Ty shrugged. "No. But what other choice do we have?"

Chapter Thirty-Four

Nilsson was high. Gloriously so. He hadn't felt so good in weeks, years maybe. And it wasn't even the spice that he'd smoked. Finally, everything was going his way.

Nilsson sat in his office high above the mine floor and watched as Florinda—under armed guard—worked with the Cereans on how to integrate her power bank into the rest of the four-seven nullifier design. She'd been incredibly helpful now that she had no choice. Nilsson almost pitied her and the rest of the scientists he'd hired. They really thought that he would let them live after they were no longer useful. Maybe he would. After all, they'd already proven they didn't mind working on weapons. Maybe he could dream up something new for them to do.

Grizela appeared at his elbow, smiling. "I have some good news. The Hutts have just put an order through. Two hundred units. They want them in the next couple of weeks."

Nilsson chuckled. "Between the Hutts and the Genetians, we've already made our money back. How's the programming of the droids coming along?"

Grizela sighed. "Better than expected. But we're probably still a couple of days from full production. I was thinking it might be a good idea to augment the workforce with a few slaves for now. The Hutts are happy to do a trade in kind if that works for you."

Nilsson waved the matter away. "Fine, as long as they come collared. I don't want to have to waste resources on making sure they don't run away."

"Hutt slaves are usually well mannered," Grizela said. "But I'll make the request anyway."

A hollow boom came from far off, and Nilsson turned toward the sound. "What was that?"

Grizela shook her head, wide-eyed. "No idea."

Erial ran into the office, expression grim. "We're under attack."

Nilsson's happy mood evaporated like smoke. "Who would dare to attack me here?"

Erial swallowed hard. "It looks like Jedi."

Nilsson pinched the bridge of his nose. "How many nullifiers do we have finished?"

Grizela consulted her datapad. "Forty-three."

"Hand them out to everyone who can wield a blaster and handle the problem. I want those Jedi dead."

Erial exchanged glances with Grizela before nodding to her and running off. Nilsson leaned over the railing separating the office where he stood from the mining floor below and gripped the metal. He was so close.

Then he turned and got ready to fight. It seemed like he was going to have to get his hands dirty if he wanted to keep the dream alive.

That was fine by him.

"Grizela," he said, calm and rational for once, the appearance of the Jedi cutting through the haze that usually clouded his mind. "Do we still have those canisters of gas we got from that old smuggler?"

Grizela nodded.

"Get them and meet me in the entryway to the mines. If Erial fails, then I will handle this myself."

And with that he strode away to plan a welcoming party for the Jedi.

Chapter Thirty-Five

Indara had read the treatises of Imri Cantaros, so she was only partly surprised when Vernestra said they were going to take one of his suggested approaches. It made perfect sense; Cantaros had argued that the Jedi should adapt more of a stance of nonviolence, leaving the lightsaber only to specific Jedi while the others relied on their command of the Force to defend life across the galaxy. It wasn't an argument that had caught on, but it was definitely a compelling one.

What Indara had not expected was that Vernestra would have a plasma shield. It was not the one once wielded by Jedi Knight Reath Silas during the Nihil conflict, but it was a brilliant replica.

"Imri gave me this as a gift, and I've never had reason to use it," she said. "I'm not sure if the nullifiers will work against it, since this one uses a ghorsian crystal as a focus source and not a kyber, but it's sturdy enough that it should provide us enough cover to get inside the mine proper."

It hadn't even required a call to Coruscant to get the information about the mines owned on Septra by Kolin Summach, the president of Pinara. A call to Master Quintana in the temple on Hynestia had gotten them the information they needed, courtesy of a story in the databank by an enterprising young journalist on Septra. She had done an exposé on a scandal a couple of years earlier, even though it seemed as though no one had much cared about it. But the record was easily accessible and gave them all the information they needed.

Septra was a planet of primarily grasslands, jagged stones jutting up out of the waving golden grasses every few kilometers. There was only a single city on the planet, and it was far from the area known for mining operations. J-6 had landed the *Cantaros* a few kilometers away from the Kolnare Mine, the one supposedly bought by a number of shell companies with government funds before going under. Indara had wondered if they had the right place as they walked across the prairie to what had to be the entrance. An article by a reporter who clearly had something against the president of Pinara seemed like a risky source of information, but as soon as the entrance to the mine came into view, she was very quickly disabused of the notion. Speeder bikes and landspeeders were parked around the facility, with armed guards standing nearby. It was definitely no ordinary mine.

"Okay, I know you explained the plan to me, but are we sure this is the best course of action?" Ty asked. She was the only one with a blaster, even though she had urged Vernestra and Indara to take one of her extras. But they were Jedi, and Indara felt using a blaster was anathema to her beliefs, even with the complication of the nullifier. "We just run in and hope for the best?"

Vernestra smiled, amused. "No, this is where Jay-Six comes in."

"I'm here. Let me just get stabilized," the droid said, walking up behind them.

Ty frowned. "What's the droid going to do?"

"I don't like blasters, but she does not feel the same way about the things," Vernestra said, and J-6's chest compartment opened up to expose a massive rocket launcher, which had replaced the blaster there previously. The compartments on her arms opened up as well to reveal several other heavy-duty blasters.

"I just find it curious that you never let me use them," J-6 said. "This is a far more efficient way to eliminate a threat."

Indara barely had time to plug her ears before J-6 launched a rocket right at the nearest landspeeder, the vehicle leaping up into the air from the explosion before landing upside down. She fired two more times, at the speeder bikes and at a nearby ship, before the launcher retracted. "And that is all I have of that."

"That was enough. Please give us as much cover as possible, Jay-Six," Vernestra said, hefting the shield. "Let's end this."

Indara fell in behind Vernestra, her hand on the woman's shoulder, while Ty maneuvered her repulsor chair behind her so that they formed a single column. As they moved forward through the smoky confusion that J-6's rockets had caused, Ty shot anyone quick to climb to their feet, while Indara used the Force to crush their blasters. The group was very quickly inside of the entrance to the mines, which branched into two tunnels.

"Left or right?" Vernestra asked, the space inside the opening eerily silent after the chaos of outside.

Blaster sounds came from behind them, and Indara turned to look back the way they had come. "Looks like Jay-Six is doing some cleanup. And the schematics I was able to pull down showed the main mine office and processing area to the right. If Nilsson is building assembly lines, it makes sense that that's where they would be."

Vernestra began to push right, but they'd gone only a few meters when blasterfire came from behind them, from the path that had branched to the left.

"Scatter!" Ty yelled and quickly reversed out of the range of fire, as Indara ducked behind an outcropping of rocks. Up ahead, Indara saw Vernestra run forward toward some goal that she could not see, but Indara was pinned down and could not follow. Not that she needed to. She had plenty to take care of right where she was.

Ty returned fire at the toughs pinning them down with blaster bolts, but Indara decided she was going to take a different tack. She held her hand out to a nearby rock and used the Force to levitate it before launching it like a missile at the nearest shooter, a Twi'lek man who grinned menacingly. The rock caught him in the face, and Indara's stomach turned as the impact turned his head to pulp.

"What the kriff?" called a voice as the man went down.

"It's a Jedi!" called another voice.

"No one told us there'd be Jedi," said another voice. There came a scrabbling sound, and Indara raised another rock, prepared to launch it at whoever fired next. But there was no more blasterfire. She stood nervously, but beyond a bit of haze from where the blaster bolts had slammed into the surrounding walls, they were completely alone, a few corpses marking the spot where their assailants had taken up their attack.

Ty stopped her chair next to Indara. "Left?"

Indara nodded. "Left."

Indara sprinted down the hallway cautiously, with Ty trailing behind. They paused, waiting for the blasterfire that never came. The path twisted back and in on itself, eventually opening up onto a cavern full of droids, all of them in an eerie sort of stasis.

"What is this place?" Indara wondered aloud.

"It's the assembly line," came a voice from somewhere near the edge of the room. Indara turned toward the sound, and there cuffed to a chair was the woman she had first seen in a bar on Haileap: Florinda Jackard. Her natural hair was red, not blue, but the curls still surrounded her head in a halo. A male and a female Cerean were strapped to chairs on either side of her.

"Please, you have to let us go before they get back," said the female Cerean, her eyes wide with fear. "They'll kill us, especially now that we're no longer useful."

As though to emphasize the statement, a blaster bolt hit the woman in the shoulder, and she cried out in pain. Indara turned back the way they had come and saw a lone shooter, and she used her lightsaber to repel the next blaster bolt right back at him.

"Let's get out of here," Ty said, "before anyone else starts shooting at us."

It was quick work to free the scientists. Florinda Jackard tried to dart off as Ty was seeing to the injured woman, who was in pain but seemed fine otherwise. Indara blocked the rogue scientist's path with her lightsaber.

"Not so fast," Indara said. "I do believe that my friend Ty would like a word with you."

"You can't stop us from leaving," she said with a sneer.

"Not them, I can't," Ty said with a tight smile. "But I have a warrant for your arrest. And since we are no longer on Pinara, you are no longer subject to a local magistrate. So on behalf of the people of Ruathi, I declare you accused of acts of chaos and disorder. You are declared detained."

Florinda looked from Ty to Indara, but the Jedi just shrugged. "She's actually right. You should've stayed on Pinara."

Ty held out a pair of binders. Indara took them and secured Florinda's wrists behind her back as Ty saw to the other scientists. Slowly, they made their way out of the caves and back to the *Cantaros*. There was no more of Nilsson's hired help to face down. They seemed to have all died or fled.

"Maybe you should go back and check on Vernestra," Ty suggested.

Indara shook her head as they escorted the trio of scientists to where J-6 was waiting. "No. She's a Jedi Master. I have a feeling she'll be fine."

As she began to walk up the boarding ramp, though, Indara turned to Ty once more. "If she isn't back in ten minutes, I'll go find her."

Chapter Thirty-Six

I ran.

I could hear the blasterfire behind me, and a bolt even caught the edge of my robes, but I could sense that what I was supposed to do was ahead of me. Indara and Ty could hold their own.

I had other enemies to face down.

The tunnel narrowed sharply before opening out into a larger area, a sort of processing center from when the mine had still been open. The equipment had been stripped away—most likely sold off once things began to go downhill—but a few empty crates were stacked around the outside edges. They were on the small side, the kind of cases that would carry something the size of a bangle that could nullify a lightsaber.

"My grandmother always said that if there was something interesting happening, the Jedi would arrive and ruin it," came a voice from behind me, and I spun around to see Nilsson standing in the entrance to another cavern. I couldn't see what was beyond him, but I was willing to bet that was where the main operation was.

"She was at the Valo Fair tragedy you know. She said the Jedi ruined everything."

I smiled. "A lot has happened since, and Valo is a very different place now. But I was there as well. We saved lives."

"Perhaps. But think of how many lives could have been saved if that senator had acquired my grandmother's design for the Republic. The Nihil conflict would've been over in days. The Soikan difficulties, the Genetian civil war, countless clashes could have been quickly avoided if the Republic had such a powerful device in their hands. Yet instead of embracing science and technology, they embraced the Jedi, a band of merry wizards with nothing but parlor tricks."

I snorted and hefted the shield. It was heavy, and I was not accustomed to carrying around such a thing, but it was my best defense. "You're an arms dealer. You really want me to believe that you care about people dying?"

"Oh, I don't care about that at all. I just like being right," he said. He hefted a sword. "This was the first prototype I built. The blade is based on an ancient Karagin design, but there's a nullifier embedded in the hilt. I thought it was the perfect weapon to eliminate a Jedi. Why don't we see?"

I stood where I was, unafraid. "You truly think you can best a Jedi Master in sword combat?" I asked. The man had to be mad.

He shrugged, and that's when I heard the footsteps behind me, attempting to be quiet. I spun just as a Pantoran woman fired a blaster shot at me, the bolt ricocheting off the plasma shield in a dazzling array of sparks. I held my hand up and reached for her with the Force, but she was already running back the way she'd come.

I spun back around as Nilsson thrust his sword right at my back, the blade instead hitting the plasma of the shield and disrupting the energy field, disabling it so that the thing was nothing more than a heavy bit of metal. I grunted as I absorbed the attack. The man was stronger than he looked. I used the Force to lend me strength of my own, pushing him backward and using the opportunity to toss the plasma shield to the side. It was too unwieldy, and it would only slow me down.

Nilsson grinned before stepping forward with a downward slash. His form was better than I'd expected, but I dodged his attack easily. I had no weapon, but as I cast around the space, I saw an ancient shovel abandoned in a bit of rockfall. The handle was made of metal, and I reached my hand out, pulling it toward me.

It would have to do.

"See? Isn't this magnificent. A fair fight. Now, Jedi, do not hold back. Because I won't."

I merely grunted. And waited for him to take the offense once more. It was simple to parry his thrusts and slashes, especially since I was not sure how strong the shovel handle might be. I recognized the form he was using, an older one once popular in royal families, back when sword fights were seen as a matter of honor. Everything about the man reeked of privilege and money.

"Why arms dealing?" I asked as I parried yet another thrust. His grin had faded by this point, and I could sense his frustration building. He had a sword. I had a mining tool. It wasn't a fair fight, and yet I was making him work for every perceived advantage. I glanced up and around the room, seeing what my options were for ending our sparring match once he lost his patience. I had no doubt it would be soon. He was sweating heavily from the effort; the too-sweet reek of spice emanated from him.

"Why not?" he said with a laugh, stepping back. "I live my life by my own rules, so why not make credits where there are credits to be made? You act like arms trading is worse than the politics of the Republic, where senators trade favors for small wins, a mine here for foodstuffs there. We are all arms dealers. Some of us are just more honest about it."

He reached inside his sleeve, pulling out a blaster. I stepped to the side as he fired, then used the Force to shove him from behind. His face slammed into the far wall, and he dropped the blaster. I immediately crushed it with the Force. When he turned around, his face was bloody and his features twisted with rage.

"No more of your tricks, Jedi!" he screamed. I waited patiently to see what he would do next. The man was no real threat to me, and I wanted him alive to face justice. But the sound of a single blaster shot rang out, and his eyes went wide as a burn appeared in the center of his chest. Nilsson fell to the ground, eyes wide with surprise and very much dead.

I had just enough time to dive out of the way before blasterfire pelted the spot where I had just been. A grunt of frustration echoed through the cavern as I took cover behind a rock outcropping.

"He is such a fool," came a feminine voice. "I did everything, *everything*, to make sure this would go off without a hitch."

I peered around the rock enough to see that the Pantoran woman who had shot at me earlier had returned. She still had her blaster, but this time she also carried a canister that looked suspiciously like poison gas.

"This isn't personal, Jedi. It's business. Do you know how many opportunities this fool has wasted over the years I've worked with him? I finally have a lucrative idea—Nilsson is usually too high to do much more than leer at me—and still he somehow ruins everything *I've* worked for. So, apologies, Jedi. I really wish it didn't have to be this way."

While the woman spoke, I judged the angle of where she was and where I'd left the shield. I reached for it with the Force, but it was just out of reach. There was a pop and a hiss from the canister as she opened it, tossing the can toward me before she fled, her footsteps echoing down the hallway.

I didn't wait. I ran in the opposite direction, back toward the way I'd come and the exit. I reached with the Force as I ran, grabbing the shield and taking it with me just in case I encountered any additional blasterfire. The plasma array was still dark. I used the Force to run away faster from the billowing poisonous cloud, and then I began to cough.

I'd escaped most of the gas, but not all of it.

By the time I exited the cave system, my steps were faltering and my coughs had grown more desperate. I fell to my knees in the sunshine, but I was helpless to do anything but struggle for breath.

A shadow fell over me, and I looked up to see the Pantoran woman once more. From her monologue, I guessed she must be Grizela. She pointed a blaster right at me, her expression hard.

But before she could fire, a rock flew into the side of her head, knocking her out.

Indara stood a few meters away, a slight smile on her lips.

"Good thing I circled back," she said.

I coughed once and then again in agreement, and then I fell backward, gazing up at the sky. My lungs burned and speech felt impossible. But none of it mattered.

The nullifiers would never see the light of day, and that was good enough.

As I began to lose consciousness, Indara's cries of alarm receded into the background of everything, and a single voice spoke, loud and clear. I would never know whether it was real or just my mind reaching for comfort, but I would remember the words for the rest of my days.

Well done, Padawan.

Chapter Thirty-Seven

It felt strange to be back on Coruscant after the past couple of weeks. Indara felt like she'd been gone a lifetime, but the entirety of her adventure with Vernestra Rwoh had taken less than a month. Still, she had changed more in that time than she had in the year before, and she wanted one last conversation with the Jedi Master before she made a life-altering decision.

She was also hoping that if she was about to make a mistake, Vernestra would be kind enough to talk her out of it.

Indara made her way out of the Jedi Temple and took a hired speeder over to a building adjacent to the massive Senate complex. It was nondescript, the kind of place where analysts and aides maintained a space. Indara took the turbolift to the top floor, and it was only when she stepped off that the significance of the space became clear: A massive Jedi seal graced the doorway leading to the office.

Indara walked up to the door expecting it to open, and when it didn't she used the Force to slide it to the side. As she entered, Vernestra came out to greet her, a smile on her face.

"Did you deactivate the automatic door?" Indara asked, incredulous.

Vernestra laughed. "Just until I get settled. I figured it would keep out the riffraff."

"By 'riffraff,' do you mean senators?"

The elder Jedi shrugged. "Perhaps. It's good to see you."

Indara smiled. "I wanted to talk to you. Do you have a moment?"

Vernestra smiled, but the expression didn't quite reach her eyes. "For you? Of course."

Vernestra led Indara past moving crates into a room with an overly large desk. A chair rose up out of the floor for Indara. Vernestra walked behind the desk and sat in the chair found there.

A droid, not J-6, appeared with a tea set, and Vernestra poured tea for both of them.

Indara waited until the droid had left, then asked, "Jay-Six?" The question was weightier than it seemed.

Vernestra smiled sadly. "Jay-Six is gone. She decided to return to Ingae. I think she was homesick, to be honest."

Indara frowned. "How can a droid be homesick?"

Vernestra shrugged, her expression inscrutable. "How indeed."

Indara sipped at her tea and put the cup down. "How are you feeling?"

"Good. I suppose a week of bacta treatment would do that for anyone. I heard you testified at Grizela's initial hearing in my place."

"Yes. It was the least I could do after she nearly killed you."

Vernestra laughed. "I appreciate it. The Senate is already asking me to investigate and verify some of her wilder claims. I think they would offer her some kind of deal if it wasn't for the fact that she was partially responsible for the assassination of a senator."

Indara nodded. She'd been following the trials of both Grizela and Florinda, and it seemed as though both women would be paying handsomely for their acts. For once, justice would prevail.

"Any news from Ty?"

Indara smiled. "She said she would be in touch ... maybe."

There was a moment of silence as she and Vernestra drank their tea.

The Jedi Master seemed happy to wait for Indara to get to the true point of her visit, and Indara was glad for the kindness. Even after working with Vernestra Rwoh, she was still a bit intimidated by the Jedi Master.

"Why did you decide to stay?" Indara finally said, opting for bluntness over niceties.

Vernestra leaned back in her chair and took a deep breath before letting it out. "There were a lot of reasons. There was the realization that perhaps sharing my experiences with younger Jedi might help them consider the galaxy in a different way. I also started to think about the kind of Jedi I have been, the kind of Jedi I still want to be, and what kind of legacy I would like to leave behind when I am gone. There was the fact that there are some people in the galaxy who must be brought to justice by the Republic, people who will always be just out of the reach of the Order. Nilsson and Grizela helped me realize that. But mostly . . . I think I can help the Order become what it needs to be by being that link with the Senate. This way, instead of the High Council being bogged down by the minutiae of politics, the Senate has a dedicated office to route all requests. I have already decided that the Order is not here for their amusement, but for serious issues. And I plan on enforcing that."

"How did the Senate take it?" Indara asked.

Vernestra smiled, this time a real smile. "I'll let you know as soon as I tell them."

Indara laughed, and Vernestra waved the matter away. "Enough about me. You came by for a reason. How can I help?"

"Well, I was thinking that I would like to become a Wayseeker. I have already put in my formal request to the Council, but I was wondering if you would be willing to give them a recommendation on my behalf."

Vernestra nodded. "Of course. But I have to ask . . . why? I thought you were happy here on Coruscant."

Indara took a deep breath and let it out, trying to carefully choose her next words. "I am. But . . . you talked about being the light in the galaxy, and then I was thinking about the idea that we are all lights, and no matter how brightly we burn, we are all chasing away at least a little of the darkness. And I want to be that person for someone, the person who pushes back the shadows just enough to make life better."

Vernestra smiled. "I wish you had gotten to meet Imri. He would have liked you. But I am also happy that my words, in some way, have led you to a new path. I am certain that as a Wayseeker, you will learn more about yourself and what it means to be a Jedi. And someday, you will pass that on to others."

There wasn't much more to be said after that. Indara finished her tea and stood to take her leave. She was almost to the door when Vernestra called after her.

"Indara, before you go . . . thank you. For being patient with me. It was a joy to work with you."

Indara smiled and inclined her head. "You, too, Vernestra." She turned to leave, excited to see what her next steps would bring. Then she paused and turned back to Vernestra once more. "Thank you for showing me what it means to be a good Jedi."

Vernestra nodded, an expression that Indara could not quite identify coming over the older woman's face. It wasn't quite sorrow, but it seemed closer to sadness than happiness. Indara again turned to go, and she was almost out of the office when Vernestra's final words floated to her, so soft that Indara would never be certain if Vernestra was speaking to her or to herself.

"Wherever you go and whatever you do, you *can* be the light. Let the Force be with you."

About the Author

JUSTINA IRELAND is the award-winning and *New York Times* bestselling author of many books, including *Dread Nation, Deathless Divide, Rust in the Root,* and *Ophie's Ghosts.* She is also the author of numerous *Star Wars* books and one of the story architects of *Star Wars: The High Republic.*

Read on for an excerpt from

LIGHT OF THE JEDI
by Charles Soule

The Force is with the galaxy.

It is the time of the High Republic: a peaceful union of like-minded worlds where all voices are heard, and governance is achieved through consensus, not coercion or fear. It is an era of ambition, of culture, of inclusion, of Great Works. Visionary Chancellor Lina Soh leads the Republic from the elegant city-world of Coruscant, located near the bright center of the Galactic Core.

But beyond the Core and its many peaceful Colonies, there is the Rim—Inner, Mid, and finally, at the border of what is known: the Outer Rim. These worlds are filled with opportunity for those brave enough to travel the few well-mapped hyperspace lanes leading to them, though there is danger as well. The Outer Rim is a haven for anyone seeking to escape the laws of the Republic, and is filled with predators of every type.

Chancellor Soh has pledged to bring the Outer Rim worlds into the embrace of the Republic through ambitious outreach programs such as the Starlight Beacon. But until it is brought online, order and justice are maintained on the galactic frontier by Jedi Knights, guardians of peace who have mastered incredible abilities stemming from a mysterious energy field known as the Force. The Jedi work closely with the Republic, and have agreed to establish outposts in the Outer Rim to help any who might require aid.

The Jedi of the frontier can be the only resource for people with nowhere else to turn. Though the outposts operate independently and without direct assistance from the great Jedi Temple on Coruscant, they act as an effective deterrent to those who would do evil in the dark.

Few can stand against the Knights of the Jedi Order.

But there are always those who will try...

PART ONE
THE GREAT DISASTER

Chapter One

HYPERSPACE. THE *LEGACY RUN*.
3 hours to impact.

All is well.

Captain Hedda Casset reviewed the readouts and displays built into her command chair for the second time. She always went over them at least twice. She had more than four decades of flying behind her, and figured the double check was a large part of the reason she'd survived all that time. The second look confirmed everything she'd seen in the first.

"All is well," she said, out loud this time, announcing it to her bridge crew. "Time for my rounds. Lieutenant Bowman, you have the bridge."

"Acknowledged, Captain," her first officer replied, standing from his own seat in preparation to occupy hers until she returned from her evening constitutional.

Not every long-haul freighter captain ran their ship like a military vessel. Hedda had seen starships with stained floors and leaking pipes and cracks in their cockpit viewports, lapses that speared her to her very soul. But Hedda Casset began her career as a fighter pilot with the Malastare–Sullust Joint Task Force, keeping order in their little sector on the border of the Mid Rim. She'd started out flying an Incom Z-24, the single-seat fighter everyone just called a Buzzbug. Mostly security missions, hunting down pirates and the like. Eventually, though, she rose to command a heavy cruiser, one of the largest vessels in the fleet. A good career, doing good work.

She'd left Mallust JTF with distinction and moved on to a job captaining merchant vessels for the Byne Guild—her version of a relaxed retirement. But thirty-plus years in the military meant order and discipline weren't just in her blood—they *were* her blood. So every ship she flew now was run like it was about to fight a decisive battle against a Hutt armada, even if it was just carrying a load of ogrut hides from world A to world B. This ship, the *Legacy Run,* was no exception.

Hedda stood, accepting and returning Lieutenant Jary Bowman's snapped salute. She stretched, feeling the bones of her spine crackle and crunch. Too many years on patrol in tiny cockpits, too many high-g maneuvers—sometimes in combat, sometimes just because it made her feel alive.

The real problem, though, she thought, tucking a stray strand of gray hair behind one ear, *is too many years.*

She left the bridge, departing the precise machine of her command deck and walking along a compact corridor into the larger, more chaotic world of the *Legacy Run.* The ship was a Kaniff Yards Class A modular freight transport, more than twice as old as Hedda herself. That put the craft a bit past her ideal operational life, but well within safe parameters if she was well maintained and regularly serviced—which she was. Her captain saw to that.

The *Run* was a mixed-use ship, rated for both cargo and passengers—hence "modular" in its designation. Most of the vessel's structure was taken up by a single gigantic compartment, shaped like a long, triangular prism, with engineering aft, the bridge fore, and the rest of the space allotted for cargo. Hollow boom arms protruded from the central "spine" at regular intervals, to which additional smaller modules could be attached. The ship could hold up to 144 of these, each customizable, to handle every kind of cargo the galaxy had to offer.

Hedda liked that the ship could haul just about anything. It meant you never knew what you were going to get, what weird challenges you might face from one job to the next. She had flown the ship once when half the cargo space in the primary compartment was reconfigured into a huge water tank, to carry a gigantic saberfish from the storm seas on Tibrin to the private aquarium of a countess on Abregado-rae. Hedda and her crew had gotten the beast there safely—not an easy gig. Even harder, though, was getting the creature back to Tibrin three cycles later, when the blasted thing got sick because the countess's people had no idea how to take care of it. She gave the woman credit, though—she paid full freight to send the saberfish home. A lot of people, nobles especially, would have just let it die.

This particular trip, in comparison, was as simple as they came. The *Legacy Run*'s cargo sections were about 80 percent filled with settlers heading to the Outer Rim from overpopulated Core and Colony worlds, seeking new lives, new opportunities, new skies. She could relate to that. Hedda Casset had been restless all her life. She had a feeling she'd die that way, too, looking out a viewport, hoping her eyes would land on something she'd never seen before.

Because this was a transport run, most of the ship's modules were basic passenger configurations, with open seating that converted into beds that were, in theory, comfortable enough to sleep in. Sanitary facilities, storage, a few holoscreens, small galleys, and that was it. For settlers willing to pay for the increased comfort and convenience, some had droid-operated auto-canteens and private sleeping compartments, but not many. These people were frugal. If they'd had credits to begin with, they probably wouldn't be heading to the Outer Rim to scrape out a future. The dark edge of the galaxy was a place of challenges both exciting and deadly. More deadly than exciting, in truth.

Even the road to get out here is tricky, Hedda thought, her gaze drawn by the swirl of hyperspace outside the large porthole she happened to be passing. She snapped her eyes away, knowing she could end up standing there for twenty minutes if she let herself get sucked in. You couldn't trust hyperspace. It was useful, sure, it got you from here to there, it was the key to the expansion of the Republic out from the Core, but no one really understood it. If your navidroid miscalculated the coordinates, even a little, you could end up off the marked route, the main road through whatever hyperspace actually was, and then you'd be on a dark path leading to who knew where. It happened even in the well-traveled hyperlanes near the galactic center, and out here, where the prospectors had barely mapped out any routes . . . well, you had to watch yourself.

She put her concerns out of her mind and continued on her way. The truth was, the *Legacy Run* was currently speeding along the best-traveled, best-known route to the Outer Rim worlds. Ships moved through this hyperlane constantly, in both directions. Nothing to worry about.

But then, more than nine thousand souls aboard this ship were depending on Captain Hedda Casset to get them safely to their destination. She worried. It was her job.

Hedda exited the corridor and entered the central hull, emerging in a large, circular space, an open spot necessitated by the ship's structure that had been repurposed as a sort of unofficial common area. A group of children kicked a ball around as adults stood and chatted nearby; all just enjoying a little break from the cramped confines of the modules where they spent most of their time. The space wasn't fancy, just a bare junction spot where several short corridors met—but it was clean. The ship employed—at its captain's insistence—an automated maintenance crew that kept its interiors neat and sanitary. One of the custodial droids was spidering its way along a wall at that very moment, performing one of the endless tasks required on a ship the size of the *Run.*

She took a moment to take stock of this group—twenty people or so, all ages, from a number of worlds. Humans, of course, but also a few four-armed, fur-covered Ardennians, a family of Givin with their distinctive triangular eyes, and even a Lannik with its pinched face, topknot, and huge, pointed ears protruding from the side of its head—you didn't see many of those around. But no matter their planet of origin, they were all just ordinary beings, biding time until their new lives could begin.

One of the kids looked up.

"Captain Casset!" the boy said, a human, olive-skinned with red hair. She knew him.

"Hello, Serj," Hedda said. "What's the good word? Everything all right here?"

The other children stopped their game and clustered around her.

"Could use some new holos," Serj said. "We've watched everything in the system."

"All we got is all we got," Hedda replied. "And stop trying to slice into the archive to see the age-restricted titles. You think I don't know? This is my ship. I know everything that happens on the *Legacy Run*."

She leaned forward.

"Everything."

Serj blushed and looked toward his friends, who had also, suddenly, found very interesting things to look at on the absolutely uninteresting floor, ceiling, and walls of the chamber.

"Don't worry about it," she said, straightening. "I get it. This is a pretty boring ride. You won't believe me, but in not too long, when your parents have you plowing fields or building fences or fighting off rancors, you'll be dreaming of the time you spent on this ship. Just relax and enjoy."

Serj rolled his eyes and returned to whatever improvised ball game he and the other kids had devised.

Hedda grinned and moved through the room, nodding and chatting as she went. People. Probably some good, some bad, but for the next few days, her people. She loved these runs. No matter what eventually happened in the lives of these folks, they were heading to the Rim to make their dreams come true. She was part of that, and it made her feel good.

Chancellor Soh's Republic wasn't perfect—no government was or ever could be—but it was a system that gave people room to dream. No, even better. It encouraged dreams, big and small. The Republic had its flaws, but really, things could be a hell of a lot worse.

Hedda's rounds took over an hour—she made her way through the passenger compartments, but also checked on a shipment of supercooled liquid Tibanna to make sure the volatile stuff was properly locked down (it was), inspected the engines (all good), investigated the status of repairs to the ship's environmental recirculation systems (in progress and proceeding nicely), and made sure fuel reserves were still more than adequate for the rest of the journey with a comfortable margin besides (they were).

The *Legacy Run* was exactly as she wanted it to be. A tiny, well-maintained world in the wilderness, a warm bubble of safety holding back the void. She couldn't vouch for what was waiting for these settlers once they dispersed into the Outer Rim, but she would make sure they got there safe and sound to find out.

Hedda returned to the bridge, where Lieutenant Bowman all but leapt to his feet the moment he saw her enter.

"Captain on the bridge," he said, and the other officers sat up straighter.

"Thank you, Jary," Hedda said as her second stepped aside and returned to his post.

Hedda settled into her command chair, automatically checking the displays, scanning for anything out of the ordinary.

All is well, she thought.

KTANG. KTANG. KTANG. KTANG. An alarm, loud and insistent. The bridge lighting flipped into its emergency configuration—bathing everything in red. Through the front viewport, the swirls of hyperspace looked off, somehow. Maybe it was the emergency lighting, but they had a . . . reddish tinge. They looked . . . sickly.

Hedda felt her pulse quicken. Her mind snapped into combat mode without thinking.

"Report!" she barked out, her eyes whipping along her own set of screens to find the source of the alarm.

"Alarm generated by the navicomp, Captain," called out her navigator, Cadet Kalwar, a young Quermian. "There's something in the hyperlane. Dead ahead. Big. Impact in ten seconds."

The cadet's voice held steady, and Hedda was proud of him. He probably wasn't that much older than Serj.

She knew this situation was impossible. The hyperlanes were empty. That was the whole point. She couldn't rattle off all the science involved, but she did know that lightspeed collisions in established lanes simply could not happen. It was "mathematically absurd," to hear the engineers talk about it.

Hedda had been flying in deep space long enough to know that impossible things happened all the time, every damn day. She also knew that ten seconds was no time at all at speeds like the *Legacy Run* was traveling.

You can't trust hyperspace, she thought.

Hedda Casset tapped two buttons on her command console.

"Brace yourselves," she said, her voice calm. "I'm taking control."

Two piloting sticks snapped up out from the armrests of her captain's chair, and Hedda grasped them, one in each hand.

She spared the time for one breath, and then she flew.

The *Legacy Run* was not an Incom Z-24 Buzzbug, or even one of the new Republic Longbeams. It had been in service for well over a century. It was a freighter at the end of—if not beyond—its operational life span, loaded to capacity, with engines designed for slow, gradual acceleration and deceleration, and docking with spaceports and orbital loading facilities. It maneuvered like a moon.

The *Legacy Run* was no warship. Not even close. But Hedda flew it like one.

She saw the obstacle in their path with her fighter pilot's eye and instincts, saw it advancing at incredible velocity, large enough that both her ship and whatever the thing was would be disintegrated into atoms, just dust drifting forever through the hyperlanes. There was no time to avoid it. The ship could not make the turn. There was no room, and there was no time.

But Captain Hedda Casset was at the helm, and she would not fail her ship.

The tiniest tweak of the left control stick, and a larger rotation of the right, and the *Legacy Run* moved. More than it wanted to, but not less than its captain believed it could. The huge freighter slipped past the obstacle in their path, the thing shooting by their hull so close Hedda was sure she felt it ruffle her hair despite the many layers of metal and shielding between them.

But they were alive. No impact. The ship was alive.

Turbulence, and Hedda fought it, feeling her way through the jagged bumps and ripples, closing her eyes, not needing to see to fly. The ship groaned, its frame complaining.

"You can do it, old gal," she said, out loud. "We're a couple of cranky old ladies and that's for sure, but we've both got a lot of life to live. I've taken damn good care of you, and you know it. I won't let you down if you won't let me down."

Hedda did not fail her ship.

It failed her.

The groan of overstressed metal became a scream. The vibrations of the ship's passage through space took on a new timbre Hedda had felt too many times before. It was the feeling of a ship that had moved beyond its limits, whether from taking too much damage in a firefight or, as here, just being asked to perform a maneuver that was more than it could give.

The *Legacy Run* was tearing itself apart. At most, it had seconds left.

Hedda opened her eyes. She released the control sticks and tapped out commands on her console, activating the bulkhead shielding that separated each cargo module in the instance of a disaster, thinking that perhaps it might give some of the people aboard a chance. She thought about Serj and his friends, playing in the common area, and how emergency doors had just slammed down at the entrance to each passenger module, possibly trapping them in a zone that was about to become vacuum. She hoped the children had gone to their families when the alarms sounded.

She didn't know.

She just didn't know.

Hedda locked eyes with her first officer, who was staring at her, knowing what was about to happen. He saluted.

"Captain," Lieutenant Bowman said, "it's been an—"

The bridge ripped open.

Hedda Casset died, not knowing if she had saved anyone at all.

Chapter Two

THE OUTER RIM. HETZAL SYSTEM.
2.5 hours to impact.

Scantech (third-class) Merven Getter was *ready*. Ready to clock out for the day, ready to get the shuttle back to the inner system, ready to hit the cantina a few streets away from the spaceport on the Rooted Moon where Sella worked tending bar, ready to see if today was the day he might find the courage to ask her out. She was Twi'lek, and he was Mirialan, but what difference did that make? *We are all the Republic.* Chancellor Soh's big slogan—but people believed it. Actually, Merven thought he did, too. Attitudes were evolving. The possibilities were endless.

And maybe, one of those possibilities revolved around a scantech (third-class) staffed on a monitoring station far out on the ecliptic of the Hetzal system, itself pretty blasted far out on the Rim, sadly distant from the bright lights and interesting worlds of the Republic Core. Perhaps that scantech (third-class), who spent his days staring at holoscreens, logging starship traffic in and out of the system, could actually catch the eye of the lovely scarlet-skinned woman who served him up a mug of the local ale, three or four nights a week. Sella usually stayed around to chat with him for a while, circling back as other customers drifted in and out of her little tavern. She seemed to find his stories about life on the far edge of the system inexplicably interesting.

Merven didn't get why she was so fascinated. Sometimes ships showed up in-system, popping in from hyperspace and appearing on his screens, and other times ships left ... at which point their little icons disappeared from his screens. Nothing interesting ever happened—flight plans were logged ahead of time, so he usually knew what was coming or going. Merven was responsible for making sure those flight plans were followed, and not much else. On the off chance something unusual occurred, his job was just to notify people significantly more important than he was.

Scantech (third-class) Merven Getter spent his days watching people go places. He, in contrast, stayed still.

But maybe not today. He thought about Sella. He thought about her smile, the way she decorated her lekku with those intricate lacings she told him she designed herself, the way she stopped whatever she was doing to pour him his mug of ale the moment he walked in, without him even having to ask for it.

Yeah. He was going to ask her to dinner. Tonight. He'd been saving up, and he knew a place not too far from the cantina. Not so far from his place, either, but that was getting ahead of himself.

He just had to get through his blasted shift.

Merven glanced over at his colleague, Scantech (second-class) Vel Carann. He wanted to ask her if he could check out a little early that day, take the shuttle back to the Rooted Moon. She was reading something on a datapad, her eyes rapt. Probably one of the Jedi romances she was always obsessed with. Merven didn't get it. He'd read a few—they were all set at outposts on the far Republic frontiers, full of unrequited love and longing glances ... the only action was the lightsaber battles that were clearly a substitute for what the characters really wanted to do. Vel wasn't supposed to be reading personal material on company time, but if he called her out on it, she'd just tap the screen and switch it to a technical manual and insist she wasn't doing anything wrong. The trouble was, she was second-class, and he was third-class, which meant that as long as he did his job, she thought she didn't have to do hers.

Nah. Not even worth asking for an early sign-off time. Not from Vel. He could get through the rest of his shift. Not long now, and—

Something appeared on one of his screens.

"Huh," Merven said.

That was odd. Nothing was scheduled to enter the system for another twenty minutes or so.

Something else appeared. A number of somethings. Ten.

"What the—?" Merven said.

"Problem, Getter?" Vel asked, not glancing up from her screen.

"I'm not sure," he said. "Got a bunch of unscheduled entries to the system, and they're not decelerating."

"Wait... what?" Vel said, setting down her datascreen and finally looking at her own monitors. "Oh, that is odd."

More icons popped up on Merven's screens, too many to count at a glance.

"Is this... do you think it's... asteroids, maybe?" Vel said, her voice unsteady.

"At that velocity? From hyperspace? I dunno. Run an analysis," Merven said. "See if you can figure out what they are."

Silence from Vel's station.

Merven glanced up.

"I... don't know how," she said. "After the latest upgrade, I never bothered to learn the systems. You seemed to have it all under control, and I'm really here to supervise, you know, and—"

"Fine," he said, utterly unsurprised. "Can you track trajectories, at least? That subroutine's been the same for like two years."

"Yeah," Vel said. "I can do that."

Merven turned back to his screens and started typing commands across his keypads.

There were now forty-two anomalies in-system, all moving at a velocity near lightspeed. Incredibly fast, in other words, much quicker than safety regulations allowed. If they were in fact ships, whoever was piloting them was in for a massive fine. But Merven didn't think they were ships. They were too small, for one thing, and didn't have drive signatures.

Asteroids, maybe? Space rocks, somehow thrown into the system? Some kind of weird space storm, or a comet swarm? It couldn't be an attack, that much he knew. The Republic was at peace, and looked like it was going to stay that way. Everyone was happy, living their lives. The Republic worked.

Besides, the Hetzal system didn't have anything worth attacking. It was just an ordinary set of planets, the primeworld and its two inhabited moons—the Fruited and the Rooted—with a deep focus on agricultural production. It had some gas giants and frozen balls of rock, but really it was just a lot of farmers and all the things they grew. Merven knew it was important, that Hetzal exported food all over the Outer Rim, and some of its output even found its way to the inner systems. There was that bacta stuff he'd been reading about, too, some kind of miracle replacement for juvan they were trying to grow on the primeworld, supposed to revolutionize medicine if they could ever figure out how to farm it in volume . . . but still, it was all just plants. It was hard to get excited about plants.

As far as he was concerned, Hetzal's biggest claim to fame was that it was the homeworld of a famous gill-singer named Illoria Daze, who could vibrate her vocal apparatus in such a way as to sing melodies in six-part harmony. That, in combination with a uniquely appealing wit and rags-to-riches backstory, had made her famous across the Republic. But Illoria wasn't even here. She lived on Alderaan now, with the fancy people.

Hetzal had nothing of any real value. None of this made sense.

Another rash of objects appeared on his screens, so many now that it was overloading his computer's ability to track them. He zoomed out the resolution, shifting to a system-wide view, making a clearer picture.

Merven could see that the things, whatever they might be, were not restricting themselves to entering the system from the safety of the hyperspace access zone. They were popping up everywhere, and some were getting awfully close to—

"Oh no," Vel said.

"I see it, too," Merven said. He didn't even have to run a trajectory analysis.

The anomalies were headed sunward, and many of them were on intercept courses with the inhabited worlds and their orbital stations. The things weren't slowing down, either. Not at all. At near-lightspeed, it didn't matter whether they were asteroids, or ships, or frothy bubbles of fizz-candy. Whatever they hit would just . . . go.

As he watched, one of the objects smashed through an uncrewed communications satellite. Both the anomaly and the satellite vanished from his screen, and the galaxy got itself a little more space dust.

Hetzal Prime was big enough that it could endure a few impacts like that and survive as a planetary body. Even the two inhabited moons might be able to take a couple of hits. But anything living on them . . .

Sella was on the Rooted Moon right now.

"We have to get out of here," he said. "We're right in the target zone, and more of these things are appearing every second. We have to get to the shuttle."

"I agree," Vel said, some semblance of command returning to her voice. "But we need to send a system-wide alert first. We have to."

Merven closed his eyes for a moment, then opened them again.

"You're right. Of course."

"The computer needs authorization codes from both of us to activate the system-wide alarm," Vel said. "We'll do it on my signal."

She tapped a few commands on her keypad. Merven did the same, then waited for her nod. She gave it, and he typed in his code.

A soft, chiming alarm rang through the operations deck as the message went out. Merven knew that a similar sound was now being heard across the Hetzal system, from the cockpits of garbage scows all the way to the minister's palace on the primeworld. Forty billion people just looked up in fear. One of them was a lovely scarlet-skinned Twi'lek probably wondering whether her favorite Mirialan was going to come by the tavern that evening.

Merven stood up.

"We've done our job. Shuttle time. We can send a message explaining what's happening on the way."

Vel nodded and levered herself up out of her seat.

"Yeah. Let's get out of—"

One of the objects leapt out of hyperspace, so near, and moving so fast, that in astronomical terms it was on them the moment it appeared.

A gout of flame, and the anomaly vanished, along with the monitoring station, its two scantechs, and all their goals, fears, skills, hopes, and dreams; the kinetic energy of the object atomizing everything it touched in less than an instant.

Chapter Three

AGUIRRE CITY, HETZAL PRIME.
2 hours to impact.

"Is this real?" Minister Ecka asked as the chimes rang through his office—consistent, insistent, impossible to ignore. Which, he supposed, was the point.

"Seems so," Counselor Daan answered, tucking a curl of hair behind his ear. "The alert originated from a monitoring station at the far edge of the system. It came in at the highest priority level, and it hit system-wide. Every computer linked to the main processing core is sounding the same alarm."

"But what's causing it?" the minister asked. "There was no message attached?"

"No," Daan replied. "We've repeatedly asked for clarification, but there's been no response. We believe . . . the monitoring station was destroyed."

Minister Ecka thought for a moment. He rotated his chair away from his advisers, the old wood creaking a little beneath his weight. He looked out through the broad picture window that made up the wall behind his desk. As far as he could see: the golden fields of Hetzal, all the way to the horizon. The world—the whole system, really—believed in using every bit of available space to grow, create, to cultivate. Buildings were roofed with cropland, rivers and lakes were used to grow helpful algae and waterweeds, towers were terraced, with fruit vines spilling from their sides. Harvester droids floated among them, plucking ripe fruits—whatever was in season. Right now, that would be honeyfruit, kingberries, and ice melons. In a month, it would be something else. On Hetzal, something was always in season.

He loved this view. The most peaceful in the galaxy, he believed. Everything just so. Productive and correct.

Now, with the alarm chimes ringing in his ears, it didn't look like that anymore. Now it all just looked . . . fragile.

"Something's happening out there," another adviser said, a Devaronian woman named Zaffa.

Ecka had known her for a long time, and this was the first time he'd ever heard her sound worried. She was staring down at a datascreen, frowning.

"A mining rig out in midsystem just went down," Zaffa said. "The satellite network's starting to show holes, too. It's like something's taking out our facilities, one by one."

"And we still don't have any images? This is madness," Ecka declared.

He pointed at his security chief, a portly middle-aged human.

"Borta, why don't your people know what's happening?"

Borta frowned. "Minister, respectfully, you know why. Your recent cuts have reduced Hetzal's security division to a tenth of its former size. We're working on it, but we can't bring much to bear."

"Is it some sort of natural anomaly? It can't be . . . we're not under attack, are we?"

"At this point, we don't know. What's happening is consistent with some sort of enemy infiltration, but we're not seeing drive signatures, and the locations being hit are pretty random. We do still have some orbital defense platforms out there, and they're all intact. If it's an attack, they should be targeting our ability to strike back, but they're not."

The chimes sounded again, and Ecka spun his chair and pointed at Counselor Daan, who cringed back.

"Will you turn off that blasted alarm? I can't think!"

Daan pulled himself up, standing a little straighter, and tapped a control on his datascreen. The chimes, blessedly, ceased.

Another adviser spoke up—a slim young man with red hair and extremely pale skin, Keven Tarr. The Ministry of Technology had sent him over. Ecka didn't have much use for tech that wasn't related to agricultural yields. In his heart, he was still a farmer—but he knew Tarr was supposed to be very smart. Probably wouldn't be long until the boy moved on, found himself a job in some more sophisticated part of the galaxy. It was the way of things on a world like Hetzal. Not everyone stayed.

"I think I can show you what's going on, Minister," Tarr said.

The man had long fingers for a human, and they danced over his datapad.

"Let me give the data to the droid—it can project the information so we can all see."

He tapped a few last commands, then unreeled a connection wire from his datapad and plugged it into the access port on the squat, hexagonal comms droid waiting in the corner of the room. It rolled forward, its single green eye lighting up as it moved.

From that eye, the machine projected an image on the large white wall in the minister's office reserved for the purpose. Normally, presentations on the vidwall would be concerned with crop yields or pest eradication programs. Now, though, it displayed the entire Hetzal system, all its worlds and stations and satellites and platforms and vessels.

And something else.

To Minister Ecka, it looked like a field overrun with a swarm of all-consuming insects. Hundreds of tiny lights moved through his system at what had to be tremendous speed, all in the same direction: sunward. More particularly, planetward. Toward Hetzal Prime and the moons Fruited and Rooted not so far away, not to mention all those stations, satellites, platforms, vessels... many of which had people on them.

"What are they?" he asked.

"Unknown," Tarr responded. "I got this image by linking together signals from the surviving satellites and monitoring stations, but they're going down quickly, and we're losing sensor capacity as they do. Whatever these anomalies are, they're moving at near-lightspeed, and it's very difficult to track them. And, of course, whenever they hit something, it's..."

"Not good," General Borta finished for him.

"Apocalyptic, I was going to say," Tarr said. "I'm tracking a good number on impact paths with the primeworld."

"Is there nothing to be done?" Ecka said, looking at Borta. "Can we... shoot them down?"

Borta gave him a helpless look. "Once, maybe, we'd have had a chance. At least some. But system defense hasn't been a priority here for... a long time."

The accusation hung in the air, but Ecka did not indulge it. He had made decisions that seemed correct at the time, with the best information he had. They were at peace! Everywhere was at peace. Why waste money that could help people in other ways? In any case, no looking back. It was time for another decision. The best he could make.

He did not hesitate. When the crops were burning, you couldn't hesitate. As bad as things might be, the longer you waited, the worse they tended to get.

"Give the evacuation order. System-wide. Then send a message to Coruscant. Let them know what's happening. They won't be able to get anyone here in time, but at least they'll know."

Counselor Zaffa looked at him, her eyes hooded.

"I don't know if we can actually implement that order effectively, Minister," she said. "We don't have enough ships here for planetary evacuations, and if these things are really moving close to lightspeed, there isn't much time until—"

"I understand, Counselor Zaffa," Ecka said, his voice steady now. "But even if the order saves just one person, then one person will be saved."

Zaffa nodded, and tapped her datascreen.

"It's done," she said. "System-wide evac in progress."

The group watched the projection on the wall, fritzes of static lancing through it now. Tarr's makeshift network was losing capacity as more satellites met fiery ends, but the message was still clear. It was like a massive gun had been fired at the Hetzal system, and there was nothing they could do to save themselves.

"You should probably all try to find yourselves a way offworld," Ecka said. "I imagine the starships we do have will be very full quite quickly."

No one moved.

"What will you do, Minister?" Counselor Daan asked.

Ecka turned back to his window, looking out at the fields, golden to the horizon. It was all so peaceful. Impossible to believe anything bad could ever happen here.

"I think I'll stay," he said. "Broadcast to the people, maybe, try to keep folks calm. Someone has to look after the harvest."

***

Across Hetzal Prime and the broad expanses of its two inhabited moons, the message of Minister Ecka traveled rapidly, appearing on datapads and holoscreens, broadcast across all communication channels, saying, in essence: *Nowhere is safe. Get as far away as you can.*

Explanation was limited, which caused speculation. What was happening? Some kind of accident? What disaster could be so huge in scope that an entire system needed to be evacuated?

Some people ignored the warning. False alarms had happened before, and sometimes slicers pulled pranks or showed off by breaking into emergency alert computer systems. True, nothing had ever happened on this scale, but really, that made it easier to dismiss the whole thing. After all, the entire system in danger? It just wasn't possible.

Those people stayed in their homes, at their workplaces. They turned off their screens and got back to their lives, because it was better than the alternative. And if they glanced to the skies from time to time, and saw starships heading up and out... well, they told themselves the people in those ships were fools, easily spooked.

Others, elsewhere, froze. They wanted to find safety but had no idea how. Not everyone had access to a way offworld. In fact, most did not. Hetzal was a system of farmers, people who lived close to the land. If they traveled anywhere else in the Republic, it was for a special occasion, a once-in-a-lifetime experience. Now, being told to find a way to space on a moment's notice... how? How could they possibly do such a thing?

But some people in Hetzal did have starships, or lived in the cities where space travel was more common. They found their children, gathered their treasures, and raced to the spaceports, hoping they would be the first to arrive, the first to book passage. They, inevitably, were not. They were greeted by crowds, queues, ticket prices spiking to unattainable levels for all but the wealthiest, thanks to unscrupulous opportunists. Tension rose. Fights broke out, and while Hetzal did have a security force to calm these squabbles, these officers also eyed the skies and wondered if they would spend their last moments alive trying to help other people to safety. A noble end, if so... but a desirable one? The security officers were people, too, with families of their own.

Order began to break down.

On the Rooted Moon, a kind trader decided to open the doors of the starship he used to transport the exceedingly fresh produce of the moon to the voracious worlds of the Outer Rim. He offered space to all who could possibly fit, and though his pilot told him the vessel was old, and the engines were a bit past their prime, the trader did not care. This was a moment for magnanimity and hope, and by the light he would save as many as he could.

The ship, holding 582 people, including the trader and his own family, managed to take off from its landing pad, once the pilot pushed its engines to maximum. It just needed to escape the moon's gravity well. Once they were in space, everything would get easier. They could get away, to safety.

The vessel achieved most of a kilometer before the overtaxed engines exploded. The fireball rained down over those left behind, and they were not sure whether they were lucky or not, considering they still had no idea what was coming for them. Minister Ecka's message did not say.

A variant on that message was sent out from Hetzal to any other systems or ships that might hear it: *We are in desperate trouble. Send aid if you can.*

It was picked up by receivers in the other worlds of the Outer Rim—Ab Dalis, Mon Cala, Eriadu, and many more, spreading outward via the Republic's relay system, and then inward to the planets of the Mid and Inner Rims, the Colonies region, and even the shining Core. Virtually everyone who heard it wanted to do something to help—but what? It was clear that whatever was happening in Hetzal would be over well before they could arrive.

But ships were sent anyway—mostly medical aid vessels, in the hope they might be able to offer treatment to injured citizens of Hetzal.

If any survived.

"Get to your nearest offworld transport facility," Minister Ecka said to a cam droid recording his words and image and broadcasting them across the system. "We will send ships to pick up people who don't have other ways to leave the planet. It might take time, but stay calm and peaceful. You have my word, we will come for you. We are all of the same crop. Hearty stock. We will survive this the way we have survived harsh winters and dry summers, by pulling together.

"We are all Hetzal. We are all the Republic," he said.

He raised a hand, and the cam droid ceased transmitting. This was the fourth message he had sent since the emergency began, and he hoped his communications were doing some good. Reports suggested they were not—riots were beginning at spaceports on all three inhabited worlds—but what else could he do? He broadcast his messages from his office in Aguirre City, demonstrating that he had not abandoned his people even though he surely could. A show of solidarity. Not much, but something.

Around him, the rest of his staff coordinated their own attempts to assist in whatever way they could. General Borta worked with his meager security fleet to both keep order and ferry people offplanet. With the help of Counselor Daan, they had organized a number of the huge crop freighters currently in transit to act as relay points, ordering them to dump their cargo and clear all space for incoming refugees. Each could hold tens of thousands of people. Not comfortably, of course, but this was not a situation where comfort mattered.

Smaller ships were ferrying Hetzalians up to the cargo vessels, offloading their people then rushing back to pick up more. It was an imperfect system, but it was what they had been able to arrange on no notice. There was no plan for something like this.

Minister Ecka blamed himself for that—but how could he have known? This wasn't supposed to happen. It was impossible, whatever it was. He was just a farmer, after all, and—

No, he thought, suddenly ashamed of himself. He was Minister Zeffren Ecka, leader of the whole blasted system. It didn't matter if he couldn't have anticipated this disaster—it was happening, and he needed to do everything he could.

As he considered that thought, he looked over at Keven Tarr, who had never stopped running his little network, trying to keep information flowing. The young man was now working with three separate datapads and a number of comms droids projecting various displays on the walls, pulling in as much data as he could about the scope of the disaster that continued to wreak havoc in the system. He still had no real answers, other than to continually confirm that Hetzal was being savaged by whatever was afflicting the system. Satellites, arrays, stations... smashed apart by the storm of death that had come calling. It was like the seasonal chewfly swarms that used to plague the Fruited Moon until they had been genetically modified out of existence.

If the swarm came, there was nothing you could do. You hunkered down, survived, and sowed your fields again once it was all done.

Ecka watched as Keven Tarr wiped sweat from his eyes, then looked back at his main datapad, the one he had propped up on the little side table he was using as a desk.

Tarr's eyes widened, and his fingers froze, hovering over the screen.

"Minister," he said. "I'm... I'm getting a signal."

"What signal?" Ecka said.

"I'll just... I'll just put it through," Tarr said, and there was an odd note in his voice, of surprise, or just something unexpected.

Words crackled into the air, one of the technician's comms droids broadcasting the message out into Minister Ecka's office. A woman's voice. Just a few words, but they brought with them, yes... the one thing most needed at that moment.

"This is Jedi Master Avar Kriss. Help is on the way."

That one thing.

Hope.

About the Type

This book was set in Hermann, a typeface created in 2019 by Chilean designers Diego Aravena and Salvador Rodriguez for W Type Foundry. Hermann was developed as a modern tribute to classic novels, taking its name from the author Hermann Hesse. It combines key legibility features from the typefaces Sabon and Garamond with more dynamic and bolder visual components.

A long time ago in a galaxy far, far away. . . .

STAR WARS

Join up! Subscribe to our newsletter at ReadStarWars.com or find us on social.

- 𝕏 @StarWarsByRHW
- 📷 @StarWarsByRHW
- f StarWarsByRHW

© 2025 Lucasfilm Ltd. & ® or ™ where indicated. All rights reserved.

Georgina Public Library
90 Wexford Drive
Keswick, ON L4P 3P7